THE ADVENTURES OF CHARLIE SMITHERS

C W Lovatt

A Wild Wolf Publication

Published by Wild Wolf Publishing in 2012

Copyright © 2012 C W Lovatt

ISBN: 978-1-907954-33-7

Also available in e-book

www.wildwolfpublishing.com

For Amber

Chapter One

"Gun, Smithers!"

Lord Brampton held his hand out expectantly, arm rigid, fingertips twiddling with impatience, all the while never taking his eyes off the fearsome black rhino grazing placidly in the distance.

I carefully handed him the heavy elephant gun, making sure the muzzle was pointing well away from either his lordship or myself. Two great bullets were loaded in those chambers. The hammers were at half-cock, but I'd learned the hard way it was always best to be safe…insofar as that was possible. I regret to say, however, that when in the company of my master, when *he* was in the company of his guns, that possibility didn't always exist.

But, so far so good; Lord Brampton's fingers curled around the polished walnut of the stock. There was a momentary unease when one digit slid unerringly past the trigger guard, but then it was out again without any harm being done.

That part of my duty successfully completed, I pulled the small brass telescope from my belt and leveled it at the beast. A moment later the head of the bull wobbled into view. He was big to the naked eye at a hundred yards, but massive in the lens, his great horns jutting up and down while he grazed. We were downwind of him and, so far, unsighted.

Lord Brampton leveled the great rifle at the brute and sited down the shiny blue steel of the twin barrels.

"Head will look good in the gunroom, what?" His lordship rumbled confidently in a voice too loud to be a whisper. The rhino's ears twitched, and I felt my grip on the telescope tighten, but he was only flicking away some flies.

My own voice was a hoarse whistle as I cautioned his grace to silence.

"Nonsense," he scoffed, "Trouble with you, Smithers, you worry too much."

I knew better, of course, but I also knew better than to remonstrate further. My master was in one of his more quarrelsome moods. It was always this way when his old wound was bothering him.

5

To accent the point, an angry growl erupted from his abdomen – the medical legacy of having so much of his intestines removed at Balaclava.

The rhino's ears twitched again, then centered, his great head rising while he peered short-sightedly in our direction. I found myself softly keening, willing Lord Brampton to pull the trigger.

At last there was a deafening report as the gun discharged. A few yards beyond and to the left of the beast a large spurt of dust heralded the usual complete miss. With a sinking heart, I focused back on him. When I did so, I saw that he, in turn, was now focusing on me, his eyes wide with surprise.

Then angrily, they narrowed.

Oh dear.

The elephant gun roared a second time. The top two inches of the rhino's front horn disappeared as if by magic, but that was all. When you stopped to consider that the tip of that horn was in a direct line between the gun's muzzle and the lethal spot between the beast's eyes, such a lack of result was really quite remarkable.

The bull took a few belligerent steps in our direction to get a better look at us, his ears fanned out and alert. I think the sun must have glinted off the lens of my telescope, for it was a mere instant before he lowered his head and charged, bellowing with rage.

"Missed, by God!" Lord Brampton roared, affronted.

"Oh hell!" quoth I, to no one but myself.

The rhinoceros had increased speed at an alarming rate. In fact, the way he was eating up the distance between us was quite impressive.

Here we bloody go again.

We'd been camped out on the great plain of the Serengeti for a week now. As usual, His Grace had failed to hit a thing, not even a wildebeest, and this, you'll note, after having worked our way to within fifty yards of a herd so vast that it stretched in every direction for as far as the eye could see!

So it was with some trepidation in my heart that, when we happened upon the small herd of rhinos, Lord Brampton had

6

decided to stop and have a go at them. When I hopefully ventured to point out an inoffensive herd of zebra a short distance away instead, he had dismissed the idea with a derisive snort. For all evidence to the contrary, my lord had a supreme confidence in his own abilities as a deadeye marksman and, misguided or not, it was his towering ambition to be accepted as such by his peers.

Now, true to form, his appalling lack of skill, or luck, or whatever else you might care to call it, had remained steadfast and not forsaken him.

So it was with a sinking feeling that I passed the other gun to his lordship. That feeling was confirmed scant seconds later when, with the bull growing larger every second, he calmly leveled the piece and let go with both barrels at once.

Those great slugs should have stopped the beast in his tracks, but he never even slowed down. Where they had got off to no one could tell, but one thing was sure: they never registered in any of the rhino's sensory apparatus. Not to worry though, he seemed quite infuriated enough already.

There was only one thing left to do.

"Get out of it, m'lord!" I cried and nudged him firmly toward where the horses were tethered some distance to the rear. Already, they were whinnying with fright and rearing back, pulling hard on their reins.

Now he turned that indignant glare upon myself. As God's my witness, I thought he was going to stand there and argue.

"There's no time, sir! You must save yourself!"

His face worked furiously for a precious moment, and then – praise be! – seemed to recognize the urgency at last; but true to his sense of dignity, there was no hurry in his step as he turned away. The very square set to his shoulders proclaimed with immense pride that a Brampton *never* ran.

It would have to do.

Now to assure his lordship's safety, my duty was to bring the brute's attention fully upon myself. Indeed, the time was so short as to be virtually nil. Already, his great bellowing form was nigh upon me, filling the very horizon with clouds of the churned-up plain in his wake.

7

I roared my own pathetic challenge and feinted a half-step toward him, then spinning away, darted off at a right angle to my master's line of escape.

It wasn't necessary to look back to know that the bull had taken the bait, and was now hard on my heels. The very ground was trembling as though I were running through an earthquake – so far, so good. Now if I could but stay ahead of him for the next twenty yards or so, to where a cliff plummeted down to the Mara River, everything was going to be jake.

Accordingly, I lowered my head, and ran for dear life.

Now, with things in hand, and all my other duties temporarily suspended, so to speak, perhaps this is as good a time as any to introduce myself.

Charlie Smithers is the name and personal attendant to John Houghton, Lord of Brampton (with five lines in Debrett) is my occupation – has been for the past thirty odd years, back to when we were just wee lads, and him and I was playmates together.

Ah, but those were the days – both of us roaming the wild Yorkshire hills with the roan deer in the sights of our wooden guns and joyful murder in our hearts! And if that didn't serve, there was always charging in amongst his mother's flower gardens (or in our eyes, obliging lines of French infantry), hacking and slashing at those prize geraniums until they were so much bloody offal. That was the life, I tell you! Plenty of mischief for a couple of mean-spirited lads, and no end of it in sight, neither!

Hold on, I think the brute's catching me up. Not to worry, I've enough left in me for a bit more speed. Ah, that's better! Now, where was I?

Right, his nibs and me was mates – well not *mates*, exactly, but as close as a peer could be to his servant, and vice-versa. I suppose that was just as well because there was never any question I was raised to be anything other than his man, just as my dear old dad was raised to be *his* dad's before us as convention demanded; and in accordance with such convention, it was through my father that I first understood what it was to be a gentleman's gentleman.

8

It must have been one of those times after having laid waste to the flowers, because it was one of those rare instances when we were immediately taken to task. Lord Brampton was hustled into the depths of Brampton Manor by his father, the earl, while my own father grabbed me by the scruff and dragged me off behind the stables. A gentle man was my dad, but duty was duty.

"Now then, Charlie," he said, and boxed my ear repeatedly 'til it rang. Then his eyes narrowed while he studied my face, searching for any sign of weakness. But I had learned at an early age that giving in to such unmanly emotions was something my guv'nor never tolerated, so I remained stolid, eyes front like a guardsman. Satisfied, he relented somewhat, and laid a heavy hand on my shoulder.

"Now my lad, I do allow that killing Frenchmen is only right and proper. After all, we're British, and that's why God put us here on this earth; but," and his voice was the rich source of reason, "destroying her ladyship's flowers is just not on, don't you see?"

"But Father," I piped, doing my best to sound man-to-man, "I was simply following orders." Which was the unvarnished truth, and I couldn't understand what all the fuss was about.

They were simple words from a simple lad, but the effect they had on my dear old dad was remarkable, and one I shall never forget. He flung himself back like he'd just taken a musket ball square in the chest. Then raising himself to his full height, eyes bulging like a surprised owl, I thought I was going to get another cuff across the head, but after a moment, his expression changed to one of paternal pride. This time more tenderly, he replaced his hand on my shoulder.

"My son," he said, his voice thick with emotion, "the day will come when you will have my position, the day, in fact, when young Master John succeeds *his* father, and all this carefree time of youth will be but a distant memory. There will be little ease in your life, and even less recognition." Then he grew even more solemn, "but though difficult, always remember there is no higher calling than to be of service to your gentleman. They are a

9

fickle race, and lack that instinct of self-preservation infused in we lesser folk. So you must see to their well-being in a thousand different ways, because they cannot see to it for themselves. Often you must place yourself in danger's path to protect them from harm. Many's the day when you must work from dawn's first light to beyond the setting of the sun, *always* with their comfort foremost in your mind. You must do all these things with a cheerful heart, and a Christian forbearance for their many strange foibles; but above all," and his eyes were flashes of stern duty, "you must *always* obey."

"Yes father," my own eyes were glued to his.

"Even when there is a certainty of punishment, you must obey – nay – even if there is a certainty of *death*, never forget your duty!"

"No, Father," I felt entranced. Like I said, a great one for duty was my dad.

"This is a sacred trust, one which has served our island race well, until it has made of us the foremost amongst all nations!" This was a favourite topic of my old man, the part about being British and all, and I thought he was just getting started, but this time he exercised some self-discipline, and contented himself by admonishing me with, "Never forget that, son!"

"I won't."

"Good lad!" he cried. Then nodding affectionately, he weighed in on the other ear.

And I never did forget, neither. Hang on – almost there!

Air rasping like hot coals in my lungs, I leapt for the precipice just as I felt the lethal end of that great horn graze my backside. I chanced to glance over my shoulder, and could have laughed aloud. The bull had pulled up just short of the brink, bellowing with rage at being frustrated in his desire to smash me to a pulp. For a brief moment I was elated to be free of that charging black nemesis…until I chanced to look down.

With some horror I realized my escape route hadn't quite been thought through in its entirety. For now I found myself poised over thin air a hundred feet above the Mara River – except, at this time of year, it was more like the Mara Trickle.

Indeed, from this height, it seemed virtually non-existent – no more than a silver thread cutting through the parched yellow of the vast grasslands below.

Down I plummeted.

Oh well, as the saying goes: it's not the fall that will hurt you....

Now, my old man certainly knew what he was talking about. Gentlemen had foibles, and by the cartload, too! And being gentlemen, their foibles were of an altogether grander nature than yours or mine. Take my master, for instance. He was always the great one for the hunt, but the problem was, no matter how hard he tried, he could never hit the broad side of a barn door. But then, neither could any of his forebears, so perhaps there may have been something inherited to it all. Yet even when marksmanship wasn't the issue – as in riding to the hounds – although he sat a horse very well, and could ride like a Red Indian, there was always the most appalling bad luck attending him. Many's the time I can recall, while the far-off belling of the hounds led the other toffs over hill and through dale, my master would invariably blunder into a wood, wild with enthusiasm, and stay hopelessly lost, until I – having witnessed, with sinking heart, the trees crashing and swaying for hours on end while he careened about in frenetic peregrination – ventured in to bring him back for tiffin.

Consequently, as the years passed, the walls of the gunroom at Brampton Manor remained bare and unadorned – had done so since time immemorial – and are so to this very day.

That came as no surprise to the common folk, for word had long since spread that, in this regard at least, the family was cursed. That in itself might not have been the end of the world (peers, after all, seldom paid much notice to the common herd) except for the fact that the subject was dear to the hearts of that ancient, blue-blooded line. For it had long been a family notion, handed down from father to son over many generations, that they were *country* nobility. Not for them was the society of London. Rather, they perceived themselves to be made of sterner stuff than those stylish fops, and fancied that the harsh nature of their northern estates fit them as naturally as a well-tailored coat.

11

While there may have been some truth to this, try as they might, they could never shake those dark whispers, and as the local superstitions eventually became accepted by some of the nobility itself, they considered it a personal disgrace.

Now all that talk of being cursed was just so much bollocks, if you ask me. However, I do have to admit there seemed to be a distressingly long list of unfortunate episodes that might appear to give credence to those whispers.

Like there was the time at the hunt when his steed accidentally trod on young Lady Wynngate's foot – poor girl, she was in plaster up to her hip for ages – and though it was never confirmed, may well have been the cause for the breaking off of their engagement.

Then there was that time when he – perhaps rashly – in an attempt to throw off the shackles of superstition, had promised his father a brace of quail for the table that evening; but the only blood to be spilled was when his gun caught on a bramble and the discharge filled a beater's backside with bird shot.

Or the time when we were hunting deer on the eastern fell…but then that was long ago, and best not spoken of. Besides, that ghillie's widow was endowed with a pension for life, so all's well that ends well.

I suppose, given the Brampton's inborn sense of bloodlust and perhaps – if my impertinence may be forgiven – a certain lack of reason rendering them unfit for much else, it was only natural that the family should have a time-honoured tradition of purchasing commissions in the military. Hence, you shall generally find that at least one of that noble family was present at some of our nation's more notable defeats. Why, milord's grandfather lost a leg at Saratoga when, at a critical moment, while bravely attempting to lead a bayonet charge into the thickest part of the fray with the last of our dwindling reserves, tripped over his sword, severing the tendons behind the knee. Many years later, in the peninsula, his father, the present earl, led a charge at Corunna – in the wrong direction – and was subsequently shot out of the saddle by some annoyed Highlanders. As the story goes, the ball caught him squarely in the forehead, but by great good fortune, was already spent. Sadly however, the blow rendered him severely cross-eyed, and looked to do so for the remainder of his days.

Of course I followed my master to the colours in our own time as well, and with thoughts firmly set on bloodshed and glory, sailed with him to the Crimea. Well, I saw enough bloodshed to last me a lifetime, and no error. And while I'm not saying there wasn't any glory, if there was I never saw it.

I suppose all the world's heard of Balaclava by now, made famous by the Light Brigade's charge, and helped along by Alfred Lord Tennyson's romantic poem – which was so much poppycock, if you ask me. It was a bloody shambles, that's what it was, and a disgrace to British arms...and my own personal disgrace foremost amongst it all.

You see, it had been pure and simple hell riding up that valley, both shot and shell screaming through our ranks, sweeping away our fellows in giant handfulls, but so far, by the grace of God, my master and I had managed to pull through unscathed. Yet even as we drew nigh the guns, I saw the Ivans wheeling that piece around to catch us in flank, and saw that bearded blighter touch his match to it, too. But the worst of it was that I saw the discharge was set to scythe directly across Lord Brampton's path, and when that happened, it would almost certainly blow him to smithereens. So, with my dad's words ringing in my ears even o'er the roar of the cannon, I'd urged my mount forward, but, lamentably, was not in time to shield him completely. The round lifted us both from the saddle, for the best I could do was to only partially absorb the charge, shredding the muscle from my shoulder, and taking a few balls of the cannister in my leg. But at length, when I came to my senses amidst all the blood-curdling thunder of hooves and cannon, and the hair-raising screams of the wounded and dying, I was able to crawl my way over to my poor master, and was horrified to see that great gaping wound in his abdomen.

That was a bad time, I can tell you. I'd thought he was a goner at first and that my failure was absolute, but then I noticed that, somehow, he was still breathing. Where there was breath there was life, as the saying goes, and where there was life there was still hope, no matter how slender. I don't rightly recollect how I was able to get him back, and with only one arm to do it with too, but I must have managed it. I remember grabbing at the reins of a horse with an empty saddle, but the rest is just so much blank confusion of coming back through all that hell, until we'd finally reached our lines and I'd summoned the surgeon.

That worthy had shaken his head with deep gravity when he saw my lord's wounds, but when he took note of the fretful state I was in, had set about them regardless of his misgivings. It had been a long and painstaking affair, with him pulling out sundered entrails by the yard, and me hovering anxiously, helping as best I could, which, I'm sorry to say, wasn't much. When at last he was finished stitching him up, there was such a pile of gory intestines on the ground beside him that I wondered if he'd left any inside my poor master. But at last, he rose to his feet and put his bloodied hand on my good shoulder.

"It's in the hands of God now, Charlie," he said, although I could see he didn't hold much hope. Then clucking his tongue in that disapproving way he always had, added, "Now let's see about saving that arm of yours."

For weeks I felt the very picture of misery while my master hovered between life and death. Many's the time I thought the fever was going to carry him away, but whatever they lack in other areas, Bramptons have the constitutions of bulls. Even so, it was a close run thing – as the old duke used to say – and when he finally did open his eyes, I was so relieved that I hobbled over with my arm in a sling, threw myself to the ground, and begged his forgiveness for having failed him so completely. He had every right to sack me, of course, or at the very least have me shot for cowardice, but believe it or not, all he murmured was, "Better luck next time," or something else along that line, before drifting back to a laudanum-induced sleep.

Now I ask you, is that, or is that not, a true gentleman?

After such a horrible experience, you'd have thought it would be nothing but Easy Street for him from then on, wouldn't you? If it were any other man I dare say you would be right, too, but my master would have none of it. Weak and wan though he was, when invalided out of the army, and having returned to England, Lord Brampton soon found that he was no

14

longer suited to the quiet country life. For once having tasted it, beneath that noble breast there burned an unquenchable thirst for adventure. So it was with little surprise when, one evening some months after our return to Brampton Manor, I was summoned to his side.

I found my lord in his rooms, pacing back and forth in evident excitement. His face was set in the way he had of showing the decision he'd come to was, as usual, the one he'd desired.

"Smithers," he cried, already showing signs of coming into the bloom of health, like a man reborn, "pack my bags! We're off to see the world!"

"Certainly, Your Grace," I bowed carefully, and somewhat awkwardly from my crutch. My arm was also still in its sling, but healing famously. "May I be so bold as to enquire where we are going?"

"Why, haven't you ears? I said '*the world*' didn't I?"

"Yes, of course, milord, but....."

His brows knit together.

"But what? Come on, man, out with it!"

"But what *part* of the world, sir, if you don't mind my asking?" I needed this information so as to reckon on which of milord's togs it was best to stash away into his travelling chests.

"Why the *world*, Smithers! The whole lot! Every last nook and cranny, every last jungle and sand dune, every last teepee and igloo, every last square inch, in fact, or," he amended slightly, "at least as much of it that's British."

"Oh," I couldn't hide my surprise, for this was doing it up handsomely, and no error. In fact, this was such a grand affair that more luggage would have to be purchased in order to transport so much of my lord's wardrobe...and his guns, too, of course.

And so, to make a long story short, seven months later – with both our wounds healing in the process – having taken a mail packet to Cairo, then overland by camel caravan to the Gulf of Suez, before taking an East Indiaman to Mombasa, here we were, with milord trundling back to camp unattended, and me plummeting to almost certain death.

Speaking of which, legs straight, arms tight to my side!

There was a tremendous splash and water engulfed me. The shock struck most of the air from my lungs and I was still sinking like a stone.

What great luck! Apparently, I had fallen into a deep eddie or a pool. I was saved!

But before I could exalt too much, my descent was suddenly arrested by a bone-jarring crunch on the gravely riverbed. A pair of sharp 'snaps' was quickly interpreted into the knowledge I had broken both my ankles.

What little air remained in my lungs was now expelled by a sub-aquatic scream of agony. Water flowed into my nostrils and into my mouth. My confused mind was so disoriented from the fall and the searing pain I didn't know which way was up. I thrashed about, but without evident effect, for with both ankles broken my legs were now useless. Yet, just as I was about to black out and give into the the river's insistence it should take me, my head miraculously broke the surface, and I found myself spluttering water from my lungs. I coughed and coughed until my stomach cramped, and I was spewing muck all over the place; but once I had retched up most of that disgusting filth, I looked up at the clear blue sky and the world all around me, and knew that I had somehow survived.

Treading water with my arms, I fairly crowed with triumph.

"They haven't got you yet, Charlie!" I cried, my voice echoing off the canyon walls. "The world's tried and tried, but you ain't bloody dead yet! Bloody *marvelous*! Bloody indestructible, that's what you are!"

I was so loud in my rejoicing that I almost didn't hear the splash, or the sound very like boulders rumbling together; but not quite like that....no, not quite. This sound was...*hungrier*, somehow.

Subdued now, I peered over my shoulder to the far shore, and was able to catch sight of the last of the leathery forms as it took to the water.

It was enormous.

"Oh crumbs," I said.

Crocodiles.

Chapter Two

I watched, horrified, as those hideous monsters glided through the oily water toward me. Even though all I could see of them was the tips of those terrible long snouts, and the mounds of their evil yellow eyes protruding above the surface, believe me, when you find yourself floundering around in their back yard, so to speak, and unable to make any headway in the bargain, that's quite enough.

The moment I found my voice again, I was screaming fit for blue murder. I turned and fairly flung myself at the near shore, thrashing the water like a paddle wheeler with a full head of steam; and don't you know, at that moment I couldn't feel any pain in my ankles one little bit.

But it was hopeless, of course. Those giants were propelling themselves along at a prodigious rate that was very disheartening, I can tell you. Try as I might, I knew they'd be on me in a very few seconds, and when they did, it would be 'bye, bye, Charlie Smithers'.

I continued splashing about, wondering if I was getting any closer to the shore, and expecting to feel those horrible jaws clamp on my leg and drag me under at any second; but then I ceased my exertions, stopping dead in the water.

It was strange, I suppose, but it was like I was so annoyed about the whole situation I forgot to be frightened. Really, not so unlike the way I felt – the way we all felt – careening into those murderous batteries at Balaclava.

This was too bad! Why, I'd already been through quite a bit today, and now this was the far side of enough. By God, it wasn't fair!

A great anger began to fill me.

I turned at bay, deciding that if I was to go down, then I would go down fighting.

"Come on, you buggers!" I cried. "I'll take the mickey out of you, you rotten swine! Come on and get your coa-coa!"

Evidently, the nearest croc thought I was bluffing because he didn't change tack in the least. He just kept coming on and on in a deadly silence, his eyes never wavering from me one jot.

Well, that made me more furious than ever. We Smithers were never much for the donnybrook, but when it was forced upon us we seldom failed to hold our own. With this thought in mind, I reared out of the water as high as I could, and came down on the tip of his snout with all my strength.

"Take that, you overgrown gecko!" I screamed.

I swear I saw his eyes widen in surprise – just like that rhino's had (good God, had that only been a minute ago?), but then, also like the rhinoceros, they narrowed into mean, little slits. Then I was gaping at his tonsils as his jaws hinged open, his upper hovering five feet above me, and I knew I was for it this time.

But then, believe it or not, one last miracle occurred. There came a whistling through the air, and as I stared, open-mouthed, waiting for the croc to finish me, something – a stick – bounced off the tip of his snout and splashed into the water only a short distance away. Surprised again, the croc's jaws crashed together prematurely, missing me by a whisker, but coming so close that I could feel the wind from the force of it, and smell the foul stench of his breath.

That great nemisis backed off, eyeing me suspiciously. It wasn't hard to tell what he was thinking: '*Why, here's this toothsome little chap splashing about in my river, looking ever so much like a little bit of something to tide me over 'til tea, and now he's banged me bongo twice without so much as a by-your-leave! Oooo! I'm really mad about that!*'

Until that moment, I suppose it had been an impersonal relationship of predator versus prey to him. Now I could see that my cheek had only served to put murder in his beady little eyes. Accordingly, he let out a mighty roar, and lunged.

Immediately the air was filled with that whistling sound again, only much larger this time, almost like the buzzing of a swarm of angry bees. Then there was a veritable drumming of club-like sticks off the brute's muzzle, each changing tone as they struck up and down his noggin.

Thrice thwarted, the enraged monster lashed backwards in retreat, hating every vile and insignificant inch of me. I never thought a croc could snarl like a dog, but this one did. He continued to hold his ground when the sound of shouting came

19

from far behind me, but as it drew nearer, he delivered me one last dirty look as if to say, 'Right chum, we'll settle you yet,' before turning and thrashing after his cronies, who had already taken flight before him.

Everything had happened so quickly there wasn't time to wonder about what had taken place. Then suddenly, there were legs churning the water all around me, and jabbering voices making the very devil of a racket. Dazed, I looked up to see all sorts of wonderful niggers, wrapped up in what looked like kilts and bedsheets – like in those paintings of those old Roman fellows – but with ears the size of beefsteaks. As dazed as I was, I noticed these men weren't like the stocky-built fuzzy-wuzzies we'd seen along the coast. Rather, these were tall, fine-boned fellows. Their hair wasn't black and bushy like those others, neither, but an unlikely shade of red, worn in elaborately long plaits, with equally elaborate headdresses of intricately linked metal, and necks similarly adorned. As to weapons, they were really fearsomely attired. Some carried brightly decorated throwing clubs the likes of which I'd just seen bouncing off my friend the croc's nose a few seconds ago. Still others carried wide bladed swords, and *all* of them carried a lethal-looking long-bladed spear and cowhide shield.

A few were chucking their clubs at the backs of the retreating crocs while another couple made threatening motions at them with their spears to keep them at bay. Meanwhile the rest were dragging me out of the river, but when my ankles touched gravel I let out a howl fit to raise the roof; so nothing would do but that they drop me then and there, while they hovered about and gabbled on as to what was best to do next.

I was wondering how long this was going to go on, when one of them began to weigh in with some effect. I think he was their leader because he had the biggest ears, and the most elaborate ornamentry depending from his forehead, so that it all but covered his face. On his ears, a multi-assortment of bangles were so pendulous they mingled with a succession of necklaces descending down his chest to well past his waist. To look at him, you would think he was all metal from the top of his head to below his knees, yet it was he who seemed to take control of the situation. A tall, thin, well-featured bloke, I could tell by the way he spoke, forcing his words to come out slow and steady, that he was someone of intelligence.

It seemed to help. Understanding began to dawn in the eyes of his mates when he jabbed a finger at my painfully swollen ankles and seemed to be explaining to them that they mustn't drag this blighter about like that 'cause he's probably got compound fractures, see? This enlightenment produced some more happy shouting and nodding, whereupon all of them abruptly scarfed off out of there like Billy-be-damned.

The boss man jabbered a further string of babble to the others watching the crocodiles – no doubt telling them to keep a steely lookout, because they just nodded without letting down their vigilance for a second. I doubted if there was much to worry about on that score though. By now the crocs were huddled about their mud flat on the other side of the river. They seemed disgruntled and peevish, but no longer showed much fight.

I was wondering what was next on the agenda, but when he knelt by my side, I wasn't at all prepared for what came.

"My fellows have gone to make a litter for you."

I was so surprised I almost soiled my breeches. And if you'll recall, it had already been a trying day, so I should think that's saying a lot.

My amazement must have shown on my face because his fine features spread into a grin before he threw back his head and bellowed out a fine basso "Hah! Hah! Hah!

"You are surprise-it that I speak the English, my friend? Hah! Hah! Hah! Why, of course you are surprise-it, and why would you not be? Here you are in the Maasai Mara, so far from your home, and you find one of the nigger peoples who speak the English as good as you. Surprise-it? You must be amaze-it!"

"Well, yes," I managed to stammer, all pop-eyed, "I am, rather."

"Jolly good!" he chuckled, then became grave but for the humour sparkling in his eyes. "Allow me to introduce the self," he said politely, "My name Musa Ole Saitoti, and you...?"

21

"Charlie Smithers," I said, still blinking incredulously, "at your service."

"How-dee-do Charlie Smithers?" Musa solemnly offered me his hand, and then smiled that huge smile of his again.

I took it and replied, "I do well, thank you."

The strangeness of the scene was not lost on me. I mean, here I was, after dodging death from a charging rhinoceros, miraculously surviving a leap from a dizzying height, and narrowly avoiding becoming a meal to a monster crocodile, I was now lying in the shallows of a riverbed in deepest darkest Africa, being formally introduced to a grinning red-headed darkie dressed in a sheet – and in the Queen's English, at that!

Yet, strange though it was, there was no doubting the little ceremony greatly pleased my benefactor. He was also not blind as to how much his stock went up with his chums when they returned bearing a rough litter and found us chatting away like old pals. Of course this caused much more excited pointing and jabbering, and through it all Musa was playing it for all it was worth, carrying on something awful, and preening about like a cock o' the hoop as if to say: weren't they just the lucky ones he was along to parley with this strange pasty-faced fellow.

But when he finally got them settled down, they lost no time putting me on the stretcher, and with a buck at each corner, hiked me up and set off like I was light as a feather. It was here I had the time to observe my bearers more closely and soon realized that what I had thought at first to be giant ears were, in fact, over-sized piercings of the lower lobe, each unnaturally stretched with large wooden plugs. As Musa's were the largest of the lot, I took this to mean it was a sign of rank.

Considering that I'm close to fourteen stone, we made good headway - my bearers nipping along famously without perspiring overmuch, and this you'll note, was at a trot over broken ground. Wherever we were going, they seemed in a great hurry to get there.

We stuck to the flat tableland for the most part, so the going was relatively easy. Still, if you've ever broken a bone, you'll know that even the slightest jar can be agony. So a great deal of my energy was being employed in clenching my jaws to

22

keep myself from crying out. After all, it had been quite good of them to save my life, so I felt it was just good manners to keep my discomfort to myself.

We had been traveling for scarcely more than an hour, the steep cliffs on either shore gradually falling away to merge with that vast and mighty plain, when Musa dropped back from the lead to jog beside me.

"You are well, Charlie Smithers?" he asked solicitously.

I replied that I was, although I was beginning to feel nauseous from the pain.

Perhaps as much was written on my face, because he said, "Not far to go now."

When I asked him our destination he pointed and said, "The village."

I craned my neck and saw in the distance some dozens of mud and wattle huts looking like so many loaves of bread set in a great circle. Around the lot was a fence fashioned from what looked like thorn bushes which, I gathered, was for protection from predators. Beyond this, to my surprise, out on the steppe on either side, I saw great herds of giant cattle, with dabs of bright red here and there amongst them signifying other warriors playing the role of stockmen. Although I had heard mention of such folk in our settlements along the coast, it was still a strange sight to find animal husbandry in the midst of such a savage land. In my astonishment, I must have blurted out as much.

But if Musa was insulted, he never let on. "Oh yes, Charlie Smithers. Enkai has said we must have all cattle."

"Enkai?"

Musa spread his arms and face up to the sky. "Enkai! Enkai!"

"You mean your god?"

Musa looked me full in the face. He did not smile. "I mean God, Charlie Smithers."

We jogged along in silence for a bit before he continued. "I know about your Lord Jesus. I heard from your mission peoples when my father sent me live with them along coast. My father was great man. For many years we had heard of your peoples, and he knew some day you would come, so he send me to learn

23

your ways." He looked pensive for a moment, as though remembering an unhappy time, "I was just little boy, and I stay-it with them for ten long years." But then he looked at me and grinned, ivory teeth gleaming against ebony skin, "Even then I found the missionaries stories very entertaining! Hah! Hah! Hah!"

I said, "But you came back?"

"Of course I come back," he said seriously, "my father was chief, but he getting old; soon it be my turn. Besides," he added, "I was not yet a man."

I was feeling too poorly to ask him what he meant by that. I really wish I had; it might have changed things.

At length we came to the village. Up close, it was pretty much as I'd described from a distasnce, except for the smell, of course, but after awhile a person tends to expect this sort of thing from native settlements. Once inside the compound, there was much consternation voiced by the congregation which instantly crowded about us. I couldn't help noticing that the women – dressed much as the men were, complete with kilts, bedsheets and lavish decoration – were rather a handsome, cheery lot. However, in contrast to their menfolk, their hair was either closely cropped or shaved completely, but what hair I could see was reassuringly black and tightly curled. From this I deduced that, far from being a natural state, the warriors had had their own flowing locks dyed. I don't know why, but that realization came as something of a relief. They really were an imposing and good-looking group of fellows, but I couldn't help thinking those red manes of theirs looked odd as the devil.

I could guess from all the jabbering they were asking Musa all about your humble obedient because he was speaking rapidly, first pointing at me, then at the great beyond, and for some reason I couldn't fathom, up at the sky. The others of our party soon got into the act as well. There was a banquet of miming as one sheltered a phantom sun from his eyes before pointing excitedly to the spot where we might find the stupid foreigner frolicking about in the water while the crocodiles were closing in for luncheon. Imaginary clubs flew through the air as the crocs' evil designs were thwarted, much nimble running on the spot as

24

they came to my rescue, and finally a spreading of the arms, palms up, as if to say, 'and *voilà*, here we are.'

The story was well received by all, and I was quite beginning to enjoy my role as a personality of some note, when there came a shouting from the back of the crowd, and a subdued hubbub as various bodies were rudely shoved aside. Presently, through the mass of goggling blacks came this leathery old cove decked out in rattles and gourds. Half his face was painted red, the other half blackened with charcoal. He held a small sort of club in his hand that looked to be fashioned from iron, and I didn't have to be told that this was their medicine man. The way he was looking at me, I also didn't need to be told he wasn't pleased I was there.

I'd noticed that, as this fellow was approaching, Musa's amiable features had begun to darken. Now, as the old bird began to harangue, first the gathering, then Musa, and finally my uncomprehending self, Musa drew himself up to the full of his considerable height, and proceeded to give back as good as he got.

The shaman shrieked at this impudence, and glared at my new friend with fierce loathing. Then he whirled on me, shaking the club under my nose, all the while beseeching Enkai to wipe me off the face of the earth, no doubt.

Musa stepped between us, gesticulating angrily.

In reply, the medicine man pawed at the red side of his face and arched his back, arms extended like claws. Whatever it was he was miming, it wasn't a pretty sight, and I noticed some of the villagers were starting to look at me uncertainly.

But Musa gave his head a violent shake. Speaking great guns now, he pointed at me, then again up to the sky. Once more the significance escaped me, but there was one word he kept repeating every now and then.

Enkai.

When he was finished, the atmosphere was of subdued astonishment. The villagers drew back with something that seemed close to frightened reverence. Even the shaman looked uncertain as to what his next step should be.

Before he could recover, however, Musa gestured to my bearers. Without a word, they picked up my stretcher and whisked me out of sight inside one of the huts.

By now, the journey had begun to catch up with me. My ankles hurt like the very dickens; my forehead felt of fever, and I had a thirst so dire I was desperate for anything that even resembled water. So presently, when a timid young woman stuck her head inside and offered me a wooden bowl brimming with a frothy liquid, I took it and drank like I hadn't just been gulping in huge amounts of the Mara River only a few short hours previously..

It had a cloyingly sweet taste, yet there seemed something about it that had the faintest resemblance to beer. I finished what she had brought and, with gestures, asked for more. When this too was provided and subsequently quaffed, I asked again. She regarded me with some exasperation and left, returning with a helper, both of them struggling with a great earthen jar of the stuff.

But even after my thirst had been quenched, I continued to imbibe, wondering how on earth I'd ever thought the taste too sweet. I was beginning to feel warm, but didn't think it was the fever. As a matter of fact, I was beginning to feel quite good really, when you stopped to consider.

Presently Musa's tall form stooped its way into the hut.

"Well," I said, "I haven't been put to death yet, so I gather everything went well?"

Musa was not smiling. "The *Laibon* does not like you."

"I gathered as much."

"He say you are evil; he say you are the Red Man."

"The Red Man?"

"Yes," Musa said, then explained. "We Maasai know Heaven is balanced with both black and red – good and evil. The black," he gestured to his own skin, "is good. The red," and here he touched my sunburned forearm, "is evil."

I wasn't liking the sound of this.

"So why wasn't I done in on the spot?"

Instead of answering, Musa began to speak of things I thought unrelated.

26

"I am chief," he said proudly, "like my father I too am great man. A chief must be wealthy, and though I have many cattles and many wives, there is one of this village who has even more."

"The *Laibon*?"

"No, the *Laibon's* son."

"Oh."

"This morning two of my cattles were missing. At first I think Parasayip had stolen them but our search was empty. It is a very serious business."

"I suppose it must be," I agreed, but as yet, had no idea just how little I knew.

"These cattles must to be found so I take my men to look for them," for the first time he grinned, "but we found you, instead."

"I'm very grateful."

But he didn't seem to hear me. "I am looking all over the place. Where are my cattles? Where are my cattles? But I do not find them. Then I look up and see you falling from the sky."

His smile broadened. I must say, he seemed very pleased with himself.

"Yes," I said slowly, "I told you I was grateful."

He waved a hand to show that it was of no account. "I start to think maybe crocodiles eat my cattles. It is a great loss, but when I see you fall from the sky, I think I have something even better."

"Me?"

"You," he agreed, then laughed, "Enkai!"

"Enkai?"

"Hah! Hah! Hah! You are the Red Man half of Enkai, he who say all of the cattles of the world are for Maasai!"

I puzzled over this for a moment. "That's rubbish, of course, but even if it weren't, I don't see-"

"You have come down from Heaven to say all Parasayip's cattles must be mine!"

"But I'm not Enkai," I cried, not at all pleased to be taking part in an intrigue, "I'm...I'm...British!"

27

Musa's smile did not waver, but I wondered, did I hear something slightly sinister in his tone?

"You will be Enkai for a day."

I tried to argue in a polite sort of way. I tried to tell him I had to get back to my own people – to Lord Brampton – which was true, but my words fell on deaf ears until finally, after I don't know how long, I was all talked out without any effect.

I lay back on the pallet with a troubled mind, let me tell you. So that was it then; I had been saved only to pretend I was their silly god – and, no doubt, place my life in grievous peril, in the bargain – just so this grinning monkey could get his hands on a few rotten cows. I didn't know what their penalty was for impersonating a deity, but I doubted if the *Laibon* would be satisfied with just shaking an iron club under my nose. It really was too bad!

But, I suppose I'm something of a philosophical fellow when I can see there's nothing else for it. I would keep my wits about me and await my chance, but in the meantime, I would just have to play along.

I gestured to my ankles, now swollen and so badly inflamed they were stretching the seams of my trouser legs, and had become quite painful. "We'll have to do something about this," I said, "I'm not much of a god being crippled and all am I? I expect even less so if I'm dead."

Musa gave a nod. "I have given this some thought, Charlie Smithers. You are correct, you must first become healed and regain your strength. It is true that the *Laibon* is the healer in our village, but I would not wish to entrust your life to him, for he is no friend to you."

"Thanks very much."

"But there is one other amongst us who carries knowledge of the healing arts." He smiled knowingly then called out, "Loiyan!"

The woman who had served me earlier reappeared from where she must have been waiting just outside the entrance. With bowed head and folded hands, she continued to wait submissively.

28

As I took closer notice of her, I saw she was rather a pretty little piece – as near as I could judge, scarcely more than twenty – all decked out in diadems and beads. And while her shaved head was a bit strange, I had to admit it allowed a clear view of the graceful curve of her neck. On her arms, I noted a novel sort of jewelry: on one a thin copper spiral coiled from her wrist to elbow, and on the other another twisted from elbow to shoulder, the low rich colour of the metal blending intriguingly with the darkness of her skin.

"Many women know of the healing herbs in our country," Musa said, ignoring her for the time being, "but Loiyan is best. She also know how to heal broken bones, maybe even better than *Laibon*, although that is secret we keep from him. Such knowledge," he told me, "is forbidden to woman."

He turned and barked a command. Without raising her head, Loiyan came forward to look at my legs. Her touch was soothing as, gently, she ran her hands over my ankles, stopping whenever I winced, waiting patiently until I had braced myself before returning to her examination. Presently she seemed satisfied because she said something to Musa and left.

"She goes to bring medicine...." He searched for a word, "...and sticks. In the meantime," he dipped the gourd into the jar and offered it to me. "Please, she say you are to drink."

I was sensing I was in for an ordeal so I didn't need to be asked twice. Besides which, my legs had been throbbing for awhile now and I found the drink helped numb the pain. By the time Loiyan returned, I was sucking up the stuff like I'd been been out in the desert for a week.

The woman's arms were full, and as I drained the gourd yet one more time, she deposited the items on the floor. I was surprised to find that what Musa had told me was accurate, for much of what she brought indeed appeared to be little more than sticks. I wondered if I should voice my concern about being treated by some sort of savage mumbo jumbo, and by a novice at that, but after considering the lack of alternatives, decided to hold my peace, at least for the moment.

Meanwhile, unknowing – or possibly, uncaring – of my concern, she set a small iron brazier on the floor by my head.

29

From a leather pouch, she took out a large handful of a dried green herb. Her eyes met my own; I suppose she was looking for some hesitation on my part. When she took note that I was indeed suspicious, she smiled gently and opened her hand under my nose so I might smell what it was. The odour was so strong that I jerked my head away, but before I could voice my disgust, images of coils of rope were conjured in my mind.

Why, these were nothing but buds from the hemp plant. For all I couldn't see how they could help, I knew they couldn't harm me. When I shrugged and nodded, she tossed the stuff on the brazier.

Immediately a pungent smoke began to rise from the coals. With hand motions, and deep breathing, she bade me inhale these fumes. Once more I thought to argue, but still couldn't find any basis for my fears. So I leaned over as far as I was able until my face was quite close to the brazier, and took a deep breath.

The coughing fit that followed was so violent that flames of agony seared up and down my legs with every convulsion. Eventually Loiyan was able to settle me with a cool cloth to my brow. Then, while she sponged the rest of my face, she signed that I was to breathe in only what I could take, then hold it in my lungs for as long as was bearable.

This time I approached the brazier with a new respect. I took a cautious inhalation, pulled a more modest amount of smoke down into my lungs, and held it. When she had indicated her satisfaction with my technique, I blew it out some seconds later, then signed to her that my throat felt raw. Could I have a drink?

Signaling that I was to continue with the hemp treatment, she took the gourd and went over to the jar. But when she saw how far down the level had become she gave me a stern look much as my mum used to do when she found me up to no good. She left the hut and came back with the bowl filled to brimming.

I drank deeply.

It was water.

All this time I had been inhaling the hemp smoke, and for some reason, now found I wasn't too disappointed to find I was getting only water. In fact, I thought it was the sweetest water ever tasted. I marveled as it coursed down my throat, cool and soothing, thrilling every inch of my body with a new vitality I'd scarcely thought existed.

"Good water, this," I said, even though I knew she couldn't understand a word. For some reason, that struck me as the funniest thing, so I started to giggle.

Her dark eyes studied me closely. When I grinned in her face, far from showing consternation – as well she might – instead she smiled and seemed pleasantly satisfied.

Now she turned her attention to my ankles. I saw there was a knife in her hand – a wicked looking thing with an edge that gleamed brightly, even in the poor light. I wondered if I should be afraid, but discovered I didn't care. I think it was the not caring that sent me into another fit of the giggles, although, again, I couldn't imagine why.

Loiyan had been poised over my leg with the blade, but when I began to convulse with muffled titters, she called to Musa who came over and put his weight on my thighs.

"Please, Charlie Smithers," his voice came from the other side of the world, "you not move."

"Right you are, then," I replied, and burst into peals of laughter.

This caused further delay, of course, with the intervening time being filled, presumably, with pleas from Loiyan for Musa to hold me, dammit, and Musa remonstrating, again presumably, that it wasn't that bloody simple controlling this great brawny oaf of a foreigner, now was it?

This went on for some time until at last my laughter subsided to the point where she felt it safe to try again.

First she cut away my boots before carefully inserting the knife between my ankle and my trousers, the inner seam parting like magic. The release of the pressure felt bloody marvelous, I can tell you. She cut up to my knee, but these pantaloons had always fit snug, so not yet satisfied, she slowly continued to work her way upwards.

The further release of the pressure was wonderful, but it was beginning to be mingled with something else. I wondered vaguely what it could be.

Musa muttered something under his breath. Loiyan offered a shy smile, exhibiting lovely white teeth, but didn't waver in her concentration. Not wishing to feel left out, I managed a weak titter as well.

By now she had cut to within a few inches of my groin, and even in my lovely state of well being, I was beginning to become nervous about a blade being in that vicinity. Yet if anything, this only served to heighten this strange excitement I was feeling.

But here she stopped – and it was strange: was it my imagination, or had there been regret? – and began the process all over again on my other leg.

For me, it was the same as before, except that now the pleasurable excitement was gaining ground with the parting of every stitch, so much so that when she reached my knee and continued on without pause, I could have wept for joy.

Slowly it dawned on me, and the understanding filled me with a world of wonder.

I was randy as a stoat!

And as I gazed with longing at the pretty little beads of perspiration on Loiyan's forehead, I realized who I was randy *for* – a native wench!

I was glad that my old folks couldn't see me now; it was right shocking, really. Staunch Church of England, was my dad, and even stauncher Church of Scotland was my mum. They'd never understand any of this, not in a million years.

Not that I understood it myself, mind you, but as that razor's edge worked its way up my inner thigh, I was finding I didn't much care if I did or didn't. By the time it had come to a stop, I was starting to pant like the town bull.

There was something else, too. It was a warm night out, but not as hot as all that. I was beginning to feel that all that perspiration on Loiyan's brow wasn't *completely* due to her dedication to her work.

As if to prove my point, she actually hesitated, the knife momentarily poised as though it had a mind of its own, and it was willing her to continue. I had said that my trousers fit snug, so there was no way that she couldn't have noticed my growing interest. But when she found her hand was shaking, she tossed the blade to the ground and did a few agitated turns about the room. Then, when that evidently didn't suffice, she left the hut altogether. By the length of time it took for her to rejoin us, she must have done a good few turns around the village.

But for a distant, amused leer, Musa held his peace.

Finally Loiyan returned, and I thought looked rather grim of purpose. If she'd had any sleeves, I swore she would have rolled them up, she seemed that determined.

She studied my face very carefully, then, apparently satisfied, slipped one of the sticks between my teeth. I took it playfully and winked at her, but she pretended not to notice. Instead she moved down to my right ankle. The dear girl must have been more agitated than she let on for she snapped something to Musa in an angrier tone than I'm sure she intended. But he never let on, either, but grasped my leg below the knee like a good boy. She, in turn, took hold of my foot.

When she began to pull, all amorous thoughts scattered from my mind like rats racing down a drainpipe; my teeth clamped down on the stick as if they were a vice while I struggled furiously to free myself, but Musa held me fast.

The agony! Oh God, the pain was a fire searing its way from my ankle all the way up my body to the center of my brain! It was torture – pure, bloody hell! I wanted to scream, but my jaws were locked tight around that stick as though they were welded shut! The room spun around and around at an ever dizzying speed while the torment washed over me in waves. Soon it became too much for human endurance, and the last sense of awareness I had before losing consciousness was the taste of blood in my mouth.

I was slipping from one world into another, never sure if I was awake or dreaming – alive or dead. I could hear Lord Brampton calling my name over and over, but try as I might, I was unable to answer. Then his face was in front of me, angry and querulous as ever, demanding to know what I meant by it.

"I'm sorry, my lord," I replied, "but I've been ill."

"Damned nonsense!" he cried angrily. "Bloody layabout, that's what you are!" His bowels rumbled their own ill humour.

"Please, my lord, I must protest….!"

But he was gone. Instead, Loiyan's face was swimming in a haze of smouldering hemp, her eyes soft and caring. When I reached for her, Musa's laughter was spinning around me as though I were in the vortex of a whirlwind.

And then it was Lord Brampton again. This time he carried a knife and looked ready to use it.

"Damned layabout! I'll teach you!"

There it was, I had failed my master, and it was time to pay the piper. I cringed, trying to anticipate that razor-sharp blade biting into my skin. But, instead, there was a soft tugging on my waist band, and there was Loiyan, once more soft and glowing. Yet, in a way I couldn't fathom, her expression changed to revulsion as her hand knuckled to her mouth, eyes filled with horror.

Then the stick was in my mouth again, and I was biting for all I was worth.

"Please! Please! Please!" I begged the pain not to come, but it wouldn't listen. It came on and on in sickening waves, washing over me like lava rain, and as I spun once more into the darkness, Musa's laughter followed me down.

Then, for a long time, there was nothing.

A cock was crowing when I opened my eyes. I noticed someone had covered me with a blanket. It took awhile to remember where I was, and why. I moved my legs, but felt only a minor discomfort.

Well, that was good, wasn't it?

I felt a burning thirst and wondered how long I had been lying there. I looked around, and saw a dipper of water on the floor beside me, but when reaching for it, there came a fiery, stinging sensation down below that caused me to hiss through my teeth.

What was this?

34

Gingerly, I lifted the blanket and turning it to the side, saw a scrap of white linen covering my loins.

In the center there was a livid red stain.

I felt my hair crawl across my scalp; cold beads of perspiration had sprung up all over my body. I ground my teeth together, bracing myself, unmindful of the dull ache in my jaws.

Carefully, I pulled the cloth aside. At first my numbed mind refused to allow me to believe what I saw. Yet even when it was possible, my horrified shriek remained frozen in my throat.

They couldn't have...

No! It just wasn't possible!

Oh, the swine!

Those bloody savages had cut off my willie!

Chapter Three

"But Charlie Smithers, why you so angry?"

Musa had come trundling in right quick when I finally found my voice. My shock was still quite fresh, so I probably wasn't thinking much about *his* reaction, but this hurt innocence he was feeding me set me back on my heels, I can tell you.

"Why am I so angry?! Why you benighted baboon! You've lopped off my tally-whacker, that's what you've done!"

"But...."

"And what've you done with it, you black bastard – eaten it, I suppose?!"

"No...."

"Of all the devilishly cruel things you savages can do to a man, this takes the cake!"

"If you would only let me..."

"There's no limit to your beastly depravity, is there?!"

"You don't under...."

"Oh, I can see through you now, Johnny! Oh yes, clear as a bell! – '*Oi,*' – you're thinking, – '*ere's this white bloke, all alone, mindin' 'is own sweet business. What say we lure 'im back to the old mud hovel, all innocent-like, an' saw off 'is pecker! We'll pop it in the soup for supper – should go well with a couple of onions, heh!? Chroist, I can taste it already!*'" I glared all the hate I could, "You're a sick bastard, that's what you are!"

"But now you are a *man*, Charlie Smithers," and so help me, it was Musa who was carrying on as if it were *me* who was being daft!

But this?! Oh, this was too much!

"Why, of all the purblind, stupid imbecilic things to say!" I lunged for him, but the sensitivity of my wound brought me up short with a yipe. I coiled protectively over my groin and said, "But that's just the point, you bloody sod, I *ain't* a man, not anymore, thanks to you! Can't you bloody well get that through your thick bloody skull?!"

"Please be calm, Charlie Smithers. You are still as you were, but now you are even better. More beautiful!"

"More beautiful!? So that's it, is it?! You're keeping me around to be a bloody poof, aren't you? You want me for your bleeding harem, don't you?! Well just you try it, you depraved sodomite. I'll see you in hell first!"

Musa seemed to have run out of words. For a moment he stood there at a loss, but then inspiration seemed to take hold. He reached down and, hiking up his kilt, pulled aside his loin cloth.

"Behold," he said.

Now I was the one at a loss for words – well, you are when another man wants to show you his dangle, aren't you? – but if he thought that just the sight of his johnson was enough to get me to hop in the sack with him and take it up my twins, he was a lot more twisted than I thought!

I was busily looking anywhere other than that particular point of interest, when I think he seemed to understand.

"Be at peace, Charlie Smithers. You are safe."

Perhaps a minute passed before I decided to take a quick peep through the corner of one narrowed, suspicious eye, and quickly looked away again. After a few more seconds I took another, slightly longer look. Then I set aside all pretense and stared.

"Why, you're Jewish!"

For there, but for a neatly trimmed foreskin, hung a perfectly normal member, with old bald Dick protruding proudly for all and sundry.

"You've been circumcised!"

I had heard about such a thing, of course, but never had I seen one, until now.

"It is the *emorata*," Musa said gravely, "the process of becoming a man."

"Right, sort of like a Bar Mitzvah," my knowledge of Judaism was somewhat imperfect.

Musa shrugged, "I do not know these words. I am Maasai, Charlie Smithers. The *emorata* is the mark by which we show Enkai we are his chosen people."

"To your men-folk, at any rate." I was so fascinated that I couldn't tear my eyes away until....

37

I experienced the dawning of hope.

I looked up at Musa. He smiled patiently.

"You mean...?"

He nodded.

In my eagerness, I pulled the cloth away too fast, yet hardly noticed the sting. Unaware that I was holding my breath, I peered down through all the gore. At first it didn't look any different than my worst fears – but wait! – as it gradually overcame its timidity of this strange new world, I was finally rewarded with the sight of my dear old friend. But for the cutting away of his fleshy hood, he was still safe and sound.

I began to weep.

"Now, Charlie Smithers," Musa spoke softly, "you are a man. You are *moran*, a warrior."

"You frightened me near to death."

"Do not be frightened, Charlie Smithers. You are whole." Then without the least trace of amusement, "Now all women will find you glorious."

But I was hardly listening; I was too busy drowning in relief. Joyous hosannas were exulting silently from my lips up to heaven. Whether there was any truth to his blather about women finding me glorious or otherwise, thank the Lord, I was still in business.

But this brought home, in a way nothing else could, just how alien this world was. Why, the liberties these people took while a fellow was asleep were truly shocking, when you thought about it. And when I did think about it – someone slicing away down there while I lay unconscious and vulnerable – was enough to make me feel quite faint, I can assure you.

I suppose that it was with this in mind when I said, "Well, I hope you were bloody careful."

And was floored by his response.

"Oh, it was not I, Charlie Smithers," he laughed as though only a stupid foreigner would think such a thing. "Oh no, no, no...it was Loiyan."

I must have gaped at him like a landed flounder, because his smile widened.

"And do not worry, for she was very careful, indeed."

I continued to gape.

"She likes you," he explained, looking pleased.

"Likes me?" I was still finding it hard to swallow that the surgery had been intended as some twisted act of kindness.

"Why do you frown, Charlie Smithers?"

"Well, I don't know," I said, "It's just that, if the lass finds me agreeable, she's got a damned rum way of showing it. I mean, I don't know about here, but back home it's quite unusual for a girl to....to....*desecrate* a fellow she likes....down there....with a *knife*."

The mere thought had got my skin crawling again.

Musa pondered this for some time. Clearly the subject interested him.

"But how do your women show their interest in a man?"

"Well, I don't know, really," I admitted, "I suppose she might drop a hanky, that sort of thing."

"Drop...a *hanky*?"

"Yes, well," I could feel my face begin to flush, "we're British, you know, *civilized*."

The moment was saved by Loiyan's timely arrival. While we hurriedly covered ourselves, she stooped through the entrance and asked Musa a question, and don't you know, I'd never realized how pretty, how like a little bird her voice was. When answered, she came over to where I lay on the pallet, and knelt at my feet.

It occurred to me then that, as incredible as it may seem, I'd been so preoccupied with...with...the other thing I'd completely forgotten about my fractured ankles. Now, as she carefully lifted the bottom of the blanket and began to conduct her examination, I took the opportunity to do the same.

I had to admit that Loiyan's doctoring was truly remarkable. The angry red swelling was much reduced, and with it most of the pain. Of the fractures themselves, each leg was neatly splinted from foot to knee with a bundle of straight green branches, each about as thick as my thumb, the lot firmly bound in place by long strips of rawhide. A bit cumbersome, perhaps, but undoubtedly effective.

After she'd examined each one carefully in turn, she asked a question in that same little bird voice, and Musa translated.

"Are the bindings too tight?"

I waggled my legs around thoughtfully. There was only a mild discomfort.

"No, they're fine."

She gave her work a last critical look. Then apparently satisfied, and before I could protest, she whipped the blanket away entirely.

I know I was blushing furiously because my toes, which had returned to being a healthy pink, were now well rouged with humiliation. The state of the rest of me you may well imagine.

Loiyan attempted to remove the pitifully inadequate square of linen from my groin, but I clutched it to my body like grim death, all the while gaping at her with a mixture of horrified indignation. Setting about a fellow while he wasn't aware was bad form indeed, but this was truly unconscionable, surely!

When she found her totally inappropriate advance was going to be thwarted, she looked up at me, voicing her question with a knitted brow. But I wasn't having it. I clung to my last line of defense with all the fervor of a fanatic.

She continued to stare steadily into my eyes. Very slowly, one of her eyebrows began to arch.

She spoke. It seemed her voice was a little less bird-like.

"She say she must check for the infection." Musa shrugged, "Sometime it happen."

"Tell her it's fine," I told him, pretending not to notice how shrill my voice was sounding. "Tell her to go away!"

"But Charlie…"

"Just tell her, damn you!"

Musa sighed, then let out a string of uncypherable gibberish. Loiyan replied heatedly, but he cut her off, and to my immense relief, impatiently gestured her to leave forthwith.

Her look of disgust was unmistakable as she let go the linen and headed for the exit, muttering along the way.

"Wait!" I called.

She stopped.

"What did she say?"

Musa hesitated. "She say that if there is the infection it is very bad. She say if she cannot see him in time maybe it need cut off."

A long moment passed.

Loiyan waited.

I lay back on the pallet, hands at my side. Then I turned my face to the wall and tried to think of England.

Soft footsteps approached, then the warmth of her leg touching mine. The air felt cool on my skin when she removed the cloth.

I closed my eyes.

An eternity passed, but still she continued to study her beastly work. Would the slut never cease her ogling? Finally I could take it no longer, I just had to look.

Her face was knit with concern, not the lascivious desire I'd imagined. She gently took my member between thumb and forefinger, carefully turning it this way and that, studying it very closely. There was a bowl of water at her knee. Into this she dipped a cloth then proceeded to wash the dried blood away with infinite care. The water was warm and soothing, and most of the grime came away easily. Even the incised area was not so bad. I accepted the sting with little more than a hitch of my breath.

My eyes found her face, divining the tenderness in her, the care with which she held me. She was bent over her work, so totally concentrated that she didn't notice when the fold in her robe came loose. Hypnotized now, my eyes remained riveted to a glimpse of the smooth roundness of her breast. It looked so delectable that I wanted to fondle it, to reach out and touch her with the same gentleness she used when touching me.

All my life, there had only been the terrible weight of my duty. I had seldom known the touch of a woman, and never one such as this.

There was a dull 'thwack' at the base of my member.

From close by Musa said, "Please, Charlie Smithers, you must not be hard. Makes bleed."

But although Loiyan wagged an admonishing finger at me, she did not look displeased.

41

Chapter Four

I was surprised how quickly I healed…in every respect.

It was a matter of days before I was deemed fit enough to be carried around on my litter. The only proviso being that I had an escort. I hadn't forgotten the *Laibon* wished ill of me, and neither had Musa. So, in addition to keeping my ankles carefully covered so as not to show Loiyan's healing application, four of his warriors were detailed as a guard every time we left the hut. As well, two more stood sentinel at its entrance twenty-four hours a day.

I suppose it was because of my being bed-ridden that I hadn't noticed the tight security earlier, but now I was out and about, it was coming home to me with a vengeance.

It didn't take long to see that the village was divided into two camps. On the one side was Musa and his supporters, on the other the *Laibon* and his.

I should explain that this was not a regimented affair. Such a thing in so small a village would have led to bloodshed long ago, and no one wanted that – the ignorant foreigner's blood being the possible exception. No, the community, as would a village of similar size in England, was tight-knit, and often interwoven with relations every which way you might care to mention. So to say the two camps were *war* camps would be a slight exaggeration. Rather, they were loosely knit groups of alliances that could, and often did, change from one party to the other as precociously as the breeze.

I had now been six weeks amongst the Maasai, although, according to Musa, I had been unconscious for much of the first two; and though my outings had been few and far between, and I was anxious to return to my old life at Lord Brampton's side, I have to admit I was keen with interest, so it didn't take long for me to see how the land lay.

I had already seen the vast herds of the giant brahmas grazing on the endless grasslands – so much larger than our own small breeds of cattle in Britain – but I had no idea how vitally central they were to the Maasai way of life.

Of course Musa had accompanied me during my outings, and did most of the talking as my bearers lugged me along. So it was from him that I first learned of the Maasai dogma – which was simple enough, heaven knows: all the cattle in the world belonged to them.

"Enkai say to Maasinta, the very first Maasai, *'I have given you the cattles. You must love them as I love you.'*" Musa looked out upon his own cows quietly grazing. You only had to look at him to see he believed every word.

Perhaps I should have, but what I hadn't quite grasped yet was the avarice burning in the Maasai soul to acquire more and more cattle – which, in addition to being a sacred gift from their god, were also their form of currency – and the way of augmenting their herds made very little difference to them.

"You see these two?" We had sauntered, unafraid, in amongst the burly brutes. Unused as I was to pastoral pursuits it took some doing on my part to cover my nervousness, I can tell you. But the cattle continued their grazing with little notice of us, very few even bothering to raise their enormously horned heads to have a quiet, soulful look. Apparently, they were as unconcerned as the Massai, neither having the least fear of the other. Musa had stopped by a mottled grey and a black with a white blaze. He scratched the grey at the base of her tail. There was a contented rumble from deep in her chest. "I took them with many others from a Yaaku village six days from here. And that one," another grey nursing a black calf, "was one of forty I took from the Aasay." He smiled, obviously relishing the memory.

And this was yet another thing I learned fairly quickly. The Yaaku and the Aasay, along with others such as the Akie, the Sengwer, Mediak and the Kisankasa just for starters, were neighbouring tribes (inclusively given the derogatory name '*Dorobo*') to whom the Maasai gleefully rendered the neighbourly service of stealing their cattle. In fact, to the Maasai, stealing cattle was equally as important on the road to manhood for the *moran* – the warrior – as was their rite of circumcision. Hence their view of the *Dorobo* as a lesser race who, with their cattle (and any others of their possessions that came to hand) were

43

natural prey, and almost as necessary to their way of life as the cattle were themselves.

Another thing that I learned was central to them – and I suppose it only made sense – was their views on grass.

Musa surveyed the scene for many miles around with evident satisfaction. "These are good grazing lands, Charlie Smithers. We have been here half a moon already and there is still much grass, and the river is near by." He seemed to wallow in his contentedness, "It is good."

Then, in our wandering, we happened to pass a wild fig tree, and wouldn't you know it, nothing would do but they set me down; whereupon everyone, Musa included, gathered a handful of the more promising green shoots and placed them amongst the tree's roots, apparently, as an offering. Then, without a word being spoken the whole time, they picked me up and we continued on our way.

I decided to query Musa on what had just happened.

"The fig tree give us the cattles. We give thanks to the fig tree," he explained.

"The fig tree? I thought it was Enkai that gave you the cattle."

"Enkai, yes," he agreed. "He give us the cattles."

Confused more than ever, I motioned back to the tree, "So, the fig tree is Enkai?"

"No," Musa shook his head, probably wondering how I'd come by such a silly notion, "it is a fig tree."

Then he sensed my confusion. "Enkai send the cattles *through* the fig tree. The fig tree – the *oreti* – is sacred. The grass, he too is sacred, you see?" He spread his hands as if to say, 'Now, wasn't that simple?'

I looked out upon that vast throng of bovine currency, then back to the gnarled old fig tree, and finally back to Musa.

"Anyway, that is the story," he said.

But as ridiculous as this story was, there could be no denying the practical importance of grass to their way of life, and I suppose it's to the Maasai's credit they realized as much, so much so that it was exalted almost to the point of being deified.

Apart from the thanksgiving ritual to the fig tree, when warriors from separate villages met – and on the off chance they weren't in a bloodthirsty mood – a switch of grass held out in the hand meant they came in peace. Grass was used to cover containers of milk to keep out evil spirits, and was shaken over heads during weddings and other rituals as a blessing. It was even forbidden to till the soil to grow vegetables because, to the Maasai, Enkai had given them the land as pasture and it was sacrilege to use it for what they considered a lesser purpose. The point is, since that time I've traveled far and wide and have borne witness to all sorts of religious mumbo jumbo: where the natives will worship a bush, or a clay figurine, or even a rock, or anything else you might care to think of. And it's not that I'm a particularly religious man myself, you understand – the Crimea saw to all that – but nothing made more practical sense than the reverence these people held for those humble and withered shoots of grass. Because without grass there was no life, pure and simple.

As we continued on, I saw still greater flocks of goats and sheep being shepherded by young boys. I hadn't noticed them before, and was surprised.

"Why do you keep these flocks," I asked. "Surely they compete with the cattle for grazing."

"But we must have," Musa explained, eyes wide with wonder at what other stupid things were going to come out of my mouth. "We need for eat."

Now, I don't mind a leg of mutton every now and then, and I suppose that goat meat will serve when there's nothing else to hand, but when I close my eyes and dream of the food back in England, the savoury smell of my mum's roast beef and gravy always seeps into my mind, to the point where I sometimes wake up drooling.

"But you have all that," I said encompassing the herds with a wave, "the best food there is."

Well, you would have thought that I'd just called his mum a slut.

"You are *savage*, Charlie Smithers! Barbarian!" Musa's chin was suddenly quivering with rage at the very thought of

45

slaughtering any one of his beloved cows. "What sort of peoples are you English!? What kind of demons would be killing my cattles?! What sort of....of....of....*monsters*?!"

He'd worked himself up into such a state I thought he was going to come at me. In fact, he was gripping his spear in such a way that I was sure of it. But as I hurriedly babbled my apologies, assuring him it was only my ignorance that had put words in my mouth, he finally managed to stop his trembling and bring himself back under control. But although he was polite to me afterwards, in a distant sort of way, for the rest of that day I caught him eyeing me warily as though wondering what sort of being he had brought amongst his people.

I derived later that he mustn't have flown into such a passion over the mere thought of slaughtering one of his precious animals; it wasn't unheard of, after all. Bullocks were regularly killed and eaten at several of their various rituals: births, deaths, weddings, graduations from child to warrior, from warrior to elder, and so on. But these were all of religious significance. The eating of the flesh of the cow or bullock, which was sacred, must have been to them akin to the eating of Enkai, himself, I suppose as a sort of blessing. Not so different, I might add, than our eating of the Host back in Britain – only much more beneficial in the terms of protein – but the very idea of doing so simply as a matter of course must have seemed to Musa as sacrilege of the highest order.

However, be that as it may, amongst other things, I couldn't regard their superstitious beliefs as being anything other than a shocking waste of good pasture, and good beef. For, except for those rituals and culling the odd beast that was sick or infirm, they never even considered thinning their herds. Nor was there ever any question of being satisfied with the numbers they had, either, or indeed, that they might have too many. For to understand the Maasai mind was to understand their literal and unquestioning acceptance of Enkai's assurance that every cow *in the entire world* belonged to them; that, in fact, they were nothing less than a gift from Heaven to his chosen people. It was the driving force to their entire existence. So you see, when they helped themselves to the herds of the *Dorobo*, in their minds they weren't stealing them so much as *liberating*. Such pursuits weren't all *just* for fun and games (although they were all that and more). To them it was a holy crusade; not just a right, but a veritable duty, no less than an obeisance to God's commandment.

When put in that sort of context, perhaps it's not so surprising to note that, while a Maasai would balk at the thought of going to any great trouble to procure medicine for a sick wife or child, it is not uncommon that he will walk many miles to do the same for a cow.

With this sort of philosophy firmly embedded, it is only logical to suppose that, as one generation of cattle rustling zealots followed the other, they succeeded in compiling herds that must have numbered in the tens of thousands.

What the *Dorobo* or anyone else who lay in their path thought of this, I could only guess.

However, having said all that, in order to disabuse you of the notion that bovine theft was of a *purely* religious significance, it should be pointed out that various sub-tribes of the Maasai – Samburu, Chamus and Arusha, to name a few – were not above stealing from one another, or, indeed one village from another, which would suggest value of a monetary nature rather than any sort of religious devotion.

But I suppose what really makes me stop and think are those plain, weathered, slow-spoken farmers back home in Yorkshire, secluded on their windswept hills, tough as nails while they quietly go about their business of tending their modest herds of equally wild and tough as nails cattle. Then just suppose, along comes Johnny Maasai with his peculiar creed and starts rounding everything up, lock stock and barrel, and when asked just what the hell he thinks he's doing, explains that this Enkai fellow has said that all their herds really belong to His chosen people.

I wonder if I can truly imagine their reaction? I mean, the sheer audacity was hard to get my mind around.

I suppose there's nothing new in believing you are of the Chosen People. The ancient Israelites of the Old Testament come to mind, and the similarity between the two races were striking – both nomadic herdsmen, both believers in the rite of

47

circumcision (for whatever that's worth), both about as inclined to peace as a war-crazed Mongol (another pastoralist of note), with all the riches of China lying within his grasp, and both shrugging off the ensuing slaughter and plunder as being nothing more than the fulfillment of God's will!

It rather takes your breath away, it really does.

Still, as their herds continued to grow and grow, using up more and more pasture in less and less time, I couldn't help thinking of all the many thousands of Maasai villages, each miserly accruing their own vast herds, and the breathtaking amount of land and water required to maintain it all, and I wondered how long it could go on. To the Maasai mind it would continue this way forever, certainly, or at least until all the cattle in all the herds in all the world were under their care. And perhaps they had a point, for this was the seemingly endless Serengeti, or the Great Rift Valley (or Maasai Mara as the Maasai themselves called it) and it was truly huge: over a hundred thousand square miles of virtually endless pastureland.

But I wondered if it was truly as endless as it seemed.

To begin with, to compare the green hills of England with these plains which were parched so much of the year was almost laughable. The acreage required to feed just one of those huge brahmas during its lifetime must have been staggering in its own right, if there was nothing else to consider, but of course there was. For the Maasai did not roam these lands alone.

Many times during my sojourn there, I literally could not see that great plain for teeming herds of wildebeest, eland, antelope, elephants, giraffes, zebra, you name it – the whole adding up to what must have been untold millions – most competing with the Maasai for that most holy of holies, the grass. And it's not that the Maasai did anything about it, either. For another curious thing about these people was that, apart from the odd wildebeest or eland (which they considered wild cattle) they refused to hunt, preferring their sheep and goats to wild game. The one major exception being lions, and then not for food, but yet one more rite for young warriors to pass on their long and arduous road to manhood. The result was that they did their level best to thin out the one species – the king of all predators – that might arguably have been more use to them alive.

I'm telling you these things not to bore you, nor to try to influence you with my own prejudices, but rather to attempt to give you some idea of this alien society I had become enmeshed in, and even then, you may take my word for it that I haven't begun to scratch the surface. Clever, cheerful, hospitable and considerate (perhaps even noble) and certainly as brave as all get out, your typical Maasai was undeniably master of his domain. Yet he had one glaring blind spot – his cattle. Although I must admit that avarice is not unique to any one race, their curious beliefs blinded them to their real wealth which was the land itself, and those same beliefs made their husbanding of it all the more likely to fail one day in the future.

However, that is all by the by, and but for an insight into these people's minds, has little to do with my humble chronicle.

The sun was just westering when we returned to the village. But instead of our normal tranquil passage to shelter, this time we were met by the *Laibon* and his usual sour expression. Behind him stood another evil looking chap decked out in rich ornaments with plugs in his ears nearly as big as Musa's. He gave the chief a look of considerable dislike before turning his malevolent eyes on me. "Hello," I thought, "this one's trouble."

And I was right, too. For it wasn't long into the ensuing conversation that I realized this was none other than Parasayip, the *Laibon*'s son.

Hitherto, there had been the odd chance run-in with the shaman – such incidents were impossible to avoid in a small community – but those times he had seemed content to show his dislike with no more than the odd sneer and a muttered curse. Now it seemed he meant business.

The old fiend started things off by shaking about what looked to be the horn of a buffalo. The way it rattled seemed to suggest it was filled with pebbles. This was confirmed shortly after when he flicked his wrist and a few were dispensed upon the ground, whereupon the old cove descended upon them with avid interest. Then, after counting them – and thereby gaining a valuable insight of the future, no doubt – he lost no time in launching a long tirade, at times pointing to heaven, then to Musa, and then, with something of a flourish, to my humble self, gibber-jabbering all the while. When that was done, he scarcely paused for breath before launching into a stream of vitriol so passionate he actually stamped his foot and shook his finger in Musa's face, looking for all the world as though he were scolding a naughty boy.

And wouldn't you know it? When the *Laibon* was waning – from lack of breath, presumably – his son took up the cause, ranting something terrible. He was pointing out to the hedged enclosure, where the cattle were just thinking of settling in for the night, and then at me and began to shake his head so vigorously his earlobes were flying around like a girl's skirts, threatening to do him an injury.

As I said earlier, I had now been six weeks amongst these folk, and they had not been completely wasted in idleness. If the sentences were brief, or the words spoken slowly and clearly, I could often understand most of what was being said. But this lot was blurted out in a long, rapid stream, so I found it was necessary to await Musa's translation.

"The *Laibon* say you are bad luck," Musa said never taking his eyes off of the charming couple. "He say you are the Red Man and will bring much suffering to our peoples."

"Nothing new there. What's the other one saying?"

"Parasayip say you not go to the cattles. Brings much misfortune. He say you are demon that Enkai push from heaven and should be kill-it."

I didn't have to be a genius to see that I was in frightful danger. The *Laibon* and his son weren't being too subtle about wanting me dead and gone. Yet if his notion of trying to sell me to the villagers as a demon was a bit of inspiration, it had also given me an idea of the best way with which to fight back.

Moving only my head, I turned slowly until I was looking Parasayip full in the face. When our eyes met, I held them.

Of course while all this was going on, the usual crowd began to gather to bear witness to this latest battle of wills. Ever since my arrival, the villagers had viewed me with uncertainty, and it was plain that *Laibon* & Son had been using the intervening time to drum up support for their agenda. In addition, they seemed to have stepped up the sabre-rattling a little by suggesting that it was, perhaps, good policy to skewer yours truly as soon as conveniently possible, and without saying so, thereby deliver a serious blow to Musa's leadership. But they didn't have to say that. It was written all over their ugly faces.

But as I had mentioned earlier, the *Laibon* had a following, and apart from that, the Maasai were among the most superstitious asses in all of Africa. When their medicine man said I was a demon, you could bet they were listening with at least half an ear, and sure enough, there was some angry muttering going on in the crowd behind him.

Well, this put me in a pretty pickle. Musa had begun to remonstrate, but I knew it was going to take a powerful lot of talking to sway this bunch, and the *Laibon* syndicate weren't listening anyway. No, words weren't going to serve this time, but I hoped I knew what would.

Even though I wasn't much more than a political pawn in their big picture, my hide happened to mean a lot to me, and when all was said and done, I'd rather keep it as not. Now, here I was, backed into a corner, and the only way out that I could see was to give these fools what they wanted. And what they wanted was a demon.

I continued to hold Parasayip's eyes with my own, willing myself not to blink.

I was relieved to see that junior seemed to have taken papa at his word that I was everything he said I was, because while Musa and the *Laibon* were verbally duking it out, the wordless duel happening between him and myself was pregnant with tension.

I could see I had him, if I could refrain from blinking, or doing anything else that was human, of course. In a way, I almost felt sorry for the blighter, because I could tell what he was thinking – '*Cor, now I've gone an' done it. I've just made 'im mad, I 'ave. Now I'm for it, sure as blazes!*' Yet at the same time, he couldn't be seen to back down. The loss of face would have been terrible.

He must have felt awfully alone.

51

I was scarcely aware when the shouting had subsided, but it registered that we were the main attraction now. All eyes were on Parasayip and the demon. And if I knew anything about anything, they were wondering what the demon was going to do next.

That's the strange thing about the supernatural. Although no one wants anything to do with it, there's still an undeniable attraction that draws people like flies to jam.

Like I was saying, the tricky part was keeping my face a mask of stone. And though it's a help to know your life's on the line if you don't, neither is it the easiest thing in the world to maintain. I had to think of something quick, because as much as they feared it, the home crowd wanted to see a show, and I couldn't very well go on like this forever.

My bearers – practical fellows that they were – had set me down when they saw the *Laibon* was in one of his more long-winded moods. I suppose they were tired of lugging me around all day as it was. So when they were faced with this further delay, they must have thought '*Sod this for a farthing, my arms already feel like spaghetti,*' and had decided to take a breather.

Which was fortunate, because if they hadn't set me down, what transpired would likely have caused them to drop me instead, and that wouldn't have done at all.

I had remembered my first confrontation with the *Laibon* and how he'd used body language to describe the evil Red Man that Musa had brought into their midst. Although it hadn't been his intention, he'd shown me how he expected a demon to act. All I had to do was give that to him.

Slowly, never taking my eyes from Parasayip, I raised my arms over my head, and drawing from memory, hooked my fingers into claws.

The crowd began to murmur; they wouldn't have been human if they didn't. And neither would it have been human if Parasayip – who really believed he was locked in a life or death struggle with a demon, the fool – didn't take a step back. When that happened everyone else took a step back as well. No one said a word. Perhaps many wanted to: some to urge Parasayip to stand up like a man, or others to curse him for being a coward, but no one was going to take the chance of bringing my attention to their own mangy carcass. Brave though the Maasai may be in all things temporal, it seemed, as I'd hoped, that a demon was another kettle of fish altogether.

I have to admit a bit of thunder would have been welcome just then. It would have made things a lot easier, and would probably have been enough to make them turn tail all on its own. But the sky was clear and tranquil, so there was no help coming from that quarter.

In lieu of that, I continued to raise my hands over my head until they could go no higher.

The villagers shuffled back a bit further, but otherwise held their ground. I burned holes into Parasayip until my eyes watered, and was rewarded when I saw his bottom lip start to tremble. When I hunched my back and lowered my head – only then breaking eye contact – you could have cut the tension with a knife.

And the damned fools weren't moving!

Dash it all! Didn't they know I was the evil Red Man?! Didn't they know that if they didn't high-tail it out of there *vite* I was going to summon all the dark forces at my command and bring them down on their stupid superstitious heads? Didn't they care a tinker's damn about saving their worthless hides?

And don't you know, when I listened to the absolute silence that was greeting my performance, I realized they did indeed want to run and hide, and never come out for a fortnight. But it seemed I'd done my job all too well, for they were rooted where they stood through sheer terror.

Silently I cursed. I was fast running out of tricks.

I was about to try an unworldly growl, just to bring home to them that the opening of the gates of Hell was imminent, when everything went dark.

"Scream," Musa whispered in my ear.

Right away I knew what had happened. Musa, that wonderful darkie, had taken the blanket from my litter when I sat up to take on Parasayip. He must have sensed what was required, and that I had nothing else up my sleeve with which to pull it off.

I let out a bellow.

53

"No you fool! Not like that, like a demon! Quick! I tell them I hold you so they can run."

I started screaming like a banshee, hoping this was more what a Maasai demon would sound like.

If it wasn't, no one was complaining. Musa gasped out a quick sentence or two while doing his best to sound as though he were Elijah wrestling with the Angel of Death. To add some verity, I began to struggle, poking the blanket all over with my fingers so all those watching might better imagine my horrible transformation into an inhuman creature trapped beneath its folds.

Thankfully, that was enough to tip them over the edge. Over my own screaming, I heard a cry of terror, and then another hard on its heels. Then all at once everyone was doing it, milling about and shouting until they'd built up a good head of steam. Then they were off, pelting into the night as hard as they could go, and letting the devil take the hindmost....literally.

I continued shrieking and punching until I feared I was losing my voice or my arms would drop off. When Musa finally lifted the blanket from my head – and I saw it was safe to desist from being a demon – I found we were alone. The *Laibon*, Parasayip, the villagers, everyone was gone, including the guards and my bearers.

For some reason Musa did not look pleased.

"You must go to hut. Can you manage?"

Well, it wouldn't be as dignified as what I'd become accustomed to, but I guessed that I could get along on my own.

"But can't you help me?" I asked, trying not to whine.

He regarded me severely.

"No, I must go."

"But, where? Why?" I was confused.

"Listen!"

I did as I was told. A nervous lowing was coming from the direction of the kraal.

Oh dear.

"You frightened cattles with *screamings*!"

Chapter Five

With that Musa was off into the night to check on his precious cattle much the same way as – periodically throughout the day – my Scottish Uncle Murchadh used to sneak up to his bedroom to count the gold he kept hidden under his mattress, supposedly to put his mind at ease that his godless English nephew hadn't been at it when he wasn't looking.

Left on my own, I had managed to hobble a short distance when I saw Loiyan hurrying towards me. She must have summoned all of her courage to come, for though she had not been a witness to what had transpired, she had to have heard my demoniacal shrieks and the subsequent stampeding of the villagers.

"Chah-lee!" she cried when she saw me, and coming on with all speed, arrived just in time. Musa had had crutches fashioned for me, but I'm afraid I had been delinquent in my exercise, and was not at all adept at using them as of yet. The short distance I had succeeded in traversing had been surprisingly exhausting, and I was on the point of falling when her shoulder appeared under my arm. I leaned on her heavily, and although staggering under my weight, she was able to help me forward.

Once we reached my hut she continued to aid me and saw further to my comfort. At length, when I was propped against the center pole and was seated upon cushions of skins, I began to feel better, and indicated to her that I wanted drink.

Ever since the day when I had first arrived, Loiyan had, more or less, been my constant attendant. Apart from being both doctor and nurse, she also cooked my meals, and by and large had assumed the role of housekeeper.

Looking back now, I suppose I should have been surprised at her attention, but for some curious reason that's not the way I remember it. She had always been there. It wasn't that I wasn't grateful, because I was, yet there was something permanent about her that seemed only natural to take for granted to a certain extent. She was there at the first; she was here now. It quite literally never entered my mind to expect anything other than that she would continue to be there when I needed her for the extent of my sojourn amongst her folk; nor, curiously, did it ever occur to me to question why.

Of course, due to his many chiefly duties, Musa was not always able to be on hand, so it was not uncommon for Loiyan and myself to spend periods of time alone together. At first there were long silences when she would come in to inspect my various injuries, and apply a salve or ointment with little communication other than signing an interrogative, 'are your bindings too tight?' or 'does this give you much discomfort', and the replies could be easily supplied with a nod or a shake of the head, or a shrug as the case may be. Yet I suppose I am a naturally gregarious fellow, and I had some interest in this world I found myself living in. So it wasn't at all out of character when she was shuffling things around, and just generally making the place shipshape, that I would point to this or that and say the English word before inquiring what the equivalent was in Maa. And such was the beginning of my education in that language. As mentioned earlier, a fair amount of progress was being made at my end, and had gotten to the point where a halting communication was possible in that language, but it was Loiyan herself, harbouring her own curiosity, who by far made the larger gains in bridging the gap between us. So, as each was familiar with the extent of the other's knowledge, we were able to carry on relatively fluent conversations in a mixture of both languages.

By now, of course, I had no illusions that she was an ignorant savage, because, savage though she may be, she was very intelligent indeed. Her knowledge of medicine alone was enough to impress anyone, whether on the Serengeti or in a modern hospital in the center of London. But that by no means exhausted her ability, or her desire, for learning.

It wasn't long before I saw she had a natural gift for languages, and although I must admit it took me a while to get used to the incongruence of this fantastic stereotype of a savage, as ever there was, addressing me in my own tongue, I found it no great hardship, in time, just as it had been with Musa.

"Not *enkiroret*," she demurred with a shake of her head, referring to that enjoyable beverage of my first night, "*nailang'a*. It better for you."

Nailang'a was a mixture of milk and cow's blood to which, as you may guess, I was not partial in the least, yet the Maasai were great believers in its invigorating powers. In fact Loiyan had made sure I took a dosage of the stuff daily, and had overruled my despairing protests with a patient ease which reminded me uncomfortably of my mum coaxing cod-liver oil down my throat when I was a young lad.

"Don't want *nailang'a*," I mumped.

"But it make you strong, Chah-lee," she said with a persuasive smile, all the while bringing the bowl nearer to my lips.

"But it tastes awful."

"It will make you a man - a great lover!" She said without a trace of coyness. Their attitude towards that sort of thing could really be unnerving at times.

"You people have some odd notions about manhood," I sulked, taking a resigned slurp. "Don't see what this has to do with making me a great….with making me stronger. Like this *emorata* thing, for instance, that's a bloody awful way of turning someone into a man."

I had healed from my circumcision some weeks earlier, but was still smarting from the memory.

"But you *are* now a man," she cried, "a *moran*, a warrior!"

"I've already been to war," I replied quietly.

"Say you so?" but then she dismissed it as of no consequence. "But you are now beautiful…except for long nose…and white skin…and great dark hair on body."

"Nonsense, how can this be?"

But Loiyan was silent.

I tried to press her, but she changed the subject.

"I heard screamings. I was frightened."

So I told her all about the incident with the *Laibon* Corporation. She took the news soberly.

"They try to kill you."

57

"Yes, well, they wanted to but they couldn't work up enough nerve, you see?"

"They will try again," she replied with a worried frown.

"I don't see how," I shrugged. "They must have lost bags of face when they turned tail."

"The *Laibon* is very powerful, Chah-lee. He hate you."

"But why?"

"In Musa's hands you are a spear. The *Laibon* see this, and think you must die."

The memory of my earlier conversation with the chief re-visited me - of his scheme to employ me as the demon Red Man in order for him to rest cattle from the *Laibon's* son, Parasayip. He hadn't brought the subject up since then, but instead appeared content to allow me the time to regain my strength. Well, tonight had seemed to have reinforced the idea to everyone that I was, indeed, a demon, and that only he could control me. So, in one sense, the episode had played squarely into his hands.

But the timing was off. I wasn't anywhere near fully recovered, and so, vulnerable should the *Laibon* recover his courage. He had shown he wasn't a fool. He'd probably known what the stakes were the moment he saw Musa and his fellows first carting me into the village. Tonight's loss of face, and Musa's corresponding gain only meant that the *Laibon's* answer had to be swift as well as final.

Hard on this thought, there came the sound of voices from outside. Wide eyed, Loiyan put her knuckles to her mouth. I grabbed the nearest weapon to hand, which was the wooden bowl, and prepared to sell my life dearly.

The hide covering the entrance was flung aside, and Musa stooped into the hut.

I made a great show of studying the bowl's exquisite craftsmanship from various angles, all the while trying to convey that flinging it at his head had been the very last thing on my mind.

"The cattles are quiet," he said wearily, "there are men guarding outside."

"Then all's well?" I asked cautiously.

58

Musa's face was grave when he looked at me. "You must leave, Charlie Smithers," he said.

Well, now he was seeing sense. It had been a mad scheme from the get-go.

"Fine," I said, "you will take me back to my own people."

"No."

Somewhere in the night, a hyena cackled at something wildly amusing. Off in the distance, a lion sleepily rumbled an angry reply.

For a moment I couldn't credit that I'd heard right. But when I stared up into his face, I was met with impassive determination. The atmosphere grew heavy with tension.

"But, are you mad?" I asked, incredulous, "I can't go out there," I gestured wildly into the darkness with all of its attendant nocturnal predators. "I wouldn't last 'til morning."

"Even more danger for you here."

"But....but...." I floundered about, aghast that this cruel nigger was thinking of chucking me out of the village to my certain, horrible death. There wouldn't be as much as a toenail left to show anyone what had become of me, let alone a headstone that read 'Charlie Smithers R.I.P'.

"But where will I go?" I asked without much hope, for of course, if I wasn't to be returned to my own kind, there was no where else *to* go.

Musa's uncertain frown plunged any last waning possibility to despair. For a fleeting second I wondered if he wasn't sure whether I might be the Red Man, after all, and that maybe it would be better for everyone if he did set me alone out on the plain so Enkai could sort out the mess. Of course it was ridiculous, but at the same time I remembered his shocked indignation when I had suggested that he should slaughter some of his precious cattle, and I wasn't so sure.

Then:

"I know a place," Loiyan said quietly.

Musa looked at her pretty sharp, and spoke rapidly in Maa. I couldn't catch what he said, but I could tell he wasn't too happy she'd decided to put her oar in.

59

But Loiyan, also speaking rapidly, answered pretty sharp herself. In fact, as the argument swayed back and forth, it seemed to me that she was giving at least as good as she got.

In no time at all, Musa was in a towering rage, but if he was expecting the usual subservience from her, he was very much mistaken, because it was nowhere in evidence. She was on her feet in a trice, hands clenched into tiny fists, jabbering at him for all she was worth. From where I was sitting, I thought she was nothing short of magnificent – her being my only hope of salvation having nothing to do with that point of view, naturally.

The battle of wills went on for some time, but Musa was already tired, and eventually showed signs of weakening. Finding himself on the defensive on all fronts, he stood helpless while she bore in and wore him down. Finally, when it was all but over, he stood there, exhausted and demoralized, but then surprised me when he threw back his head and gave a great bellow of laughter. He arched an eyebrow at her, then with a knowing look, murmured a question, motioning towards me with his head.

If you think that a darkie can't blush, well, they can...I assure you.

But whatever the question was, Loiyan answered neither nay nor yea. Instead, having got her way, she briskly returned to the business at hand.

"There is a place to the north, perhaps one moon away."

"What place is that, little cheetah?" Musa inquired sarcastically. Perhaps he was smarting from losing the argument more than he let on.

"It is safe," she said, motioning silently to the entrance. The point was well taken. The guards outside had ears, the extent of their loyalty unknown.

But Musa shook his head, "There is nothing to fear. Sakuda and Tepilit are sound men." Then, perhaps for my benefit, added, "They are my brothers."

Yet in spite of his own assurance, Musa lowered his voice and asked, "And how will you bring Charlie Smithers to this wonderful place, oh wise one. Or have you forgotten that he cannot walk?"

"We will take the Angry One."

60

For a long moment the quiet was deafening. When comprehension finally registered, he was incredulous.

"I see now that for all of your clever plans, you are but a foolish woman! What do you know of the Angry One? How will you control him? Most assuredly, you will be killed!"

Unperturbed, she replied, "The slave woman, Kakenya, is of the Samburu. She will know the Angry One's ways."

"Kakenya?" Musa ejaculated as though wondering what other nonsense would assail his ears this night, "but she is a stupid crazy woman, a mere slave!"

He was slack-jawed with amazement before he regained enough control of himself to address Heaven.

"Enkai! Why have You sent this foolish woman to torment me? She proposes to take the Angry One and the stupid crazy Samburu slave and make an end of Charlie Smithers, and thereby my hopes of Parasayip's cattles. Please! I beg You, strike her down with your thunder!"

Personally, I couldn't see what he was on about. Just minutes ago he, himself, had seemed willing to surrender the political advantage of keeping me alive for no better purpose than as a form of damage control. But I suspect those in the halls of power are like that all over the world; if it's not their own idea, it's not worth considering.

When, after a pregnant pause, neither Enkai, nor any other god, appeared willing to strike anyone down, he began to pace back and forth, muttering under his breath.

Once more the submissive woman, Loiyan waited with bowed head, folded hands, and a placid smirk. On the other hand, I looked from one to the other, totally at sea. Who was this Angry One fellow, anyway? And how would he make escape possible?

At length Musa ceased his mutterings and swung on Loiyan. "Well?" by the look on his face, I wasn't so sure but that there might be some thunder after all, "What are you waiting for, foolish woman? Run and get the stupid crazy slave!"

After Loiyan left, Musa resumed his muttering and pacing. I thought to venture to ask what all this was about, but taking

61

note of his far from serene brow, decided it could wait for a bit longer.

She was gone no more than a minute before returning with a withered hag in tow. The woman, apparently Kakenya, the Samburu slave, was of an indeterminate age, but it was clear she was well past her prime when – if, in fact, that time had ever been – she could attract a man's eye. She was dressed in rags, and with dirt ground into every one of her numerous wrinkles, and patches of baldness showing through her ill-kempt and kinky gray hair, looked much ill-used by those years she had experienced. Yet, even though she found herself in the presence of the chief, and the demon Red Man, she was gazing about her surroundings with curiosity, but not fear.

She was the first to speak.

"*Enkirore!*" she demanded, thirstily smacking her toothless gums together.

Given his mood, I thought her impudence was going to drive Musa to apoplexy, so dark did his visage grow. Indeed, he leapt across the room with a bellow of rage and would have brained her with his *orinka* – his throwing club – had Loiyan not intervened.

"Please lord," she said calmly, "she will be of no use if you kill her."

Meanwhile, Kakenya, who had taken no apparent notice of Musa's fury, began to show some of her own for what she apparently considered an appalling lack of good manners from those she obviously considered not as masters, but as her hosts.

"By the hairy balls of Enkai, I said I want *enkirore!* Or are you deaf?"

Musa ground his teeth in fury, the combating struggles - one of his desire to kill this stupid crazy slave, and the other his greed for Parasayip's cattle - playing across his face. He swung around and strode to the far end of the room. There, still with his back to the rest of us, he shouted, "Well, don't just sit there, get it for her!"

Loiyan rose and went to the earthen jar. She filled a bowl and brought it to the crone.

"Well," I ventured, "if this is going to be a drinking affair, I wouldn't mind a drop." I wobbled my own empty bowl suggestively, but to my disappointment, was ignored.

The hag snatched the bowl from Loiyan's hands and drank greedily, rivulets of the honey beer streaming down her chin, onto the withered dugs of her chest. For a long moment there was silence but for her cow-like gulping. When the bowl was empty, she wiped her mouth with a scrawny forearm, and demanded, "More! My throat's as dry as my...." It was a word with which I was not familiar, but her grimy finger was pointing in the general area of her nether regions.

Nervously my eyes ventured to where Musa was standing with his back to us in the corner; except for an agitated pistoning up and down on the tips of his toes, he remained as a statue. Even Loiyan hesitated, but in the end, with an exasperated frown, did as the slave directed. This act was repeated twice more, punctuated by croaks of profanity, before she finally rested the bowl on her lap, belched, and allowed, "By the holy turds of Maasinta, that wasn't bad, though," she added, "not as good as Samburu."

Slowly Musa turned, his eyes burning coals. "Have you no wits, slave! Do you not fear for your life?!"

The hag cackled drily. "I do not fear you, chief."

I could have sworn he was trying to grind his teeth into dust. "Oh, and why is that, oh stupid one?"

"I am no fool," she countered with a bleary eye, "In the middle of the night I am summoned. You have need of me – that is as plain as the nose on your face – something this girl," she motioned dismissively to Loiyan, "remembered even if you did not."

"If you are so wise," Musa glowered sarcastically, "then tell me what I want from you."

"But that is easy!" She cackled then, making a lewd gesture, shook her dusty paps at him. "You want me for..." again, my vocabulary hadn't evolved quite that far, as of yet.

For a long time the air was filled with the crone's screeches of laughter while Musa strove to control himself, and I tried not

63

to retch at the very idea. But when the laughter had subsided into mirthful whimpers, it was Loiyan who spoke.

"We want you to help us."

Kakenya turned on her, eyes narrowing suspiciously.

"How can a mere slave help you, girl?"

The silence was heavy when she replied, "There is danger for the Red Man if he continues to stay here, so he must be away. But he is crippled and cannot walk. I want you to help with the Angry One."

Kakenya's shrewd eyes narrowed even further.

"Well, slave," Musa asked quietly, but there was danger in that quiet, "can you do this?" I thought that a sizeable portion of him hoped she would say no. If that were the case, she would no longer be of use to him, and he would be free to brain her after all.

The hag peered thoughtfully at him. Then, understanding, she said with dawning avaricious wonder, "I am the only one who can help you," and started to cackle all over again.

She stopped abruptly when she felt Loiyan's knife at her throat.

"Cease your noise, witch!" Loiyan hissed icily. "I have an end to my patience. Answer your lord's question!"

Kakenya peered down the length of Loiyan's arm, wincing slightly, as the point of the knife was embedded in her flesh. She seemed to be giving the younger woman a quick re-appraisal. A thin trickle of blood ran down her chest to mingle with the dirt and stale beer.

"I can help you," she said.

My crutches were digging into my armpits while I hobbled along, trying my best to keep up with the others. If aid had been offered, I would have accepted gladly, but such was not the case. Leading the way, Musa was deep in whispered conversation with his brothers, Sakuda and Tepilit, whom he had decided should accompany us. Beside me, Loiyan was burdened with our supplies, and so, unable. Kakenya was too frail, and did not offer in any case. In fact, she hadn't let on that I, a novel white man, and a demon to boot, even existed.

64

To maintain secrecy, we had stolen silently into the night. I had no idea where we were going, had little idea, in fact, as to what we were doing. So much of the immediate past was such a bewildering mystery that I was feeling a bit dizzy, but when I asked either Musa or Loiyan for any sort of enlightenment, they were too preoccupied to supply me with an answer outside of the fact they were taking me to the Angry One – who and wherever that was. It all sounded rather ominous, though. I mean, the *Angry One*? He didn't quite sound like Father Christmas, now did he?

At length I was able to make out giant shadows in the pale moonlight, and realized we had come to the cattle enclosure. A lurking wraith and a barking laugh signaled the presence of at least one hyena close by, no doubt testing the thorned corral for any weakness.

Unconcerned, Musa led the way past the cattle to where the herds of smaller animals were kept. He pulled aside the bush that acted as a gate and entered.

Silently we made our way past the dark, wooly forms, the occasional sleepy bleat the only acknowledgement from them that we were there. In my mind, I tried to put the monicker, Angry One on any of this lot, and almost laughed aloud. Sheep? Angry One? You get my point. In the dark more than ever, I kept my peace, and hobbled on.

Without warning, a huge specter loomed directly in front of me.

Unconcerned, it casually leaned forward and spat in my face.

I started to cry out with surprise, and reeling backwards, would have fallen if Musa hadn't caught me and clamped a hand over my mouth.

"Shhhhh!" He cautioned, "Scares sheeps!"

I nodded mutely and he let me go.

"The Angry One," he whispered with a tremulous gesture.

Myopically, I peered closer at the ominous form. Immediately, there was a bad tempered hiss and the unpleasant sensation of teeth being sunk into my arm.

65

Mindful of the sheep, I squeaked about frantically until I heard a thud, and the teeth removed themselves from my bicep. Kakenya now stood between myself and the beast. In the weak light, I could just make out the club in her hand. Without a word, she took from her shoulder the coil of rawhide I'd seen her take up at my hut. It had been braided into a rope, and one end fastened into a noose. Now I watched while, with amazing dexterity for someone of her years, she tossed the noose over the brute's head, and pulled the line taut.

"Why, it's a camel!" I squeaked, so surprised that I almost forgot about the bloody sheep.

It was, in fact, a dromedary, and how it got to be here, the Lord only knew. One thing was sure, it wasn't about to tell me because, among other things, at the moment its attention was elsewhere. It received the noose with extreme ill humour and tried to bolt. Kakenya held on for dear life, but it was evident the contest wasn't equal.

"Grab the rope!" she hissed to Musa, and that worthy, too stunned to do anything else, obeyed.

Finding his escape thwarted, the Angry One (now a lot of things had become clearer) lunged towards the crone, teeth bared, but was brought up short by the club. He continued to struggle mightily until she shouted something in her language that gave him pause, as though uncertain that he had heard aright. She shouted again, and his neck stretched suspiciously forward as though to study her more closely. Almost, in fact, like someone who believes he may have recognized something from his past, but the incongruency of the time and place had rendered him unsure without taking a second gander.

Unnoticed, the sheep shuffled about, still in their dreams.

Insistently, she commanded a third time. The camel shuffled grumpily, like a brat determined to avoid correction. Then, to my surprise, he slowly sank to his knees like a mountain descending into a crater.

Speaking softly now – who would have thought she was able? – Kakenya crept closer and stroked his muzzle. Quick as a flash, he whipped his head around to bite, but she must have anticipated such mutinous behaviour and was ready. She leapt back and delivered him a whack with the club. He groaned and spat at her for spite. Then, finally at a loss as to what else might be done, was quiet.

More cautiously this time, once again Kakenya approached the beast, crooning reassurance as she advanced.

The Angry One regarded her narrowly, took hateful note of the club, snorted his disgust, and with immense dignity under trying times, submitted to having his poll ruffled.

Without undo haste, she loosened the noose and fastened it into a halter, continuing to speak softly and scratching his tawny head all the while. When at length there came a rumble from deep in his chest that might have been something other than total annoyance, she beckoned me over.

I approached a cautious step on my crutches.

She reached out and patted the great hump, motioning for me to mount.

"Not bloody likely!" I hissed, rubbing the teeth marks on my arm. I'd taken a closer look at the brute and decided that he was only pretending docility.

"Please Chah-lee," Loiyan's whispered at my side, "we must hurry!"

I regarded the creature with considerable dislike. Unconcerned, his head swiveled on that ridiculous neck, held my eyes just long enough to convey his undying contempt, before dismissing me without further interest.

I took a breath and approached nearer, but I was beneath his notice. Turning, I handed my crutches to Loiyan before gingerly climbing aboard, ready at an instant to abandon ship at the first sign of trouble. However, somewhat to my surprise, all remained tranquil until, at last settled, I motioned I was ready. Kakenya uttered a word of command, and with much loud complaining, the Angry One rose to his feet.

As a last eloquent gesture of protest, he broke wind and copiously stooled.

Chapter Six

Tepilit and Sakuda motioned for silence, their heads atilt, listening. For a time we all stopped breathing. I strained my ears, but there was only the wind.

Then Sakuda motioned us onwards with an urgency that seemed to suggest he didn't agree with my findings.

No one spoke, but we broke into a trot.

We had been four days on our journey, and I was finding the going difficult. My previous neglect at maintaining at least a semblance of physical fitness – preferring instead the novelty of being carried around in a litter – had caught up with me. I was finding that the long neglected muscles were now crying out in protest while I did my best to adjust to the Angry One's gait. This was made even more difficult because I was beginning to suspect that the beast didn't have one. I had heard that a camel has a different stride than a horse, and that it took some getting used to, but nothing could have prepared me for the stiff-legged jouncing he provided with such nefarious good humour. I had three falls the first day, and two more on the second, narrowly avoiding re-injuring my ankles. I had managed to hold on throughout the third, but the strain on my body had been merciless. Kakenya told me it would have been much easier with a saddle, but I doubted it; he probably would have jolted that off, too.

I had insisted on making a detour that first morning. I wanted to return to the place where we had fought the crocodiles, the place were the Maasai had saved my life. I'd always planned on doing so as soon as possible, but as yet hadn't the chance. Now my fortunes had taken a turn for the better, and there was even help should the crocodiles still be in residence.

The reason why I wanted to go back was not to conjure up old memories, but to find the gun. As you'll recall, Lord Brampton and I had brought two of them with us that morning when he'd had a go at the rhinos. We'd each had one when we went our separate ways, but mine had become lost during my fall from the cliff. I'd had this in mind when I slung the strap of the cartridge case over my shoulder while preparing to leave the village. On its own it was useless, but vitally necessary should the gun ever be found in one piece.

The crocodiles had, indeed, still been close by when we came to call. I could even pick out the ugly features of my old foe. His malevolent glare said that he recognized me as well. The brothers had been detailed to keep an eye on the monsters while the women and I splashed about in the river, looking for the gun. That is to say, that the women splashed about while I, too infirm to be of much help in that regard, sat on the shore and shouted out helpful suggestions as to where to look. But, after an hour's searching, it was I who found it after all, when the sun glinted off the barrel tucked beneath a shrub some few yards away. I was relieved to see it was still in one piece – the soft mud of the shingle having absorbed most of the impact – and in fact, had survived the fall better than myself. Like me, it had been banged up a bit, but unlike myself, was still serviceable. Once I had it cleaned and oiled, and slung across my back, I'd felt more secure than I had in a long while.

We had barely resumed our journey on the morning of the fourth day when the two warriors began to have suspicions we were being followed.

I would like to think that Musa had sent Sakuda and Tepilit with us out of an act of kindness, but I rather suspected he had been seeking only to protect his investment. But, whatever the reason, their strong bodies and long, wicked spears were a welcome addition to our party.

Not that they were all that enthused, you understand. Traipsing off into the wilderness to play nursemaid to a couple of women and this crippled 'water youth' (white man) was not their idea of a good time. It wasn't as much fun as, say, a good old cattle raid where one could indulge in one's natural bloodlust, and rape to his heart's content. Still there was at least some promise of adventure, and a break from the dull routine of stockman besides. So I suppose it wasn't too bad for them.

At first, Musa's vague promise of adventure had proved uninspiring as there was very little to be found outside of chasing away a pack of hyenas that first night, and a lioness the next day; but that morning, with his ear to the ground, listening to the

69

distant drumming of approaching footsteps, Sakuda had begun to look more interested.

I couldn't grasp the stream of words that subsequently flew between the two warriors, and had to rely on Loiyan.

"Men coming," she said, "perhaps..." she held up all her fingers in both hands, then the thumb and forefinger on her right.

"Twelve men? But how do they know?" I asked.

She shrugged and pointed to the ground. "They listen."

I thought that was so much poppycock, but to humour her, I lay flat on my belly with my ear to the ground, aping Sakuda.

At first, all I got was some dirt in my ear, and the next time I wasn't sure if I was listening to the sound of anything but my own heart beating. But when Sakuda, seeing my interest, took me in hand and lay me down on what he felt was a likely looking spot, I was able to calm my breathing enough to be rewarded with the shadow of a whisper of something that could have been the staccato beat of heavy sandals, or a family of hippopotami wallowing in a pool nearby.

Still, Sakuda seemed to know what he was about. Obviously no stranger to active duty, he was a likely looking fellow somewhere in his mid-twenties with a jagged scar on his left cheek that stretched from eye to jaw, giving him a rather evil rakish look that would have set off all the ladies back in England, had he been white. On the other hand, Tepilit, perhaps a year or so younger, had those typically striking features of the Maasai that were so fine-boned you actually had to look quite closely to see whether he was a male or a female. Not that I ever mentioned that to him, of course. You could never tell just how he would take it.

Up until this point, both young men had refrained from having much to do with me. Perhaps that was because they were naturally shy, but more likely they looked down on me as someone who was inferior – proud as Lucifer, those warriors were. So it was with no small sense of gratification that, after I'd picked myself off the ground and dusted myself off, Sakuda looked at me and slowly – like someone speaking to a half-wit – said, "We go."

Somehow he'd managed for it to sound neither like a question nor a command, but somewhere in between. At any rate, I knew better than to argue.

They had set off in the lead at a faster pace, Loiyan keeping up easily enough, while Kakenya, leading the Angry One, grumbling almost as much as the camel was himself, behaved as though every step was her last, but managed not to fall behind.

After four days, I was pleased that my body was finally coming into its own. I won't say I was staying aboard that woefully erratic creature with anything resembling ease, nor will I say that at the end of the day I wasn't feeling fire and broken glass in every joint, but I was coping, at least, and every day was just a little less arduous than the one before.

I soon found that sitting a camel was nothing like sitting astride a horse. I had tried that at first, but found that I was continually sliding either forwards onto his withers or backwards onto his rump. It had been Kakenya who had shown me how to crook my right leg over the hump and anchor it with my left. Then, with both hands gripped firmly onto the coarse hair inside the crook, I was able to keep my place, although the strain on my arms and back were torture. With the faster pace, the pain was searing.

We didn't stop at noon, but pressed on so as to maximize the separation between ourselves and the party behind. For this was Africa, and I wouldn't have given a brass farthing on the odds that they – whosoever *they* might be – were friendly.

It wasn't until much later that Sakuda called a halt to listen, this time without bothering to put his ear to the ground. As I said, I couldn't hear a thing, but if he could, that meant that those behind us were closing fast.

We trotted along with some urgency for a mile or so when both warriors veered towards the river. Now I could hear the wind rasping from Kakenya's lungs with every breath, even Loiyan was starting to tire, and I knew we couldn't last much longer.

We had been heading north, more or less, always with the Mara on our left, but when we reached the water, Sakuda splashed into the shallows without hesitation and backtracked to the south. We continued on thus for some ways, with me looking anxiously for our pursuers to appear suddenly over the next rise. For while I appreciated that our reversing direction in the water was designed to obfuscate our passage, I also knew we were now heading on an intersecting course with those following. Every moment was fraught with danger.

I was considering calling out to the men that we must change course when we came to a shallow ford with well trampled mud on either shore. Evidently this was a crossing that was common to herds both wild as well as domestic. Our trail would be easily lost in that churned up quagmire.

We struggled through the mud and a short distance up a gentle rise, being careful to stay below the horizon. Then we turned north again and kept on for a few hundred yards until we came to a grove of date palms. At last, the warriors felt that it was sufficiently safe to call a halt.

By now Kakenya had taught me how to command the Angry One to kneel, and that was just as well for, as soon as we stopped, the old woman collapsed into the elephant grass, dead to the world. When the camel had finished grumbling his way to his knees, I slid thankfully to the ground and almost joined the crone. My legs were as rubber, and there was such a deep ache low in my back that I despaired of ever standing straight again.

Foregoing my crutches, I unslung Lord Brampton's gun and crawled over to where Sakuda and Tepilit crouched silently, hidden by the grass and the boles of the trees.

Fingers scrambling from lack of practice, I bit off the wax paper from a cartridge and poured the powder down the muzzle of one of the barrels. Then I pushed the heavy slug in and rammed it down until it was well seated. By the time I had fitted the percussion cap over the nipple of the firelock, heads had begun to appear over a hillock on the other side of the river.

Five….ten….thirteen figures, a baker's dozen – I glanced at Sakuda with growing respect – were swarming over the rise at a run. They were Maasai, even I could tell from this distance. But for their weapons, daubs of paint and fearsome lion mane headdresses, they were naked – a war party.

Without hesitation, they glided over the ground like angels of death, seemingly without effort, their shields held high so as not to tangle with the vegetation, the sun glinting off the razor edges of their long-bladed spears held parallel to the ground, ready for instant use. Yet even more frightening was how they were able to move so quickly over the ground without making a sound, or at least any that my untrained ears might catch. Instead, they slid over the land like deadly black phantoms, floating along with liquid ease until, at length, they disappeared over the next rise, leaving no trace that they had ever been.

I lay motionless long after they were gone. Whichever one of us was to move first, it wasn't going to be me.

That was just as well, for just when I was thinking of asking if it was safe, one of the devils popped up from whence they'd just disappeared.

The beggar seemed to be staring straight at me!

I hugged the ground like a grog-sodden sailor hugging a whore. I believe I forgot to breathe.

Tepilit told me later that this was a common ruse when on the warpath, to check if they were being pursued, or to surprise a backtracking quarry.

Well, I wished he'd told me sooner, because it surprised *me*, right enough, so much so I nearly ruptured myself! The sight of that savage, painted and predatory face was one that I won't soon forget.

The fiend stood there for what seemed an eternity, scanning every inch of ground, listening, perhaps even *smelling*. Even though we were a good three hundred yards off and well hidden, I was convinced those all-seeing eyes had been boring right through me all along. It took a supreme effort of will not to jump up and blaze away at him, but that wouldn't have done at all.

And then he was gone again, melting away like a wraith to catch up his chums.

For a long while after Sakuda and Tepilit had relaxed their vigilance, I didn't dare move so much as a whisker. I didn't trust that bastard one little bit. Even when Tipilit touched my arm and said, "Come, we go," I crawled back to where Loiyan was holding the Angry One with more than a few fearful glancess over my shoulder, I can tell you.

I motioned to where the war party had disappeared, and asked, "Looking for us, you think?"

"They from our village," Tepilit said, his handsome face troubled.

I could see why. If they had been from the village – and the brothers would certainly know – that meant that the *Laibon* still held sway over many of them, enough to send those men all this way to find us. Further to that, it was obvious that they hadn't pursued us this far to enquire about our health. The *Laibon* wanted me dead, and their war dress stated, plain as day, that they were to see to it, come hell or high water. It also meant that Sakuda and Tepilit now found themselves in the unenviable position of defending me – someone whom they had no reason to love – from men they had known from childhood. That knowledge couldn't have made them very happy.

By this time Kakenya was sitting up, but her head was sunk low on her chest, exhausted. Plainly she was done for the day. Yet the two brothers wanted to move farther west, well away from the river. Tepilit prodded her with the butt of his spear, but with no effect. Neither did the point produce any better results. Muttering angrily, he was about to skewer the crone where she lay when I felt it best to intervene.

"Stop," I whispered, for the sight of those devils was still fresh in my mind, "I will help her."

Tepilit regarded me with disgusted disbelief before turning away in a dark dudgeon. Clearly, he didn't believe in mollycoddling slaves, but then, he wasn't British, so he had no way of knowing what was or wasn't done.

Loiyan helped me lift the old woman to her feet. When she looked her question at me, I nodded towards the Angry One.

"But Chah-lee," she protested, "for *you* to ride."

I lifted my crutches from where they straddled by a thong across the camel's back. "I can use the exercise," I said with a smile, but I fear it was rather a weak one.

She looked to be on the point of arguing further, yet for a wonder she didn't, but shrugged instead, and helped Kakenya onto the hump.

"Thank you, kind lady," the old woman's voice was no louder than a whisper, "thank you, kind lord." She was able to cling to the hump as the Angry One rose to his feet, with scarcely a complaint for a change. "I am tired; a worthless old woman, despised by everyone, wanted by none." A sob hitched in her throat and a tear shone in her rheumy old eye. "May your cattle be plentiful, and may you bear many sons for the mercy you have shown me."

Embarrassed by her gratitude, I cleared my throat, and feeling some response was called for, muttered a few words I thought were appropriate.

"And may you have much jigga-jigging in the making of your sons," she continued.

"Oh, think nothing of....pardon?"

"And may your toes curl often in ecstasy."

"Now see here!"

"And may your balls be filled with much…"

"Silence!" I hissed, too scandalized for any other words. But she just kept on voicing her gratitude in her own peculiar way until I felt quite faint. I had thought, somehow, to lead the Angry One, but in the end, unable to listen to any more of her lascivious nonsense, I simply tossed her the rein and let her ramble off on her own.

What with that and struggling along on my crutches, it was a good long while before I could steal a peek at Loiyan.

She was walking beside me, lost in her own thoughts, yet for all that had just transpired, I thought the peaceful serenity on her face was not that of a woman insulted.

We continued west for a few miles until we came to a stream with a grove of sausage trees nearby.

"We camp here," Sakuda said, once more making it sound like something between a statement and a question.

I don't think he quite knew what to make of me. I'm sure that Musa had filled him in, at least to some degree, and neither brother could have been ignorant of the *Laibon*'s opinion, nor of

75

what had transpired four nights ago either, for that matter. So they must have had their suspicions about me, about whether I was a man or a demon. But if they did, aside from that peculiar rising inflection whenever they spoke to me, there was neither deference nor fear in their treatment. In fact, if anything, it was the opposite. They were Maasai, while demon or no, I was a 'water youth'. *Ergo*, I was inferior. Yet, to complicate the issue, I was important enough for them to be roused from their beds so that they might play nursemaid, and as I was the only other man in the party, by far the most preferred individual to communicate with. In the end, they put up with and even indulged me to a degree, but of subservience there was no sign.

Whatever the case, I thankfully agreed to stop. Those few miles had been quite grueling for me. Outside of being on the point of collapse, my ribs were much chafed from the crutches, and my ankles were hurting like the seventh circle of Hell. Besides which, we were far enough away from the river in that rolling country to make any chance of discovery quite miniscule, if we could do without a fire.

With the last of my strength, I hobbled over to the bole of one of the trees and sat down. Ever attendant, Loiyan accompanied me with her bag. She bade me take off my shirt and clucked over the raw sores below my armpits. With her typical gentleness, she applied a salve which was remarkably soothing. Then there was a dressing of leaves – of a species with which I wasn't familiar – bound in place by a thong. That seen to, she now turned her attention to my legs.

Since my trousers had been ruined when she had first set the broken bones, I had since adopted the loin cloth and kilt of the natives. I found that, as well as being wonderfully cool, it served admirably for a convalescing patient as there was no impediment for her frequent inspections of my injuries.

Now placing one of my feet on her lap, she undid the rawhide binding the splints together. There was some swelling in the ankle, but little enough when you considered the punishment I'd put it through. Finding the other to be no worse, she bathed them both in the cool water before applying a different salve from her bag. Finally, she took out rolls of soft leather bandages and wound them expertly from my feet up to my calves, binding them tightly to offer my ankles maximum support.

"They heal well, Chah-lee," she said with approval. Then after a moment's consideration, "Maybe now don't need crutch?" Smiling encouragement, she rose to her feet, holding out her arms, "Come, you stand."

Considering that the last time any significant weight had been put on my ankles had been when they had snapped like dry twigs, just the notion of my standing unaided was enough to make me want to faint.

It must have been written on my face because her smile deepened in that reassuring way she had. "It will be all right."

So, overcoming my misgivings, I took her hands, and she supported me while I slid my back up the trunk of the tree, my feet shifting about unsteadily, trying to recall their role in life. At last I was standing, leaning only slightly against the tree. My brain sent inquiries to my legs. They came back with the surprising news that there wasn't any pain. It would seem that, having outlived their usefulness, the splints themselves had been the contributors to my discomfort.

I grinned.

I pushed myself away from the tree.

I took a step.

I wobbled dangerously and would have fallen, had not Loiyan caught me. She settled my back against the tree and bade me wait. Then knife in hand, she disappeared into the grove, coming back some minutes later with a crude but serviceable cane.

"Here," she said, "you try."

The tri-pod effect made an amazing difference. I took a step, then another, then more and more, not stopping until I was happily exhausted.

Loiyan was standing before me, her satisfaction matching my own.

I gazed deeply into her beautiful, gentle face, and remembered a time when I had not trusted her ability. What a fool I'd been.

"Thank you," I said with deep reverence.

77

"You are welcome, Chah-lee," she said as though my gratitude was ample payment for having given me back my legs. "Now," she said happily, "must makes strong."

For the first time I noticed she held a bowl in her hands. My stomach lurched. It was worse this time. The muck had been dried into pellets.

"It is time for your *nailang'a!*"

Chapter Seven

We continued west for another half day before we thought it safe to turn once more to the north. When we re-made contact with the Mara, we turned to follow it downstream. Our detour had forced an increase in caution and so a delay to our destination, wherever that destination might be.

Kakenya and I were now taking turns riding the Angry One. In truth, I didn't mind not having my ribs crushed like an accordion with every erratic step that cursed beast took, and though I could only go short distances before I had to switch with her, as the days followed, those distances gradually became farther and farther apart as my legs grew ever stronger.

All this time Loiyan had not spoken of where she was taking us, but when I asked her later the next day, she was not reticent.

It's strange that, while I was well aware of the dangers and the travail of the journey, what I remember most of that particular time is her gentle presence close beside me while we trekked along that vast savannah, under the even greater immensity of the warm African sky.

As always, Loiyan.

"We go to the place of the great water," she told me.

"What great water?" I was interested. Often had I overheard Lord Brampton's friends speak of rumours of a great lake deep in the heart of the Dark Continent. Some even claimed that it might very well be the fabled source of the Nile.

She shrugged, "Mbatian, my father, went there when he was young man. He told me many times in his stories."

"Did he travel alone?"

"Yes, I think so. He say he went to find the hard metal," she smiled indulgently, "but I think he was young and wanted to find great adventure instead."

"Hard metal?"

We were strolling along amongst the rich verdancy and extravagant fauna of the country. Sakuda was on point some hundred yards to the front, followed by Kakenya on the Angry One – both occasionally muttering drowzily to themselves – then

79

Loiyan and myself, with Tepilit maintaining an alert watch some distance to the rear.

I found that I wasn't leaning on my cane quite so much, and there was hardly a trace of a limp anymore. It was one of those pleasant days you might remember thirty years later as a time when moments were idylls.

"Yes," she said, then struggling for the word, put her hand to the ornate metal necklace about her throat, and said, "Okiek.".

"Iron?" I asked.

"Ire-on," she repeated, taking evident pleasure as the unfamiliar vowels and consonants played over her tongue. She smiled up at me.

"So *okiek* means 'iron' in Maa?"

"Okiek are a *people* who live many moons to the east by Kirinyaga, the great mountain," she explained. "They work the ire-on."

"And your father, Mbatian, went to the great water seeking iron?"

She laughed. "I think no. There is much ire-on in the rocks at Kirinyaga. He did not need to go to the great water to find more."

I too smiled at the thought of such an adventurous spirit, and contemplated how much his daughter must resemble him.

"Do you know what this great water is called?"

Again she shrugged. "My father told me the people there call it Ukerewe, but he does not know what it means."

We walked further in silence. Over to our right, a small herd of gazelles nibbled daintily amongst a field of hibiscus. Much closer, a sunbird, invisible but for its scarlet throat, flitted here and there amongst the flowers like a nymph, as though finding each new bloom more beautiful than the last.

As we strolled, the conversation continued without much meaning. I think my only goal was to continue hearing the sound of her voice.

"So you are Okiek?" I asked.

She looked at me, still smiling. "Yes, I am Okiek."

"Are the Okiek Maasai?"

Her brow dimpled prettily. "We are...*near* the Maasai."

80

"And the Okiek work the iron."

"Not just ire-on," she held up her arm for me to admire the copper band coiling from wrist to elbow, "but yes, they make tools and weapons and…" again she put her hand to the metalwork necklace.

The Okiek were very skilled, indeed.

"When you say *near*, do you mean the Okiek are related to the Maasai?"

"We are part of the Maasai," once more her brow dimpled. "Just as the Maasai are a part of us. We make things of metal, things they need…and other things."

"What other things?"

"Well," with a glint of mischief, "the *emorata*, for one."

I realized I was staring when she put a hand over her face to hide her giggling.

"The *emorata*." Just the word by itself prompted a phantom stinging sensation in my loins.

"Yes," she said, with an evil grin, "the Okiek are very skilled. That is how I know how to perform this operation for you."

"But why did you?" I was walking hunched over, and it had nothing to do with my limp.

"I have already told you."

"No you haven't, not really." As much as I quailed whenever the subject was mentioned, I have to admit I was curious about what it was that had driven her to disfigure me. Perhaps it was a harmless disfigurement, perhaps not even a disfigurement at all, but whatever it was, the fright it had given me had taken years off my life.

Her smile faded, and the sunlight with it. She walked on a long time in silence. Wretchedly, I thought I had said something that had offended her, for such things were easy to do – Musa's horrified reaction when I'd suggested eating his cattle coming to mind. She had become submissive again, smaller somehow, a contradiction of the woman from moments before. When she spoke her head was bowed, as though ashamed.

"That night after Musa and I…" a small swirl of her wrist while she searched for the words, "fix your legs, you are asleep."

81

"I had fainted."

"Yes," she nodded absently, but I didn't think she was listening. "After Musa leave, I lay in my bed, but I cannot sleep." Her voice was very low. I had to bend closer to listen.

"I was...upset."

"But why?" I asked, "Were you upset with me?"

"Not upset," she said, shaking her head, "but...*upset*."

I waited.

"When I cut your...." She moved her hand up and down her leg.

"My trousers?"

"Yes," she nodded, "When I cut...."

She stopped and raised her head, her face troubled. She took a deep breath. When she continued, there was an aura of determination about her.

"When I first see you, Chah-lee, I think you are very...ugly."

I smiled, but it wasn't returned.

"I think you are so pale, and big," her hands fanned out across her chest, "and all over is the hair; your chest, your arms, your face. I think you are...*dorobo*."

I was silent. '*Dorobo*' meant literally 'a person without cattle', which was to say, someone who was beneath contempt.

"I don't want to be near you, but Musa say I must fix legs. I don't want, but Musa is a man, I cannot say no. So I give you medicine," her eyes met mine, deep and searching, "and then for first time I see you smile. I see your soul, and I think I am a foolish woman because I am so wrong. You are *not dorobo*, you are..." another gentle swirl of her wrist, "...you are the *sun*!"

My eyes were the first to look away.

"I was not myself, Loiyan."

She placed her hand on my arm, and said quietly, "Oh, but you were, Chah-lee. The medicine does not lie. It show you to me. I see. I know."

I lacked the courage to contradict her, so did not reply.

"And yes," she continued, "when I cut the... the...*trousers*, I feel something, but I do not know what. I am curious. I want to

82

know. I am so upset that the knife makes…" She made her hand shake, as though trembling.

I remembered the moment and nodded that I understood.

"When I go to my bed, I am still upset, you understand?"

I wasn't certain that I did, but I nodded again anyway.

"I lie in my bed, I cannot sleep. Musa is gone, you are asleep. No," she corrected herself, "You are…*faint*. The night becomes so long, and still I want to know."

Far in the distance across the river, elephants browsed the fruit off of the sausage trees while a giraffe nursed her calf. It butted her greedily, tail wagging, full of life.

She continued:

"I cannot sleep. The night is too long. I cannot lie still for one moment. My face, my body, it burn. At last, it is too much. I can take no more." Another deep breath, "So, I take my knife. I cut your trousers, and finally I see."

I remembered her in my vision, hands knuckled to her mouth, eyes wide with horror.

"Now I am…I am *confused*. I still do not know. You are beautiful, and yet you are…"

I finished for her, trying to keep the bitterness from my voice.

"Still *dorobo*."

She nodded faintly, then whispered, "Yes."

When she finished, her voice was hollow, without passion.

"Then I remember my father show me the *emorata*. I see many times, but I am woman, never have I done. It is forbidden. But then I remember, too, that I fix leg. This is also forbidden, but am I still not woman? Yet, if I can do this for Musa, why can I not do *emorata* for *me*?" She lifted her chin, but there was not much defiance in her voice. "If it is forbidden, I do not care. I am on fire. I must do." She shrugged. "Such a small thing, and now I think you are beautiful." But she would not look at me.

"But what if I'd struggled, and the knife had slipped?" Just the thought was enough to make me feel ill.

"I was very careful, Chah-lee. Musa put the stakes in the ground to hold your legs…"

"Musa?!"

83

"Yes, and then he hold you while I…" she mimed a meticulous cutting procedure, and I felt cold perspiration pebbling my brow.

"Musa *knew* before…*before* you….operated?"

But of course he had known. I didn't know what the penalty was for mutilating a guest without permission – of his host – but I thought it was probably more than a slap on the wrist.

"Yes," she said, still not meeting my eyes, "I show him, and he agree you must have the *emorata*. He say we must make you as close to Maasai as we can."

I continued on in silence. It made sense, in a barbaric sort of way. For, as were the Maasai, so too, must be their god, and Musa would want me to bear the mark of his people. Not that there had been much chance of anyone noticing, but it was best to leave as few things to chance as possible. So, that had been the official purpose of that wily cattle thief, regardless of Loiyan's having a very different reason in mind. Few things were as they seemed with that fellow. A natural born politician as ever there was.

But, whatever had been the reason, it would serve no purpose to dwell any further. What was done was done.

And yet, I dwelled.

We talked no more that day. I was tired and needed my turn on the Angry One. And so we continued on until the sun began to set, and made camp under the boughs of a giant acacia.

I didn't have much appetite, and made little of the evening meal. As a consequence, while the others were so occupied, I took my cane and walked some distance toward the river. It was wider here, much wider, with shallows and swampland home to dozens – perhaps hundreds – of different species of creatures. My thoughts, as they often do, went back to England. I did some mental calculation and realized it was December; soon it would be Christmas – roast goose and plum pudding, caroling in the snow. It all seemed so far away.

The grass rustled behind me and I turned. There was Loiyan with her bag of medicine. I sat down without a word while she unwrapped my bandages and applied the salve, her

84

fingers working quickly and expertly, as if they wanted to be away.

"Do you...." I cleared my throat and tried again. "Do you really think I'm beautiful....down there?"

Her head was bowed over her work, her forehead knit with concentration. "Yes." The bandage fumbled. It rolled into the deeper grass, uncoiling as it went.

I felt her eyes searching. They were beautiful and gentle....and *there*....always there.

Much later the cicadas where lulling me into the land of dreams. Night beasts were abroad as if let out of their kennels. I kept the gun close by, yet I wasn't worried, someone always stood watch. My turn wasn't until much later.

"You are beautiful," she said. Her arm draped sleepily across my chest, the deep glow of her coiled bracelet rich in the moonlight. As the cicadas carried me away, I heard her once more.

"Yes, *very* beautiful."

Three weeks later we came to Ukerewe, the great water.

More than once we'd had to detour around villages along the river. For, although pursuit now seemed unlikely, we thought it best to avoid witnesses to our passing. But as we drew closer to the end of the Mara, there were so many settlements that we left the river altogether, and continued on several miles inland until, at last, we breasted a rise, and there it was before us.

Our little band halted, very much in awe. Loiyan perhaps glowing with pride, as well, that she had succeeded in retracing her father's footsteps.

It was, indeed, a great water. In fact, as we stood there, staring in amazement, it seemed infinite, stretching on to all points of the horizon, and still remained endless. At first I was sure such a vast body must be the ocean, or at least an inland sea, but once we'd collected ourselves and proceeded cautiously down to the shore, the Angry One didn't hesitate, but dipped his muzzle to the surface and drank deeply, and with obvious relish, signifying that Ukerewe was a fresh water lake.

A mile offshore a fisherman stood on the bow of his boat casting a net. With the land behind us we were invisible to him.

A hand touched my arm.

"It is as my father said," Loiyan was full of wonder, "the water, the strange craft that float, everything."

I put my arm around her. She leaned against me, comfortable in my embrace. From the corner of my eye, I saw Kakenya observing shrewdly.

"Your father spoke the truth," I said.

"Yes he did," she replied, "although I was not completely sure until now."

"You mean you doubted his word?"

She laughed, her teeth flashing in the sun. "My father used to tell many stories," she said by way of answering. "Of course I always believed him, but I thought perhaps he loved the stories more than he loved the truth."

We made camp that night in the shelter of the jungle coming down to the water's edge. The density of the vegetation and our isolated position – the nearest village being a mile distant on the far side of a natural promontory – was such that it allowed us to build a fire. The cheery flames added to our feelings of celebration.

But for one of our number.

"By the balls of Enkai, my throat is dry," Kakenya grumped in her usual irreverent fashion. "I'm so thirsty I could lick the sweat off his bag!"

Our sense of well-being continued to hold sway, for apart from our cringing at the thought, by now no one took particular exception to the cantankerous old crone.

"How can your throat be dry, old woman?" Tepilit, the youngest, and therefore the most easily gulled, asked her. "Why, there is all the water in the world but a few steps away. Surely even your ancient legs can carry you that far."

She gave him a baleful look, silently commiserating with him on the ignorance of youth.

"I've drank enough water to piss rain for a week," she declared, "but that's not what I mean, stupid boy. I'm *thirsty*, I tell you!"

86

Tepilit shifted uncomfortably, his youth allowing him to forget temporarily who was master and who the slave.

Then to my surprise, Sakuda spoke up.

"The hag is right." He was on his feet. "I, too, have been dry too long." He jerked his head at Tepilit. "Come."

"Where are we going?" the youth asked, taking hold of his spear.

"To a place where we can slake our thirst."

"But Sakuda, all this water..."

The older brother delivered a glare remarkably similar to that of the Samburu woman. "Come!"

Without another word, for he had found them to be unprofitable, Tepilit took up his spear and, although puzzled, followed his older brother out into the darkness.

When they were gone I asked Loiyan where they were going.

She looked worried. "I think to the village."

"But that's dangerous, surely!"

"Oh no," she said. "No one will know they were there." Yet I wondered if I might not have heard a trace of unease in her voice.

I should have inquired further, but decided, instead, to let it go. I didn't want anything to upset this surge of elation inside me. Gad, I couldn't remember ever feeling so good! The memory of those nights, of lying naked under the moon, my body entwined with Loiyan's, had continually played across my mind. And then later, spent and tired, I couldn't remember ever feeling such bliss as when coiling myself around her while she slept.

When I looked to her, with those memories ever present, I saw she was already looking at me, her face aglow. If there had ever been unease, it was gone now, lost in her own memories. I smiled. She blushed and looked away, offering a free view of the curve of her neck. I wanted to kiss it.

"I *thought* I heard something last night," Kakenya smirked, eyeing each of us in turn with her evil little eyes. "I was drifting away when I thought I heard a jackal, only no jackal ever sounded like a woman with a pecker inside her."

I was so shocked I was speechless. But such talk could not go unanswered. Still, I felt a certain lack of adequacy with my, "Must you *really*?"

She cackled, "You think I'm bad, don't you, white man. You think I'm *dorobo*?"

"*Very dorobo!*" I seethed. "You are lewd and crass and....and....and a dirty, dirty woman, so there!"

She crowed with laughter as if I'd just given her the biggest compliment in her life. Knowing her, I just might well have done.

"You think I was always old?" She wiped a mirthful tear from her eye. "You think I was always so?" She indicated her own filthy emaciated body with a sweep of her gnarled fingers. "Such a big handsome man as you could never look twice at a woman like me."

"Never!" I shuddered at the very idea.

"Well, my fine young man," her taunting laughter disappeared as if by magic. In its place was a voice hardened by years of anger and bitterness, "you may be surprised to know I was not always as you see me. Once I was beautiful, the daughter of a great chieftain, a princess! I had my pick of strong young men, and I picked well and often." Her lip had curled into a sneer. It made her look even more like a slattern. "The people hated me behind my back, they whispered that I was *orkirekenyi* – a transgressor – but what did I care what their little minds thought? I was beautiful! I held power in the palm of my hand! My father was a mighty chief!"

"Where is your father now, witch?" Loiyan asked, quietly interrupting.

Kakenya's eyes narrowed to burning slits. She regarded Loiyan with years of pent up hatred and loathing.

"Aye, well you know, you Okiek slut. My father was killed the night the Maasai came, murdered trying to defend the cowards that were his people! We were many, and they were few, but still the people hung back and let the Maasai kill him. Six spears they drove into his body! Six spears! And they let him die alone in the middle of the kraal while they ran away to save

88

themselves, and the Maasai took our cattle….and me, they also took me, the only one who tried to help my father.

"They used me, those warriors," she sneered, "those *brave* Maasai who needed six of their own to take the life of one man. They used me until they tore me apart inside, and the blood was flowing like a river between my legs. They hit me, and kicked me, and beat me and they used me until I begged for mercy, but there is no mercy in a Maasai. What I had once taken for my pleasure I now received as my punishment for living. They broke my bones, they knocked my teeth from my head, they shoved their pricks into so many parts of me that, by the time we came to their village, I am nothing; no longer beautiful, no longer powerful…nothing. Even the lowest of you could look down on me with contempt. And you did, every one of you!" Her voice grated hoarsely, "I should have died that night the Maasai came. I should have *died*!"

Well, the silence was long and uncomfortable after that, I can tell you. Kakenya had turned away from us, and was sobbing in great unseemly snuffles on the other side of the fire; the Angry One, on his knees behind her, was lost in his own thoughts.

Much to my surprise, her words seemed to have a dark effect on Loiyan. I had thought that, being of this savage land, she would remain untouched by things that might upset a European lady, but I was finding, more and more, that her nature was often at odds with her culture, and often as not, the emotions that surfaced were distinctly civilized.

She put her hand in mine and leaned closer. "That could be me," she said miserably, hiding her face in my chest. Then she, too, began to sob.

Well, once more I was at a loss for words. I held her like that, feeling helpless as all get out. Finally I took her face in my hands and said, rather stern, "Now see here, what's all this about?"

But Kakenya's words had struck a deep chord in her, and she wasn't so easily shaken from her dumps.

"Oh Chah-lee," she said tears streaming down her face, "don't you see? A woman is nothing! Even if she is the daughter of a great chief, still she is nothing!"

"Oh, stuff and nonsense!" I said, still all stern, "Why, you aren't nothing, are you? At least not to me you aren't."

She snuffled prettily. "I'm not?"

"'Course you're not," I couldn't keep up the stern facade any longer. "Look old girl, you must know that I…that I….well….that I have feelings for you, don't you see? You know, *tender* feelings, and all that."

"But Kakenya…."

"Now don't you worry about Kakenya, 'cause she ain't you, and I'm not the king of China, neither. The point is it don't do no good fretting about things you can't change, now does it? You're…well…you're beautiful, aren't you, and Kakenya's just a Samburu slut, so there you are!"

That brightened her up considerably.

"Do you really think I am beautiful, Chah-lee?"

"What? 'Course I do. Why, you're the best looking nigger wench this side of Cairo, I don't mind telling you!" I gazed tenderly into that beautiful teary-eyed face. "Dash it all! You're a credit to your race, that's what you are!"

She flung her arms around me. "Oh Chah-lee!" She started crying again, "I want to be your beautiful nigger wench!"

"There, there," I said, patting her back. "There, there. Not to worry, old thing." I began to dab at her eyes with my shirt sleeve, "Let's dry your tears, shall we? There's a good girl." Then I held her at arm's length. "Now, let's have a smile."

She managed a teary grimace that quite pulled at the strings of my old heart.

"That's better," I said.

Then I lowered my head to kiss her.

Chapter Eight

"This stuff tastes like rancid piss!"

Startled, we whirled around to see Sakuda and Tepilit come running into our small clearing, both looking tired, but cheerful. Tepilit was the first to see us and immediately, putting two and two together, blushed and commenced to look everywhere else. At his brother's side, Sakuda's scar grinned sourly.

Tepilit had just taken a long pull from something in a goatskin bag. He grimaced then took another pull, pausing to taste, before allowing that it might not be as bad as he first thought.

Sakuda took a long drink from a skin of his own and swallowed without demur. He paused to consider before offering the sack to me.

I'd tasted arrack in Cairo, and as the fiery liquor burned its way into my stomach, I wondered how it had come to be here, in the very bowels of the unknown world, for it was inconceivable that it was distilled locally. Was the great lake connected to the north by some distant waterway, and was it serving as a trade route? Once more I remembered Lord Brampton's friends discussing the source of the Nile. Could it be?

The brothers-not-so-grim took their places around the fire. I offered the skin to Loiyan, and she took a sip, made a face, then convulsed into a fit of coughing.

Meanwhile, Kakenya had roused herself from her dark depths the instant she'd heard footsteps returning. "Me! Me!" she demanded as soon as her eyes had lit on the skins, arms outstretched as a child to a favoured toy.

When Loiyan had recovered sufficiently, she proffered the skin - not so much as a nicety, I thought, but as to be rid of the stuff as soon as possible.

"No!"

Sakuda was glaring angrily.

"It is not for a slave!"

But Loiyan didn't retract the offer. Truth be told, I think that after hearing Kakenya's story, she saw the Samburu woman more as a sister in suffering than as anything else. I think she intended only to show her a sister's kindness.

Kakenya lunged for the skin, snatching it from Loiyan's hands as a person close to starvation might snatch at food.

Sakuda was on his feet, spear in hand. "Woman, this is unseemly!" he protested, "The slave does not drink!"

Now I was on my feet, the gun in my hands. The sound of its hammers being cocked was heavy over the crackling of the fire.

"It is her wish," I said quietly.

Meanwhile, Kakenya was hungrily sucking at the skin as though she was expecting it to be ripped from her grasp at any moment.

Tepilit stood grimly beside his brother, ready to follow his lead. The air grew thick with tension.

Sakuda riveted me with his eyes. "What do I care of a woman's wish? Did I go to the village and risk my life that a slave might drink?!"

The two spears were leveled, threatening. I thought my first bullet would be for Sakuda, but wasn't sure if there would be time to bring the second barrel to bear before Tepilit struck.

But it was Loiyan who broke the tension. Her voice was quietly confident, the very soul of reason, "No, Lord Sakuda, you went to the village because you were bored."

The scar-faced demon looked as though he were on the very brink of murder. I felt my finger take up the slack on the trigger. Only Kakenya and the Angry One seemed unaware of the tension.

Then Sakuda, sounding very much like his older brother, threw back his head and howled laughter.

He roared a throaty bellow and grounded his spear. Tepilit, more cautiously, followed suit.

"Loiyan speaks true!" Sakuda cried, tears running down his cheeks. "I have been too long playing nursemaid to women and a crippled water youth! My spear thirsted for blood!"

Well, I suspected as much. A Maasai was never happier than when he was up to mischief, but it took Loiyan to say it to his face.

"And is your spear sated, Lord?" she asked quietly.

"Oh yes," the brothers resumed their seats, Sakuda still chuckling appreciatively, "When we find this fiery spirit, I see it has value, and if we take, there will be a search." He wiped the tears from his eyes, still smiling. "So we killed one of the fellows, and put his body into one of their floating craft and let it drift away. Every one will think it was he who was the thief."

"The notion was mine," Tepilit boasted, joining in on the general feeling of *bonhomie*.

I was grinning and laughing as much as the rest of them – I was taking great care to – but the blood was running cold under my skin. I had to mask the horror washing over me at the sight of those two grinning devils relishing the memory of having conceived and carried out their plan to murder an innocent man over nothing more than a couple of wineskins. No, I corrected myself, the arrack had been an excuse. They had slaughtered the poor fellow for the pure unmitigated fun of it!

"If only they had cattle," Sakuda shook his head wistfully, and that was enough to set them off again - falling over each other at the merry thought of making off with the villagers' herds, no doubt, amidst even greater slaughter.

Eventually their glee subsided to the point where there was but a weak chuckle every so often from one or the other. The tension seemed to have gone, and Tepilit's arrack was passed around companionably – for once having touched a slave's lips, Sakuda's was deemed unclean.

Well, no wonder he'd been so put out.

Meanwhile, the slave in question had not been idle.

"Oh brave warriors!" Kakenya sneered at them from across the fire. The goatskin had been gurgling constantly ever since she'd got her claws on it. Having a full half of the arrack to herself, she was determined not to let it go to waste. "Oh, brave fighters of the Maasai! How boldly did you sneak into the night! Tell us of your courage while you murdered a man as he slept, then stole away with your ill-gotten goods!"

The brothers had listened indulgently, believing themselves to be praised. But as the old crone continued, their expectant smiles slowly faded.

"Oh, if there were but a woman to steal!" She lamented ironically, "If only there was not some willowy young wench for you to snatch from her father's house and despoil! How mighty would be your triumph!"

"And who is to say there was not?" Sakuda replied with a lightness that never reached his eyes. "There were many, but they all smelled of fish."

Tepilit chortled. "That is so, old hag. They smelled almost as bad as you."

"Brave warriors!" She glared at them blearily, taking another suck at the skin. "Brave Maasai murderers! You could have stolen a girl, but you did not. Why? Were you afraid their mothers might waken and beat you?" The thought struck her as funny. She started to cackle. "Yes! That is it! You were afraid of being chased away by a woman! Ha! Ha! Ha!"

Sakuda had his spear across his knees. Slowly, almost lovingly, he ran his fingers up and down the length of its blade. He seemed terribly engrossed.

"Have a care, old woman," he said in that same light voice.

"Or what?" She spat, too far gone with hatred and arrack to take heed. "Will you carry *me* into the bushes instead?" She wriggled her useless chest at him. "Will you make a man of yourself with a helpless old slave?" Her tongue taunted suggestively from the wrinkled folds of her mouth. "Or are you afraid that your loins aren't up to the task?"

When Sakuda rose to his feet, there was a casualness about his movements that was unsettling. Without giving pause, he walked over to where Kakenya sat cross-legged on the ground.

"Ohhhh!" The old woman chortled, clutching the goatskin possessively to her chest, "Here comes the brave warrior! Perchance he is man enough after all! Ha! Ha! Ha!"

Without a word, he stooped and knotted his fist in Kakenya's girdle, hoisting her up as if she were nothing more than a bundle of sticks. Still not speaking, he set off towards the lake.

Too late, sober recognition of her peril dawned on the crone's face.

"I take it back," she whispered. "Please, master, I take it back!"

Sakuda appeared not to have heard her, but continued his stroll to the shore.

"I am a foolish old woman!" Kakenya wailed. "Forgive me!"

The water splashed heavily around the Maasai's feet. It was very shallow, scarcely two inches deep, but Sakuda seemed satisfied. He dropped the old woman. She landed in the mud with a wet splat.

"Please, master!" But she had run out of time.

Sakuda placed his sandaled foot on the back of her head. Almost gently, he forced her face down into those few scant inches of water.

Kakenya gargled and sputtered, trying to draw breath for one more plea for mercy. But it was wasted, for there was no mercy in a Maasai….she'd said so herself.

Her feet drummed the ground, splashing water in all directions, her fingers clawing frantically through the mud as though she were making a ridiculous effort to swim in what was nothing more than a puddle. Her body wriggled and convulsed, struggling to break free, but Sakuda held her without effort.

A long string of bubbles broke the surface beside her cheeks, and ran on for a surprisingly long time. When at last they stopped, there was another prolonged, but weaker struggle, until eventually, she was still.

Sakuda lifted his foot from the back of Kakenya's head. He carefully wiped the sole of his sandal on the dry sand of the shore before coming back to the fire.

Sometime during all this, Loiyan had come into my arms.

"I say!" I was too shocked by what I'd just seen to formulate anything more.

Sakuda accepted the wineskin from Tepilit and drank thirstily.

I tried again.

"Look here," I said.

He looked at me, the scar on his face dancing shadows in the firelight.

95

"You can't just go around doing that sort of thing, you know? I mean, Due Process, and all that."

Even before they were out, I realized how ridiculous my words were, even to my ear. It was useless to speculate how they sounded to his.

Of course he could do what he had just done; he was Maasai.

But Sakuda didn't appear angry. In fact, if anything, he was courteous.

"How are your legs?" He asked with a terrible gentleness.

"What? My legs? Why, they're fine," I answered, somewhat bewildered, "getting better every day."

He received this information with a sober nod. "That is good."

"I suppose so, but I don't see what it has to do with…."

"That," he indicated the corpse with a careless toss of his head, "was needed because the Samburu knew the ways of the Angry One. We needed the Angry One to bring you away from the village."

He leaned forward with some significance. "Do you still need to ride him, the Angry One?"

I glanced at the cantankerous camel where he knelt, drowsily oblivious of being discussed. Then I turned to watch as the waves began to lap at Kakenya's body, already pulling it further out into the darkness of the lake.

"Well, sometimes," I said.

"And you understand his ways?"

"Yes, I think so. But," I added just in case he was thinking of trying to do her in next, "Loiyan knows him better than I do, much better, in fact. Then there's her medicine, too, of course." I finished lamely.

"Musa, my brother, told me no harm must come to you. He said it was a matter of much honour." He looked at me, very serious, "I would die to protect my honour."

"Yes, but can't you see…"

"For reasons I do not know, you are important to my brother." Then, once more, he offered a last dismissive nod to

96

the corpse fast disappearing in the shimmering moonlight, "She was a mere slave, a nothing."

Well, she'd said *that* herself, too, when you got right down to it.

In all this time Loiyan had been silent, and continued to remain so. Thus far her only action had been to seek the protective circle of my arms. I suppose that, if I'd taken the time, I'd have been surprised at her reaction to the crone's death and the warrior's cruelty that had brought it about. After all, she had lived her entire life amongst these people - was one of them herself, in fact. Such unfeeling acts must have been common, hardly noticeable even. Yet, once more, as she had upon hearing Kakenya's woefull tale, she huddled against my shoulder, trembling with the horror of what she'd just witnessed, as though it were all new to her.

As for me, the night had suddenly taken on an entirely new meaning. Gone were any feelings of elation or sense of complacency, and above all, any notion I was safe amongst these folk. I suppose that, up until that moment, I'd lived in a sort of dream world, probably because it *was* a dream world: a world so totally alien from my own that my mind simply wasn't capable of accepting it on any other terms. But now, sitting across a fire in the wilderness, sharing an amiable skin of arrack with savages, who were contentedly reminiscing about their most recent acts of barbarity – intermingling the story with other fondly remembered instances when their baser instincts had got the better of them – it came home to me with a vengeance just how grave was our danger. Loiyan's and my life was no more foreseeable than the gratification of these bloodthirsty creatures' curious sense of honour. Once that had been satisfied, once I had ceased to be of value, they may well come to the conclusion that the demon Red Man and his Okiek woman were worth more to them dead than alive. For in my clearer vision, I now saw how greatly Loiyan had compromised herself by succumbing to her curiosity about me.

It was with no appreciable sense of direction that I now proceeded, merely the sense of one whom, upon finding his head beneath the water, was striving to rise once more to the surface.

"I am grateful for Musa's concern," I said with humility, "and I am grateful to you for having carried out his wishes so well."

The wineskin gurgled, both warriors relaxed. "I have told you," Sakuda said with a magnanimous wave, "that it was a matter of honour. I am to keep you safe and near until it is time for your return."

'*Safe and near.*' It was as I had suspected. In addition to my being kept from harm, I was also being held prisoner. The two brothers were both my protectors and jailers.

"May I ask when that time might be?" I was trying to keep my tone light and unconcerned, but if there was any note of anxiety, it was lost on the warriors as the liquor began to run its course.

"Let me see," Sakuda reflected with dry playfulness, "was it one moon or two? I cannot remember. It was dark, and Musa's words were hurried."

"Mayhap it was the time of Mangla giving birth," Tepilit suggested, and both brothers roared good-heartedly. Mangla was Musa's favourite cow, and was pregnant, a fact that kept him in a constant state of agitation, and looked to continue to do so until she freshened.

"Or perhaps it is the passing of *Oladalu*," Sakuda conceded, "and the rains of *Oeniong'ok* have begun."

Oladalu was the month of dryness, *Oeniong'ok* the one of light rains. There had been very little precipitation for some time now, and none at all for the past, let's see, three weeks, was it? Maybe more? That would mean that the dry season was due to end almost any time. Was it possible that, having no sooner arrived at the great water, Musa intended for us to turn around and come back?

Yes, I thought, it was possible. Our journey meant nothing more to him than that I should be safely away from the village long enough for him to strengthen his position against the *Laibon*. He probably imagined that he might require a few months to achieve this aim, but not much longer.

I rose to my feet, pulling Loiyan up beside me. Far off in the distance, a single bolt of lightning scorched across the sky.

98

Several seconds later, thunder rumbled its assertion that it had ever been. Was it the precursor to the rains? It seemed likely.

I feigned tiredness and bade them both good night, but when turning to leave was brought up short.

"You take the woman to your bed?" Sakuda asked without much apparent interest. When I told him that I was, however, he gazed myopically up from his place by the fire, the goatskin clutched in his fist. "What would you say if I told you the woman was ours?" The danger appeared in his voice the same way a demon might rise from the dark depths.

Tepilit dove in with his tuppence worth. "She is Maasai," he said, his head bobbing all over the place as the arrack worked on him. "She wants something more than a water youth."

Both brothers chortled at the thought of getting up to more mischief.

Loiyan shoved herself away from me, suddenly all spirit and defiance.

"You would not dare touch me!" She grated, "Have you forgotten that Musa is my husband?"

Well, this got a reaction, all right. While the warriors grew sullen, I found myself gaping in astonishment.

"Yet you would sleep with the water youth," Sakuda muttered angrily.

"It is an affront to Maasai manhood," Tepilit confirmed.

"What do you mean by '*husband*'?" I asked.

"I will sleep with whosoever I choose!" she flared. "It is my affair, Sakuda, not yours!"

"Oh, you have grown very high," Sakuda growled in that same, dangerous voice, "and very mighty, too, little Loiyan of the Okiek. What do you think Musa would say of your sleeping with a water youth?"

These were my thoughts exactly. My horrified imagination was racing as to what might be the Maasai punishment for this sort of *laisse-majesté*. Why hadn't the stupid bitch told me earlier? Why hadn't *anyone* mentioned it to me earlier? Of all the designing hussies, this one had to take the cake! It was too fantastic for words!

"Musa knows the law as well as you do," Loiyan answered with a shocking lack of contrition, all things considered. "If I fancy a man, then I am free to choose him. Musa cannot interfere."

I couldn't believe what I was hearing, and so I'm afraid I did a good deal of foolish gaping. What was the woman yammering about? Why wasn't she worried about the punishment that was sure to be her due instead of tying into these two like a bosun would a couple of recalcitrant landlubbers?

"The law is for the Maasai," Tepilit howled indignantly, "He is not Maasai!"

And then, wouldn't you know it, that got them wrangling on the finer points of Serengeti jurisprudence. I doubt if, but for the setting, and the colour of their skin, it was much different than our own barristers back in England – the state of the men's sobriety notwithstanding.

But I was still pretty baffled when Loiyan finally, after loosing a last defiant broadside, took hold of my hand and dragged me off into the undergrowth leaving the prosecution muttering mutinously in the background.

"You are *orkirekenyi* – a fallen woman!" Sakuda roared.

"Why, because I have chosen a *man*, and not an *Olksiodoi*?" she spat over her shoulder. I happened to know that an *Olksiodoi*, or a 'knife kicker' was a boy who struggled and cried out during the *emorata* ceremony, thereby bringing shame upon his family. It was a blot on the old copy book, no doubt about that, but it was also considered bad form for anyone to dig up the episode once it had become safely buried in the past.

Sakuda blanched at the insult. Then, with a roar he was on his feet and charging, spear in hand. But he'd taken on more of the puggle than was good for him, and tripped over the fire before he'd gone two steps. He went sprawling, embers flying in every direction, and lay babbling incoherently, while Tepilit clucked over him like a mother hen.

"We'll get you, you bitch!" he howled, weaving mightily in the still night air, but his anger was steady enough. "Just remember, Loiyan, a dead wife tells no tales! So mayhap we will have some fun with you after all!"

But Loiyan, apparently considering that the discourse had been seen to a satisfactory conclusion, continued to lead me away from the fire without another word. Yet once we were well clear, she turned about and flung herself into my arms. Only when I felt the sobs wracking her body did I realize just how frightening the ordeal had been for her.

"Oh Chah-lee," she cried, "we are in great danger!"

"There, there," I said for the second time that night, "I'm sure that was nothing but the booze talking. They won't have remembered a thing, come morning." Then I tucked my finger under her chin, "Now what's this about your being married?"

"It is true," she snuffled back some fresh tears, "for almost one year I have been Musa's wife."

"But...but...why?" I realized it was a bloody stupid question, but I don't think I was thinking quite clearly.

"I was seventeen, an old woman with no husband. The men in my village do not want me: they say I have a demon because my father allows me things that are forbidden for a woman – the practice of healing, my refusal of *emorata*...."

"Wait," I interrupted her, "let me get this straight. *Women* are given the *emorata* too?"

"Yes, of course. It is the law. If we do not, men say we will be bad women."

As shocked and revolted as I was upon learning this, I felt I needed confirmation. "But you refused it?"

"Yes, I refuse. I will not be like....like a hole in a log for a man," she flared with proud defiance.

"But how could you refuse if it's the law?"

Still proud, she said, "Mbatian, my father was *Laibon* of our village. He was a good and wise man. When it was time for me to take the *emorata,* he told me of a time when he was young, he had a woman of the Luo people, perhaps here on Ukerewe. It was a long time ago, but he remembered it well. He said that the woman had been whole, and had seemed to taste the experience as much as he." Then, without the least bit embarrassment, she added, "My father claimed it was a very good experience."

101

I could imagine having the same sort of conversation with my guv'nor, couldn't I just?

She continued:

"Even though he know it will cause problem, he say, 'Loiyan, my daughter, I will let you decide: will you be a good woman or will you taste your life?'" She shrugged angrily, as someone would who is pulled in two directions, "It is not much choice, almost no choice at all," then her expression changed, became more introspective, "but I remember my father's eyes when he tell the story of the Luo woman, how they sparkled with the memory. Then I think to myself that some day I would like a man to remember me that way. In the end, there is no choice; I decide I do not care if I am bad woman, I would taste my life."

Then the defiance waned in the face of sad memory.

"I bring shame to my mother because she has raised such a bad daughter. She try to pressure me to take the *emorata*, but my mind is made up. 'No man will touch you,' she warns, and this is true, no man wants such a willful girl. But I refuse to live as an unfeeling vessel for their pleasure alone, and because my father is *Laibon*, none dare force what I do not wish. But years go by and I do not marry. No man will have me, nor I them because they are not worthy of my respect. I feel I am a stranger in my own village.

"But Musa is friend with my father, and he knows of my mother's shame. He tells my father that for a bullock and two goats he will marry me, and take me away. At first my father said no because the bride price is shamefully low, but my mother tells him that Musa is a chief and that it is an honour to give me to him. She says that her shame has been hard to bear, but that it will be gone when he takes me away. She would not let him alone until his mind was changed."

"I see." I was deflated. Was it only hours before that the world had seemed so full?

"Musa was kind," she continued on quietly, "but he did not want to be near a woman with a demon. I try to be a good wife, I try very hard. I cook, I milk the cows, I fetch the water, I try to be humble, but I cannot be other than who I am. There is so much in the world, and so little that is allowed to a woman.

With this my spirit will never be easy, and the people hate me for it. Very soon it is as it was in my father's village."

"But you came to me knowing you were already married."

"Yes," she said, yet again without shame. "It is my right, just as I told Sakuda. I am free to choose any man I want, if he will have me." Then, after a pause, "Is this not so in Ingle-land?"

"Good God, no! Not for a married woman!"

"But if she does not want her husband, or if he does not want her? What is she to do?"

"Eh? Well, let's see. There's cold baths, I suppose, and they can fill their time with needlepoint, that sort of thing…and there's always the children, of course."

But she didn't seem to be listening. Instead, she looked at me. "And you, Chah-lee, are you free to choose?"

"'Course I am, I'm a man, you see?"

Her teeth glowed like pretty little pearls. She came closer, curling her arms around my waist, and laid her head on my chest.

"If we are both free to choose, then let it be so."

At that, she took my hand and lay down in the sweet smelling grass, pulling me down beside her.

"I choose you, Chah-lee."

To give me my due, I remained undecided for more than a heartbeat before the inevitable thought, 'Oh well, when in Rome…'

Some while later, her feverish lips whispered in my ear, "I choose you, Chah-lee! I choose you!"

All in all, I was glad she hadn't been forced to endure the *emorata*.

Yet, I was still bothered, afterwards. Whilst coiled around her, in readiness for sleep, I thought of Musa, with his amused smile, telling me, 'She likes you'. I remembered his ill-tempered acquiescence our last night in the village. Had at least part of his anger been jealousy? Just because he was too fastidious to touch his new wife didn't mean he would gladly suffer another man to do so.

Yet although she, too, was anxious, Loiyan was on an altogether different tack.

"I think there will be trouble."

103

"Mmmm?"

Her body was drawn up fetally, with her back to me, the nakedness of her shoulder marvelous in its ebony marble-like perfection. I thought she must be as tired as I was, yet her voice was alert.

"With Sakuda and Tepilit."

"Oh no, I don't think so. I told you, that was just the booze talking. Besides," I could feel myself beginning to drift off, "I've got the gun, just in case."

"You really think so, Chah-lee?"

"Yes, now go to sleep."

I slid further and further into slumber. Just as it took me completely, I heard her voice clearly over the night sounds.

"There will be trouble."

Chapter Nine

I awoke in the morning feeling very fine and refreshed. I stretched luxuriously and then, feeling the call of nature, went a discreet distance off into the jungle to relieve myself. It wasn't until after I returned that I noticed I was alone.

I called out her name but my only answer was from a small green and yellow parrot chirruping in a tree high above me. Still half-muddled from just having woken, I grabbed the gun and slung it over my shoulder, guessing she had gone to rekindle the fire for our morning meal.

As I drew nearer the campsite, I felt no alarm at the absence of voices. Undoubtedly the brothers had imbibed well into the evening, and were still deep in sleep. My mind had turned to what was going to happen when the rains came, and it was time to return to the village. There was a world of problems to face then. Naturally Musa would have come up with some sort of plan to convince the village, once and for all, I was the Red Man, and thereby bleed Parasayip's cattle from his herds. That was, presumably, if he had been able to call off the *Laibon's* war party that were after my hide. Then I thought uncomfortably about Musa himself, and how he might receive the news I was having it on with one of his wives while we were away. Try as I might, I couldn't bring myself around to Loiyan's view that this wasn't cause for worry. Musa was an acquisitive fellow, and it wasn't in such people's nature to share, no matter what the local customs stated to the contrary.

I was ruminating along these lines when I came upon the campsite. The first thing I noticed were the cold embers of last night's fire. The second was Loiyan.

She was sitting on the ground, pale in the early morning light, her eyes wide and unseeing. Her knife was in her right hand, her arms covered in blood.

That was when I noticed the awful stillness.

"Loiyan?"

But she didn't answer.

Then I noticed the brothers.

Sakuda lay on his side where he had obviously passed out some time during the night. His knees were curled up to his chest, while his lower arm stretched out towards something unseen, the other trailed loosely by his side. A vast pool of blood, already coagulating, had spread on the ground by his throat. I took a step closer and saw the deep slice that spread from one ear to the other. He was quite pale beneath his black skin, as though he'd been covered in ashes.

Tepilit, on the other hand, was sitting with his back to the bole of a tree, his eyes staring a horrible accusation. His throat had also been cut, but Loiyan must have inadvertently woken him because he'd been able to put up enough of a struggle for her to have thought it necessary to disembowel him as well. His intestines and organs lay in a heap on the ground by his feet. Flies had already begun to gather on them.

A high, thin keening brought me back to Loiyan.

The knife started to tremble and waver. I had a flash of the vision of lying back in the hut, boiling with passion while that very same knife trembled over my body in that very same hand. Even as I stared, it fell from fingers that might have been lifeless, the dull thud muted as it landed amongst the ashes.

Then the keening became a wail.

I rushed forward and took her in my arms, but it was as though she were fashioned of stone, so rigid was her body, the very same body that was so soft and yielding but a few short hours ago. When she started to scream, I placed my hand over her mouth and held her close, mindful that there might be others close by. When the muffled sounds turned into great, heaving sobs, I took away my hand and placed my arm around her. The sun was well up in the sky by the time I let her go, and well past its zenith before she could speak.

In the meantime, I had not been idle. First, having released my hold on her, I went to the lake and wet a cloth to wash her arms and face. Then, one by one, I dragged the bodies deeper into the undergrowth and, for some reason, covered them with fronds. The chances of a passerby stumbling upon them were small, yet the fronds would be no protection from the discerning nose of a hyena or jackal. I had thought of consigning them to the lake instead, but thought of Kakenya and the poor fellow from the village. Too much death had already been buried in those waters.

When I returned to the campsite, Loiyan had moved to the extent she was hugging her knees, with her head draped to her chest.

I covered up the bloodied earth and rekindled the fire. Then, searching through her bag, found a packet of wormwood leaves with which she'd used to make tea upon occasion. Closer inspection produced another packet, this one of hemp, with which she'd used to dose me the night my broken ankles had been set. Perhaps it was my British instincts that made me take a measure of both and put them in a clay pot, for I knew that few things offered so much comfort as tea. I filled the pot with water from the lake and nestled it amongst the coals to steep.

When it came to a boil, I fished it out with a stick and poured the contents into the same bowl she'd used when it was time for my *nailang'a*. I took it to her and held it to her lips.

At first there was no sign of life, the bowl's rim brushing against lips that might have been fashioned of rubber. But as the magic of the tea's essence penetrated her mind, demanding preeminence over the horrors dwelling within, her head gradually began to rise, and the lips parted, accepting a sip, followed by a tiny grimace over its bitterness. Whether or not the tea held any reviving properties I couldn't say, but she continued to sip and, after a time, her eyes began to focus until, eventually, she was able to drink on her own. I put the bowl in her hands, and set it on her lap. Then I sat down by her side, but not so close as to suffocate. If I saw signs that she wanted me to draw nearer, I would, but until then I would give her room to breathe.

All of my old worries of the early morning had been erased in an instant. Musa and Parasayip's cattle now seemed as foolish as the thought of myself as a demon. All of them seemed distant and unimportant as though they were events that might have happened to someone else – some minor character in a bad play.

We could never go back, that much was certain. I wondered how much of this had been on Loiyan's mind when she took up her knife and left my side while I slept.

"I have never killed anyone before." Her words were dead and empty, but at least they were words, a reaching out. "I never knew how it would feel."

"It's a rum business," I said quietly.

"The blood has a smell."

I remembered the Crimea.

"Yes, it does."

"I wanted it to be done quickly, cleanly, but there was so much blood. I never knew one man could hold so much blood."

I was silent, waiting.

"I had my knife in Tepilit when he woke. The artery was already severed, but he awoke before I could pull my hand away."

"I know."

"He tried to cry out, but there was just this….this *sound*. We struggled, but he was soon weak from loss of blood. I was stabbing him, again and again, ripping out his stomach."

Still I waited.

"I knew there would be trouble. Sakuda always wanted me. I knew from the way his eyes would follow me everywhere I went, but I feel that he is a bad man, and I do not want him. In the village he could do nothing, and out here I was safe as long as you needed me. But once you were healthy, he would be free to do what he wanted, and Tepilit is easily led. The Maasai Mara has many pitfalls for a defenseless woman. One of them would have befallen me before we returned to the village."

For the first time, she looked at me, eager to make eye contact.

"I know this, Chah-lee!"

"Yes."

"Please, Chah-lee," she begged, "I know this."

"Yes."

"I know this, Chah-lee, I know this." And then, as though it were a fixation, "I know this! I know this! I know this!" Over and over.

I held out my arms.

She came to me.

Later that evening the rains started.

We had not stayed in that place where so many of our party had met their end. Loiyan had said that it was an evil place, and I didn't argue, but had taken up the Angry One's rein and led the way to a secluded spot some miles distant, yet still on the shore. We made camp in the jungle as before, only this time I had the foresight to fashion a crude shelter, with a roof of thatched fronds, to protect us from the weather.

These were not yet the rains of *Olodoyiorie*; the deluge rains that flooded the rivers into raging torrents – those were some time off as yet – but a light squall that had blown in from the lake. It was no great hardship, and we were snug and dry under the shelter, warmed by a fire.

Our plight had struggled with concern for Loiyan for control over my thoughts. I wanted to make her health my sole occupation as she had done for me. Yet there were decisions to be made, and now, no one else to attend them.

We could never return to the village; our bridges had been burned in the blood spilt by the cold ashes of a fire. We were alone now, a lost tribe of one man and one woman, doomed to wander and hide ourselves away from those who would destroy us. Yet, if Loiyan was to be believed, and I saw no reason why I should not, we had been doomed by Sakuda's desire for her even as we took our first reckless step away from the village.

Loiyan was more herself now, to the point where she would look about and see the world around her, yet after her confessional, after her tear-stained explanation as to why she had felt driven to act as she had done, and the frantic desperation of her need for me to believe her, she had largely resumed her silence, filling her ears instead with the workings of her inner thoughts.

I allowed it, for the most part. For one thing, I didn't know what else to do. For another, I had some hope that, if left to herself, her mind would be able to come to terms with itself all the sooner without my own clumsy words to cloud the issue.

But as I said, our future needed to be planned, and as the raindrops patted softly on the roof of our shelter, an idea began to form in my mind.

Lost we might be, but for the first time we were also free. Free of the village, free from intrigue, free of protectors, free from jailers, free, in fact, to go wherever we would. That had to be somewhere on the plus side. Now, all that needed deciding was what we were to do with it, this freedom.

I asked Loiyan, "Is there a place you have in mind where we can go?"

"It matters not, Chah-lee," she shrugged, disinterested. "There is no place I can go. I will not be welcomed back to my family's village. And Musa's…" she let the obvious trail off into nothing.

"Then would you come with me?"

This was enough inducement to spark some light in her eyes, however little that might be.

"But where would we go, Chah-lee?"

"Well," I began carefully, formulating the thoughts even as I voiced them, "I've been thinking. That strong drink came from somewhere, and it didn't come from the village where Sakuda and Tepilit found it, that's flat."

"No," she agreed slowly, "I had not tasted such a drink before."

"Well, I have; in a place called Cairo."

In spite of herself, this roused some interest. "Where is this Cairo?"

"To the north somewhere," I said, motioning with my arm. "Perhaps far, I don't know. But wherever that arrack – that strong drink – was made, it must have been from a place that is accessible to Ukerewe. In fact, I think this great water is a hub for a vast inland trading center in the very heart of Africa!"

"Please, Chah-lee," she frowned, "I do not understand."

"Look, somebody brought the arrack here, to Ukerewe, and I'll bet my last farthing that if one of its shores doesn't touch on that place, then there is a river flowing from here that does. All we have to do is find it!"

Loiyan turned to gaze at the endless reaches of the great water. "But where do we look?"

"Well, I know it's not much to go on, but Cairo is to the north. I say we try there."

She shrugged. "But how?"

"By boat — by the craft that floats."

I could tell this appealed to her. For although she was still reeling with shock, I knew adventure still lay hidden in her depths, as it had with her father, and for a moment her eyes did light up in a way I hadn't dared hope for. She'd never been on a water craft in her life, and I knew the very idea was appealing in a way that only something new and exciting can be. But then the cloud was back, and chased the light away.

"Where would we come by one of these boats?"

"That village had them, didn't they?"

"Yes, Chah-lee, but how will we get one? I think the village will not give one to us. These boats must be very prized."

Well, that was a question, and no error. How would we get a boat? Even if I was inclined to do so — which I was not — I doubted that my skills at thievery were on the same scale as the Maasai, even on a bad day. I also doubted that anyone would go easy on us if we were caught in the act. But even if, by a miracle, we did succeed in purloining one of those vessels, the villagers knew the lake and we did not, and would quickly hunt us down. Plainly put, such a course of action was bound to end in failure, and more than likely some form of hideous death to follow.

"We could purchase one," I said, but not too hopefully.

"With what, Chah-lee? We have nothing."

Well, strictly speaking, that wasn't true. I had the gun, and that would probably bring enough to buy a whole fleet of boats. But I didn't dare part with it. For one thing it was Lord Brampton's property, and I had a duty to return it to him — just as soon as I could return myself. For another, I had no idea how far we had to go, or what sort of dangers we might meet, but in every one that I could imagine, the gun played a prominent role. No, Loiyan was right, we had nothing, we would be reduced to begging, and something told me that wouldn't suffice.

But wait!

"We're not so bad off as all that," I said.

Puzzled, she frowned at my excitement, but followed the direction of my gaze.

111

The Angry One looked his eternal contempt at me, spat, missed, and then, losing interest, turned away.

Loiyan actually smiled.

"Where did Musa get this beast, anyway?"

I wasn't particularly interested in the answer, but Loiyan had started to talk, and I wanted her to continue, to give her mind a rest from fighting with itself.

It was mid-morning of the next day. We had broke camp at first light, and were making our way to the fishing village. There we hoped to trade the Angry One for a canoe, which was what the lake craft amounted to - a sort of a high-prowed dugout affair. We had been walking for hours, and the lake traffic, while not heavy, had been constant. Mostly the craft had been in the distance, but once we'd happened upon a fisherman trying his luck inshore, and been able to catch a glimpse up close. While I was no seaman, I thought the vessel looked sturdy enough, although the fisherman had paddled away at great speed when he saw us.

"The Angry One come from a cattle raid on a Samburu village," Loiyan said. She had observed the boat with much interest, and it had animated her somewhat. "Musa had seen them riding such creatures before, so when he see the Angry One, he take him with many cattle. I think he plan to ride some day, but he did not know the Angry One's ways, and was too proud to ask." She smiled softly, "For many moons the Angry One is the company for sheep."

We rounded a promontory and saw another dugout bobbing in the shallows. Its owner was standing in the bow with a forked fish spear in hand. As he was concentrating on the waters at his feet, he didn't see us until we were quite close. But, after that, it was a repeat of our first reception, to whit: wide-eyed surprise, then beating a hasty retreat with neither greeting nor curse to stimulate a conversation.

"Come back, you stupid wog!" I shouted. "We come in peace!"

112

But man and craft sped away without a word, as though we were lepers.

In disgust, Loiyan threw down the handful of grass she'd been holding as a signal of our pacific intentions. "*Dorobo!*" she spat.

Although I was equally disappointed, it was reassuring to see her show so much spirit. It was a good sign, surely.

"Are they *Dorobo?*" I asked.

She shrugged. "They are afraid like sheep," and that was *Dorobo* enough for her.

These fisher-folk were not tall and fine featured like the Maasai, but more like the Bantu along the seacoast with their thick-set bodies, fuzzy hair, large lips and flat noses. If they were of one of those despised *Dorobo* tribes, their lack of friendliness might now be easier to understand – given Loiyan's unmistakable attire branding her as a Maasai. Even if they had never felt the wrath of those robbing cattle barons (Sakuda had said they had no livestock to speak of) their cousins further inland probably would have, and the stories they, no doubt, related would have been enough to do the rest.

But Loiyan was right; they really were a timid crew.

We had already passed our old campsite and its many unhappy memories. I'd taken her by the hand and steered her steadily along, keeping up a brisk conversation to keep her mind off things. It seemed to be working well enough, for more and more she seemed to be coming out of herself.

"Where are your people from?" I asked.

"I told you, from Kirinyaga, the great mountain, far to the east."

"No, I meant where did you come from originally? Surely your *Oloiboni* – your elders – had the stories handed down to them?"

"Oh, I see." She knitted her brow as she recollected the ancient tales. "There was a story of a time, long, long ago that said we were once a people who lived far to the north, beyond the Ndoto Mountains, along a great river at a place called Oto."

113

"Well, we're going north," I pointed out, "and we're looking for a river. In fact, chances are the biggest river would be the one we want. It just stands to reason."

"But it is just a story, and very old."

"Yes, but still, wouldn't it be something if you were to retrace your people's footsteps all the way back to where they originated? And I'll tell you something else," the idea had just struck me, "during our stay in Cairo, we saw many people from many places, from all over the world, or so it seemed. But what's really interesting is there were some who resembled the Maasai, not *Dorobo* at all."

"But they were not Maasai?"

"No. Well, I don't think so, anyway. They didn't dress like your folk, more like Arabs, really. They said that they were from a province to the south, place called the Sudan."

Loiyan shook her head. Obviously the name held about as much meaning for her as it had for me. It was something of a miracle that I'd managed to remember the occasion at all.

"But suppose they were once part of your people. Suppose they are some sort of distant cousin."

"How will we know?"

I had to admit that my anthropological leanings were causing myself more excitement than they were for her.

"Well, we might meet some of them, and then we might find someone who can speak civilized, or maybe even Maasai, or something close to it. Then we could ask them. Surely they'll have their own stories, and we can compare notes, so to speak."

But Loiyan didn't answer. In fact, she'd stopped, eyes staring to her front, her mouth wide open in a silent scream. I thought, at first, she'd had some sort of relapse, but as things became clearer, I'm sure my own expression was quite similar. For this was something altogether new.

By this time we'd passed the last promontory to where we knew the village lay in a small inlet on the other side. I blame myself for not having noticed earlier, but Loiyan was my first concern, and I was excited by the prospect of exploration and of making some great discovery, so failed to notice when we'd come to the headland.

The village was just where I remembered it to be, about a half mile distant: a quiet sleepy sort of place, it had looked quite peaceful.

Now, while we stared with growing unease, there were flames licking at the thatched roofs of the huts, smoke boiling up into the sky. I suppose the reason why we hadn't noticed the smoke earlier was that the day was overcast, and it mingled well with the clouds. Although why I hadn't noticed the smell, I can't think.

Small lifeless forms lay littered about the lakeside. They looked suspiciously like bodies.

Confirmation came a moment later when a woman burst out of the jungle a scant few hundred yards away. She was naked and there was blood streaming from what must have been a score of wounds. Even as I stared, dumb and uncomprehending, she came streaking blindly in our direction, screaming hysterically.

The reason was soon made clear enough.

For, erupting out of the forest, hard on her heels and bent on butchery, came men covered in paint, and armed with those too familiar spears, all of them with that distinctive lion mane headdress.

Our missing war party.

Chapter Ten

It had been assumed by all that our pursuers had given up the chase once they found we'd given them the slip. Yet apparently, such was not the case. It seemed they had followed the Mara down to its mouth, hoping – correctly – that we'd done the same. But not knowing how accurate their thinking was, and angry at finding their efforts had seemingly come to nought, they were taking their frustrations out on this peaceful village.

I don't know how long I stood there, gaping like the town idiot, while those screaming devils bore down on us at that sickening speed I remembered so well, but it seems hellish long in the nightmares I still have every now and then. It was as though we had grown roots, so incapable were we of movement.

It was all one to take in the shambles of the burning homes and lifeless forms scattered about, but quite another to act with the required alacrity. If I've learned one thing, it's that horrifying encounters always take time to register, and we simply didn't have that opportunity before the poor girl came running out of the bush. I mean, scant seconds before, there I was up to my eyeballs in speculation and interesting theories about the origins of the Maasai of all things, when, speak of the devil, here they were, naked as the day they were born, charging across the sand like so many ghastly demons, and screaming bloody murder.

Even while we stood frozen with shock, I saw an *orinka* come flying through the air, and the girl went down like a felled ox.

The brutes were on her in an instant, the foremost whipping her legs apart and plunging in even while his mates gathered around to form a cheering section, and to offer him pointers on technique, no doubt.

My mind was struggling mightily to function, but here was another point of contention. The brutes were preoccupied with rape and murder, and there was just the possibility that we might steal away unnoticed. Yet, if I wasn't a gentleman, exactly, at least I was a gentleman's gentleman, and British to boot. Clearly, here was someone in distress, and it didn't seem right just to run off and leave her.

I'm sure it took but a moment, but my indecision was enough to render both actions impracticable.

It was Loiyan's wail of despair that drew their attention to us; not that I blame her, mind you. She'd already had a pretty trying time of it over the past few days, and the scenario playing out in front of our eyes just then might have been enough to unbalance the poor girl. But still, I wish she'd been able to hold off long enough for me to get my wits about me. It would have helped a great deal.

As one man, they all looked up from their vicious fun and saw Loiyan and myself, her screaming hysterically, and me gawping at them for all the world like some sort of deranged voyeur.

It seems to me there might have been another pause, but I could be mistaken. Yet their looks of surprise, changing to dark recognition, and finally to joyful rage at having found their prey at long last, could not have happened in an instant.

And *still* we didn't move!

It wasn't until they let up a howl fit to raise the dead, and came on like a pack of wolves, that I realized some sort of motor function might be called for, and the sooner the better.

Evidently Loiyan had the same understanding, for we both set off at once…in opposite directions. I suppose it was only natural for her to want to get away from those fiends as quickly as possible, and that's exactly what she tried to do, setting off like a bullet back the way we had come. But when my body started working, my brain decided it was time to join in, too. Quick as a flash, I saw there was no hope trying to outrun the fleet-footed bastards; they'd be on us before you could say 'would that be nuts or a cigar?' Our only chance, slim as it was, lay in the other direction, straight at them.

It was fortunate I'd taken hold of Loiyan's hand while we had been strolling along, planning our future, for no time was lost when I jerked her around and pointed.

"Come on!" I cried, starting off at a lively sprint up the beach. It was also extremely fortunate she was such an intelligent girl, because after feeling her struggle for the first few strides, she

117

suddenly understood what I hadn't dared take the time to explain, and was pelting along beside me like a good'un.

There was a canoe pulled up on the beach a scant hundred yards away. It seemed silly, even then, but such things will often register during moments of stress, I suppose. For I recognized the bright vermillion craft as the one which had sped away from us, what, an hour earlier? There too, lying in the shallows at its bow, was the owner, still and forever, with that same look of surprised stupidity on his face, his entrails spreading gore in the water all around him.

I reckoned we would beat them to the craft, but only just, for the swine were closing at a disheartening rate.

"We've got to run for it!" I urged, but might as well have saved my breath, for Loiyan didn't need telling. In fact, as the distance to the boat halved, she was pulling slightly into the lead.

Meanwhile, that hellish band of brothers were charging in at a pace fit to incapacitate your mind, let me tell you. My God, but those fellows could move when they wanted! And shout, too! For they were screaming out what I assumed was their war cry (I doubted if they were entreaties of friendship and everlasting brotherhood) in blood-curdling ululations as they came, and they were getting louder by the second.

All that hate being spat at us was numbing, really. It tended to lull my brain, freezing it with the utter hopelessness of the situation. And for a split second, I did feel my limbs begin to lag, but then I was aware of the presence of that marvelous black beauty churning up the sand beside me. Something about her indomitable spirit stiffened my own resolve to see things through to the end.

My breath was rasping in and out of my lungs now, searing them like hot coals fresh out of the furnace. My chest was heaving like a beached whale, and a stitch began to stab into my side, tearing at me with every frantic stride.

There was a thud at my feet, and I caught a glimpse of a brightly decorated *orinka* half buried in the sand as I streaked past. Another followed hard on its heels, and then another, each missing by a whisker. It was amazing they could throw so accurately from what was now a hundred yards away, and at a

118

dead run, too. But any admiration for their prowess was overwhelmed by my rage.

For, clever fellows that they were, they had discerned our plan, and seeing we were going to beat them to the mark, were trying to bring us down beforehand. It struck me as being a singularly unsporting thing to do.

"You black fiends!" I roared shaking my fist, foolishly wasting time, breath and energy, all in one go. "That's not bloody cricket!" The gun was unslung in my hands, "Well, two can play at that game, you rotten savages!" I let off a round without taking the time to aim. It was a fantastically stupid thing to do, but my blood was up, you see?

The discharge let out a mighty roar that quite overwhelmed their ghastly cries, and I was sincerely gratified to see one of their number tumble headlong into the dust.

That brought them up short, right enough. At first they cringed from the thunderous blast, then, seeing their mate writhing in the sand with gouts of blood spewing from where most of his shoulder used to be, they turned to me with a new respect, which was also quite gratifying.

But any hopes that what must have been their introduction to modern weaponry, would frighten them off, quickly dissipated when, after some muttered consultation, they brought up their shields and came cautiously on. Say what you like about them, bloodthirsty and cruel as Hades though they may be, you couldn't fault them for their courage.

Meanwhile, we had reached the canoe and, dancing quickly around the erstwhile owner's corpse, hit the prow at a dead run, propelling it deeper into the lake. But the bloody thing only skidded back a few feet before jarring to a halt. Beside myself, I gave another mighty heave and got another foot or so, yet the wretched craft was obstinately stuck in the mud. I invested an anxious moment to peer over my shoulder. The warriors were less than thirty yards away, and with some of their confidence restored, looked ready to make a dash at us.

Forcing myself to remain calm, I grabbed the gun from where it had been flung into the canoe. I leveled it, taking careful

119

aim at the very center of the leader's shield, and squeezed the trigger.

Two thirds of their number hit the ground, most of them from sheer fright, but when those who could had regained their feet and taken stock, three had not risen. At that range the elephant gun's heavy slug had, of course, passed through the shield with ridiculous ease, continuing on through the man behind it, tearing out his heart, on through the breast of the man behind him, and finally shattering the thigh of the third with a force still far from spent.

It seemed that this latest black magic from the Red Man called for another council of war, and while the survivors mulled things over amongst themselves – ignoring the screams of their comrades while they flailed about in agony – I was determined that the opportunity they'd so thoughtfully provided would not go wasted.

Meanwhile, Loiyan, clever girl, conceiving the crux of the problem, had scampered around to the stern of the boat, and began to excavate the keel from the mud by lifting and pulling at the same time. It worked wonderfully well, and shifted the craft another three feet. Now with my assistance, our next effort left the stern wobbling about as it took on buoyancy. One more heave and it was free! I continued to propel the craft out into deeper water as I shouted at Loiyan to climb aboard. She cocked a nimble leg over the gunwale, looked up and screamed.

I turned and found one of the lion-maned fiends scant feet away, eyes ablaze with the clear intention of skewering me.

I had barely enough time to grab the gun and parry the spear thrust, its deadly blade shrieking sparks up the barrel. I reversed the weapon and smashed his face with the butt. He disappeared with a howl of hate liberally intermingled with pain, only to be replaced by two others. These boys were soldiers, and no error, because they were going at it like professionals, with one addressing my front while the other circled around to take me in flank.

I might have hesitated, but even though the odds were hopeless, I don't think I did. I lunged a feint to the left, causing the one to my front to bring up his shield. Spinning hard on my heel, I brought the gun around, braining him with the barrel on his exposed side. Even as he sank without a sound, I twisted frantically to parry the one coming in on my flank, but was only partly successful. The thrust was aimed for my kidneys and I caught it a glancing blow on the stock, veering it away, yet a searing pain scored up my ribs. The brute followed with a blow from the haft, and I was flung backwards onto the bows, leaving my body exposed.

It must have been but a split second, but it seemed an eternity while he, shouting with triumph, raised that horrible weapon and lunged in to run me through.

His lion-maned head filled my vision, grinning like a satyr. Off balance as I was, I was helpless to riposte, but could only stand waiting for that sickening bite of cold steel to bring about my end.

Then, out of the blue, there came a roar of rage, and something tawny struck the back of the bugger's neck. In a series of instances his glee switched to shock, then to pain, and then fear as, suddenly, his body was whipped backwards.

Even now, all these years later, I cannot believe that it was any affection for me that caused him to strike, because he simply didn't have any – for anyone – but for whatever reason the Angry One had chosen that moment to live up to his name, and thank heaven he did. He spun the warrior around so fast I swear his feet never touched the ground. Then releasing him, the fellow splashed, screaming, into the shallows, whereupon that belligerent camel proceeded to stomp him with a particular frenzy that was beyond mere mean-spiritedness, and caused me to wonder if there was not something personal between them.

But whatever the reason, I wasn't about to let such sacrifice go wasted, so, chock full of adrenaline, I launched myself into the boat with a single bound, almost capsizing us with the effort. After a few alarming rolls, the sturdy little craft managed to right itself again.

Three of their remaining number veered off, racing to the aid of their comrade, who appeared to be coming in second best in his struggles with the surly brute. And quite a help they were, too. They hovered around anxiously, shouting and waving their arms to distract the beast, but they might as well have been on the moon for all the good they did. For the Angry One was worrying the poor sod as a dog would a rat, and didn't take the least notice of the others. He had his victim and wouldn't be swayed, kicking out an irate hind leg at any who ventured too close. It's quite astonishing, really, when you think about it, but none of those fellows made any attempt to spear the beast. Looking back, I think that, due to a lifetime of devoted pastoral husbandry, the idea quite simply never entered their minds. To them, although he held no particular sacred value like their cattle, perhaps because of his rarity, the camel did have worth, and that was all there was to it. However much of this view their friend shared, while he lay bleeding, bruised and howling by the shore, I couldn't say.

Meanwhile, the remaining four came charging in at the run. They had seen their chums come to grips with me, and saw me wounded in the bargain. It was obvious they hoped to rush in and make an end of it.

But Loiyan, having witnessed earlier how the craft was propelled, had seized a paddle and was now splashing about in a lubberly fashion, but pulling us inexorably backwards, away from the shore. Still, the water was shallow, scarcely up to their thighs, so the brutes kept floundering on. Inexpertly handled as the boat was, there was a chance they might still reach us.

I suppose I could have taken hold of a paddle myself, but as I said, my blood was up, and with the village burning in the background, I felt I had a score to settle.

I took my time while I reloaded, taking care to keep the powder dry. An *orinka* clattered against the gunwale. I leveled the gun at the culprit and pulled the trigger, feeling great satisfaction as the top of his head disappeared in a pink frothy haze.

Seeing the demon revived, the others came on more cautiously, masking grimaces of disgust while they gingerly skirted the involuntary spasms of their less fortunate comrade.

I took advantage of the lull to reload the empty chamber.

"Loiyan!" One of them called, "Why do you run? Bring him to us!"

"Go away!" she cried, "Leave us alone!"

It wasn't until then that I realized she was weeping. The effect was sobering.

Suddenly I understood that she must know these men, perchance had laughed with them, for as long as she had lived amongst their village. Raping murderers though they might be, they were still her people, not far removed from being her family, in fact. She couldn't be feeling much joy about any of this. Whatever her sympathies for the fisher-folk, she was still Maasai, and her treatment of Sakuda and Tepilit notwithstanding, it must have pained her to see it come to this.

There was silence from our pursuers while they mulled over her reply, but they kept on coming.

Then, "Why do you say these words, Loiyan? Do you not recognize me? It is I, Sabore! Bring us the demon!"

"Go away, Sabore!" she sobbed. "I will not do as you ask!"

"You are bewitched, Loiyan! The Red Man has put an evil spell on you!"

"I am *not* bewitched! And he is *not* a demon! He is a man!"

After feeling the indignity of being discussed as if I were so much chattel, I felt it incumbent to dip in my own oar, so to speak.

"Go away, you stupid niggers! Can't you see you're upsetting the lady?! Go on, get out of it, or you'll get what's coming!"

But of course they ignored me.

Gad but this lake was shallow. We were better than a quarter mile out and still the water wasn't much higher than their waists.

"Oh to blazes with this!" I muttered, setting the gun down and picking up a paddle. I think, when I first realized we were safely afloat, I had some thought to killing the lot of them, should they be so obliging as to keep themselves within range. But it's one thing killing someone in the heat of battle, quite another when they're passing time with the missus, so to speak. So the only reasonable course of action lay in making good our escape.

I turned the bow around and set off at a good pace. It didn't matter if the lake was never any deeper than this clear to

123

the other side – wherever that other side was – they were hardly likely to wade all that distance.

But no sooner had we started when something hit me a terrific blow on my right shoulder, numbing my arm all the way down to my fingertips. The paddle slipped from my grasp, and I found myself gazing stupidly at the *orinka* bobbing in the water along side.

"Back-shot, by God!" I thought, reaching for the gun, but only my left hand would answer. Suddenly I felt dazed and confused, no doubt from the shock of the blow, and had soon stretched my length on the bottom of the boat.

"Chah-lee!" Loiyan was at my head, cradling it in her lap.

"Get us out of here," I cried, but the words were thick and heavy, coming out of my mouth in an indecipherable mutter.

"Where are you hurt?"

It was vital that we keep moving, but she had flung her paddle aside and grabbed for her medicine bag, not seeming to care for anything other than my welfare, and I was helpless to tell her to do otherwise

It took quite a bit of effort, but I managed to push myself up on my good elbow. Sabore and his chums were scant yards away. I fumbled for the gun, managing to pull back the hammers, and endeavored to bring it to bear.

Lord, the thing felt as heavy as Aunt Hilda's sow. I leveled the barrels, but now my vision was blurring. I felt I was going to faint again.

The gun was knocked out of my hand, and Loiyan let out a fresh scream. It brought me around enough to see Sabore, one hand on the bow, the other hefting his spear with obvious intent. In a dazed funk, I flung myself at him, and fancied I caught his head a clip as I went over the side.

The water was wonderfully invigorating, and I hoped we might be on equal terms when I regained my feet. But as my head broached the surface I found that my right arm was still dead to the world.

I must have knocked Sabore's spear away in my desperate lunge for it was nowhere in sight. I took a swing at him with my fist, but my reflexes were slow, and he dodged the blow easily.

124

Then I felt his fingers around my throat, and my head being forced back into the water. I struggled, but I fear it was a feeble effort. I barely had time to take a breath before I was under again.

My God, but it was agony! His fingers tightened their grip forcing me ever further downward. My already feeble struggles became more pathetic still as my strength began to wane. I tried to claw for his face, but already I was seeing stars before my eyes and knew I was losing consciousness. My lungs felt as though they were ready to burst. It couldn't be long before I succumbed.

Then there came to my ears a muffled roar, and amazingly, the pressure on my throat was gone. I had just enough strength to force my way to the surface, and then I was gasping and coughing, spewing up everything that was inside. I raked in air by the lungful and retched some more when it grated across the searing pain of my bruised larynx.

Sabore lay on his back, his body fluctuating gently on the choppy waves. His face was the very caricature of surprise and amazement. Also, I took note that there was a hole as big as my thumb where his left eye should have been, and blood was blossoming around what was left of his head like some sort of strange water flower.

I looked to the boat and saw Loiyan plunked down amidships, the barrel of the gun – smoke curling lazily from one of the muzzles – resting on the gunwale. Her face was also a caricature of surprise and amazement. But when a sound came from behind me, she pulled herself together with a quickness that was a relief to see.

She motioned to the lifeless corpse with the heavy gun, and said, cool and hard as you please, "Take him and go."

I turned to see the remaining two warriors, angry and vengeful, yet apparently afraid to renew the assault.

I shoved the body forward. It drifted over to them like a water-laden bear skin. The warriors hesitated and then, one after the other, lowered their spears.

"There will be a reckoning, Loiyan," one vowed, laying hold of one of Sabore's arms.

"You can never return to the village," his mate growled, taking hold of the other.

To this one Loiyan replied, "Be grateful that you still can, Isaya."

"You have murdered him," said the first, which I thought was a bit hard, when you considered what they themselves had just been up to. Still, I didn't doubt that the charge would hold up in a Maasai court, if they had such a thing.

"Yes," she replied evenly, "I have murdered him, Kuya." She aimed carefully before adding, "Each time it becomes easier."

The boy – for he was scarcely more than that – had guts, I'll say that for him. Had that great gun been pointed at me, and its wielder having just displayed her willingness to use it, I would have been high-tailing it out of there just as fast as my legs could carry me, but the oaf just looked puzzled and asked, "Each...time?"

She observed. "You have not enquired about Sakuda or Tepilit."

You could almost hear the gears grinding around in the lad's head. Then slowly his eyes began to bulge.

"You mean....?"

"I slit their throats while they slept." Her voice was cold...dreadfully cold. "It was them or me. I chose me. Now," she pointed the gun at his chest, "how shall I chose, *you* or me?"

The silence weighed heavy while the idiots ran through their options. If they had been white, I daresay they would have made excellent Guards material; sense of duty fairly bursting out of them, and not overly burdened with intelligence, they were of the stuff that I'd seen a belly-full of in the Crimea, quite possibly even the same fabric officers were made from, if they came from a good enough family.

Then I noticed Kuya take the most surreptitious of peeks towards the shore, and I wondered if they were as stupid as I had first thought.

The Angry One having done his worst with regards to his victim, and notwithstanding the efforts of the erstwhile rescue party, was disappearing into the jungle as fast as he could go,

126

lashing his tail joyfully as he went, and that was the last I ever saw of him. Meanwhile, said party, finding themselves free to consider other options, had decided to make their way out to where we sat at a deadlock to see if they could lend a hand.

No, they weren't fools; they were buying time.

"We cannot return without his blood on our spears," Isaya said in an ominous tone. "It is a matter of honour."

"Loiyan," I called, pointing to the reinforcements making their way up from the rear.

As if that were a signal, both Kuya and Isaya chose that moment to strike. The former, bringing his weapon on guard, made a sudden lunge at me, the latter launching his spear at Loiyan.

I'd barely enough time to position myself before he struck, and with one arm useless, and no weapon to hand, it looked grim. But for all of his bravery, Kuya was a handless clown with a spear. At the same time that I heard the gun roar, I was able to buffet the point aside with my good hand, and close with him. He tried to pull back for a second go at me, but I butted him in the face with my head. He fell back with a splash, his spear flying out of his hands, and I was on him with my superior weight and strength – for he was only a lad, still in his teens. Then, convinced as to the effectiveness of such a move (for Sabore had used it on myself only a minute before) I locked the fingers of my good hand around his throat, forcing him beneath the water. When he was low enough, I put my foot on his chest and pressed down for all I was worth, forcing the air from his lungs. It broke the surface in an eruption of bubbles.

Meanwhile, unaware of how the other altercation was shaping up, I took stock of what had been happening around me. My first thought was to brace myself for an attack from Isaya, but none came. In fact, he hadn't moved from where he'd been standing, though now he was staring in astonished shock at the grisly remains of his arm. I then spun around to see if his hurled spear had found Loiyan. With immense relief, I saw it hadn't. Those heavy weapons were not made with casting in mind, and proved what a desperate ploy it had been in the first place.

127

Loiyan was a picture of infinite woe. She dropped the gun into the bottom of the boat and covered her face with her hands.

"Oh, why would you not listen!?" she wailed.

I struggled over to the canoe, convinced that all opposition must now cease. The last three warriors were still a good distance off, so we were safe from their bloody *orinkas* for the time being. If I could just climb aboard, we could make good our escape.

But I was up to my waist in water and it would take a goodly heave to bring myself athwart the hawser, or whatever the nautical term was. With only one good arm, I would need Loiyan's assistance if I were not to capsize us into the lake.

"Loiyan," I called as softly as I dared, but she made no indication of having heard. I tried again, "Loiyan!" and splashed some water in her face.

It seemed to do the trick. She shook herself and got her bearings before coming over to lend a hand.

I heaved myself up as high as I could, and felt her hands grip the back of my shirt. The craft was tilting dangerously, but I was thinking I just might make it, when I heard her cry, "No, Isaya!"

Another hand gripped my belt, pulling me back into the lake. I couldn't risk tipping the boat over, and had to allow myself to be so drawn.

Isaya was pale, deathly pale, but there was a grim determination about his set that made my heart plummet.

"I cannot let you go," he said. "It is a matter of honour."

"Look, lad," I said slowly, "you're hurt bad. No one's going to hold it against you if you let us go. Now be a good fellow and bugger off."

I turned to make a second effort to board, but he said, "No!" and tried to drag me back.

It was ridiculous, and if the last three hadn't seen what was afoot, and were now setting a more urgent pace to come to his assistance, I would have said it was downright farcical. I couldn't board with him tugging away at me, and he being too weak from loss of blood, was capable of little else.

I had to make up my mind, and I didn't have all that much time to do it. If those fellows ever caught up we were done for.

The gun was empty, and I could scarcely hope to take on even one of them, let alone all three. By the way his blood was pumping into the lake, I knew Isaya was a goner if he didn't get help soon, but I reckoned he could hold on just long enough for the others to get here.

It was no good.

Earlier, I'd felt my foot come into contact with something on the lake bottom. I'd realized it must be Sabore's spear. So, after having weighed our options, and realizing there was nothing else for it, I reached down and took hold. Bringing it to the surface, I leveled it at him and said, "For the last time, you damned fool, just turn around and walk away!"

But he just stared at me – too weak to bring himself to his full height – and shook his head.

I'm afraid I made rather a hash of it. The spear was awkward in my left hand, so it took half a dozen lunges before he finally keeled over.

Loiyan was a fright when it was done. Her hands were fluttering like leaves, and her mouth wide open, but emitting no sound.

I tried splashing water on her again, but without any effect, just that shocked catatonia.

I dared to look back and saw the last three were now within a few hundred yards. Whatever was to be done, I had to do it now.

I reached up and grabbed her by the front of her robe, pulling for all I was worth. She came over the side like a shot, and plummeted to the bottom with a mighty splash, then came up sputtering, and agog, but coherent, at least.

"Help me up," I said, and added for emphasis, "we've got to hurry."

At first she looked at me as though I were from another planet. I was afraid I'd have to give her another dunking, but then she collected herself and came over to assist me.

I was surprised at how strong she was, for when I heaved upward, I was aboard before I knew it. After that, it was a simple matter for her to climb in; she didn't even need my help.

"You'll have to paddle." I rubbed my shoulder; it was beginning to ache abominably.

She nodded, and settled into the stern, paddle in hand.

It felt anticlimactic when the three remaining Maasai finally grew smaller as the canoe sped away, leaving them in the distance. They had slowed to a walk, for there was no longer any need to hurry.

All that was left for them was to retrieve their dead.

Chapter Eleven

After skirting a long promontory, stretching far to the west, we followed the coast to the northeast, finally making camp on the beach while there was still plenty of light.

We passed other villages along the way, but had taken care to give them and their boats a wide berth. We were safe now, but the day's experience had left us with a distaste for the company of humans.

Loiyan, with robotic efficiency, dressed my wounds with the predictable salves and poultices. In truth, I was already feeling sensations at the ends of my fingertips by the end of the day, and was thankful the nerve damage hadn't been permanent. By the time she had finished binding both poultices in place, I was feeling pins and needles up and down my arm, the cut in my side proving to be little more than a scratch.

"It is just a bruise," she referred to my injured shoulder in a hollow voice, "but it has gone to the bone. One week, maybe two, the pain will pass." She sounded wistful, as though I were the lucky one.

I took her hand in mine. "Yours will pass, too."

I thought she would be too far gone to reply, for she had been silent for the rest of the day, but she looked at me with great sadness and said, "I wish I could believe you, Chah-lee, but it goes deep inside me." She looked down at her hands folded in her lap, "I *knew* them…all of them."

"Look here, I know it's hard, but you did what you had to do. Why, you saved my life, didn't you? Anyway, what other choice did you have? If you hadn't killed them, they would have killed us. It's that simple. That has to count for something, don't it?"

"Yes, of course that counts," she smiled a sad smile and gave me a hug – taking care to keep clear of my injuries – but it was a listless embrace, as one might give to a stranger. Still, she was doing her best, brave girl.

"I want to forget."

It was good she was willing to talk. That was the first step towards drawing out the poison.

131

"You won't forget; I don't think it's possible," I admitted. "I know you may not believe me now, but after awhile, when your mind has exhausted itself to the point where it can come to terms with the fact there was nothing else you could have done, you will learn at least to accept what happened. And then you can get on, you'll see."

We had kindled a fire, but somewhere along the line most of our food supplies must have gone over the side leaving only a bag of jerky, of which we were both heartily sick. So I went to see if there was anything in the canoe.

The fisherman had thoughtfully left his boat fully stocked with his gear, but more important to our immediate needs, there were three of his morning's catch lying fresh in a basket. I filleted them, and lay them on the coals.

"I am not hungry," she said moments later, when I offered one to her.

"But you must eat something."

"I can't."

"Look, you've done so much already," I cajoled, holding out a small piece in my fingers. "Go on, have a bite."

She hesitated, but then took it and placed a tiny piece in her mouth, then another, chewing slowly. She grimaced when she swallowed, as though the very act had choked her, and would take no more after that.

Defeated, I put the fish down and was silent. It was a hard go, but there was nothing to be done until she reached out. It was my job to see that I was there when she did.

We were bound together, she and I. For better or worse, something had started between us, probably from the moment we first met. Like a boulder rolling down a mountain, and we had given it that first, necessary shove. Now it had a momentum of its own, and would go where it would. Until it came to rest, we were joined by the very capriciousness of its journey. In spite of the need I felt to return to my duty at Lord Brampton's side, and in spite of my desire for all the familiarities of England, I do admit there was a yearning in me that longed for that journey never to end.

132

The next day was better as we continued following the littoral to the northeast, and her indomitable spirit, though battered and bruised, began to regain its rightful place, as I should have known it would, and the next day was better still, and so on. My ribs and shoulder still hurt like the devil, but at least my arm was of some use, to the point where I could grip a paddle. I took over that chore from her, and taking my place in the stern, found the stiffness of the bruise would ease after a few minutes, although it was an agony that had me grinding my teeth until it passed.

I loved to sit there watching her with her back to me – sometimes paddling, sometimes not – until, unaware that I was watching, she began to take an interest in the world again. It was as though I was witnessing the rebirth of a phoenix, rising anew from discarded ashes – or the blossoming of a dark rose in the morning's first light; and as one day followed another, she continued to rise and bloom. In time, but for a haunting that scarred the depths of her eyes, a sadness so subtle you might think it had never been, that vision of her remained true.

We never stopped in one place for long, but neither did we hurry overmuch. The boat became our home, the land a curious place to visit and make love; the flames of our campfire were pitiful and small compared to that which burned within us.

We fished for our supper along the way, and soon became proficient. That is to say, she became proficient while I continued to paddle. It was a reversal in gender – she providing the meat, I the haven – into which she took some delight, although she was too sensitive of my feelings to admit as much. But I didn't care, it was worth far more than a bruised ego to see her come alive again.

She taught herself how to use the cast net. I had always managed to tie the thing in knots whenever I tried, and was ready to give it up as a lost cause, but she never did.

At first it was amusing, watching from my place in the stern while she stood wobbly legged in the bow, and my greatest chore was to not laugh too hard when her best efforts produced an impressive splash that merely served to frighten the shore birds, but supplied us with no catch. Yet gradually her legs

133

became more agile on the water, and her hands more adept with the net. It wasn't long, too, before she found her robe to be an encumbrance while casting, and so, set it aside with pragmatic ease – a Maasai woman not being overly modest in regards to her breasts, youthful and firm though they might be.

That was something, I can tell you, and if, one day, some marvelous photographic moving machine should ever be invented that could capture such moments, it will be as one to me. For I have only to close my eyes and see her still: legs spread, balancing nimbly in the bow. Then with a graceful twist of her body, the net flies high and wide, tracing golden circles in the air as the sunlight catches the water racing from its strands; and there she stands in startling profile: back arched, breasts upthrust and proud, arms stretched high and away from her body, neck twisting, graceful, as she follows the trajectory, frozen in time...and beautiful beyond words.

For me, that was the real prize; the fish she caught were perhaps necessary, but seemed the lesser benefit.

Sometimes, when the weather was easy, we'd head out further from the shore, and from that vantage point could see the land much farther inland. In the distance, to the east, there was a long range of mountains, volcanic in origin, I should think, their effluvia forming great drifts sliding down to the water's edge, long ago repossessed by jungle. I realized these must be those that formed the eastern barrier of the Great Rift Valley. I had taken note of them earlier, when Lord Brampton and myself had originally set forth to seek adventure – how trite those words seemed to me now. It felt odd to be viewing them here, from the opposite direction, an ever present reminder of just how far I had traveled, into the very heart of this continent.

Then too, there were birds in their virtual millions, in species too many to describe, often forming vast artificial clouds – many of them criss-crossing above and below one another – as they wended their way, hither and thither, for reasons best known only to themselves. It was seldom quiet on the lake. Seldom could you sit back and listen but there would be some call, some twitter, or more often, a veritable cascade of avian exaltation assaulting you in waves, urging some visceral part of you to rise up and take flight with them, to soar to the furthest reaches of the world – to be freer than any other man since the beginning of time.

And villages. Many, many villages, and often as not protected by walls of stone. I was intrigued by these, for they seemed to be without mortar and very old; as old as, and not at all dissimilar to, the dry stone walls bordering our own fields back in Yorkshire. Such a way of building was fast becoming a lost art in Britain, and judging by the haphazard reparations I saw, so too, it seemed, was it here. From this, I deduced that the people who lived within their protective enclosures must have been doing so for a very long time. Realizing their apparent lack of evolutionary progress in any other field, it seemed to me that these were now societies in decline, merely subsisting in their days, waiting for some unknown nemesis to come bearing down upon them and sweep them from the face of the earth.

In spite of the heat of the day, I felt a chill pass over me when I realized these sentiments, for they had not been cold deduction. Rather they had visited themselves upon me in a way that was more of a premonition than anything else. I was reminded of my Scottish mother, and the way my father and I had used to indulge her when she lay claim to having the gift of the sight. Her folk were from the wild, untamed hills to the north where such superstitions often held sway, and contact with civilization had not completely succeeded in breeding it out of them. Indeed, I wondered if I had not inherited some small part of that from her – whether superstition or fact.

I hugged myself until the chill had passed. Then once more conscious of the sun's rays, I took hold of my paddle and continued on. Soon the premonition, if that was what it was, became as a distant memory, and was forgotten.

In the end, it turned out that I was right, and that, too, I was wrong. For nemesis there was, yet the fisher-folk were not waiting. It was already upon them.

We had been a month upon Ukerewe, and as the days passed, one after the other without incident, I confess we had grown more and more complacent with our situation. The episode at the fishing village now seemed far away, and with but very little imagination I think we might even have convinced ourselves it was something that had happened to other wayfarers, as in a story, but not to us. So idyllic had our ensuing time become that such ugly memories seemed not to have been possible. And too, so timid were these local villagers that fear, that vital instinct of survival, had been left gradually to decay, the keenness of its edge to become corroded with disuse.

We had been continuing to follow the coast to the northeast; then gradually, it bent more to true north, until finally, after many days, there seemed to be a heading somewhat to the west. It appeared that we were now approaching the furthest northern perimeter of some great bowl or hollow, and that if there existed a conduit over its rim, we might expect soon to discover it.

Loiyan's fishing had proved profitable in the early afternoon, and as I had mentioned earlier, we were not pursuing our goal with any great urgency, so it was decided to make camp about a mile distant from a village we had just passed.

Our habits had begun to fall into a comfortable routine. Loiyan took the coals from the previous day's fire from the metal pot and kindled a new one while I busied myself gathering fuel. Neither chore being very arduous as the jungle continued to come down to the water's edge in most places, bringing with it an abundance of deadfall. Soon the flames were lapping merrily away while I prepared the day's catch, and Loiyan, being more knowledgeable in such pursuits, ventured into the forest to see if there were fruits or other edibles nearby for the harvesting so as to guard against our diet becoming tedious.

Just as I was thinking the coals ready for the filets she returned.

"Any luck?" I asked.

She smiled and offered a view of the contents of her basket: some mangoes and the pods and roots of a moringa tree. To a meat and potatoes man like myself, the roots I had found to be especially tasty, not at all unlike horseradish, really.

"Fit for a king," I said, nodding approval.

"Fit for *my* king," she laughed.

She was always saying that sort of thing, and though it never ceased secretly to please me, I found it impossible not to become embarrassed by it. Not that she wasn't aware, the little imp. I think she did it for no better reason than it pleased *her* to see me blush.

More and more, also because it pleased me, I think, she had taken to leaving her robe aside, allowing me to drink to the full the sight her nubile young body. After weeks of this, I doubted if I could ever look at a woman in quite the same way I used to, when a mere glimpse of an ankle had been a memory to be treasured. This more primitive form of *haute couture* never failed to work its wiles on me, of course, and I found it a most delicious way to string out the day.

After I wrapped the filets together with the roots in some leaves, and placed them on the coals, I accepted a mango she offered and, leaning back in the sun, luxuriated in the tranquility.

"Chah-lee?"

"Mmm?"

"Tell me about your world, this Ingle-land."

"What do you want to know?"

"Everything. I want to know everything about you."

"Not much to tell, really. I'm my Lord Brampton's servant, and that's about it." I struggled with a twinge of guilt that I was not currently at my place to attend him.

"But this Ingle-land, what is it like?"

"Best country in the world. Cricket, rugby, that sort of thing. Then there's the Empire too, of course, but you can't be interested in all that, surely?"

"Yes, I want to know."

So I told her all about the vast fleets of mighty vessels under sail to the farthest reaches of the world, and all of the far off lands and different races of people under the protection of the Empire. I told her about Lords and the cricket matches I had seen there whilst in my master's service. I told her about Yorkshire and the Brampton's estates; of Brampton Manor, itself. I told her about the theater and the pursuits of gentlemen as well as warm evenings spent amongst my peers at the *Stag's Arms*, the local tavern, with a pot of ale, cheerful company, and

137

rosy cheeked, and saucy tongued barmaids with which to while away the hours.

"Are the women there pretty?" It must have been the mentioning of the barmaids that prompted her to ask.

"Oh yes, quite pretty."

"Are they white like you?"

"Mmm hmm."

"Perhaps, some day, you will take one of them for your wife? Perhaps you will have many wives?"

"Mmm…what? Of course not! In civilized society we have only one wife."

"Say you so?" she mused. "It is because you are a slave and not a great chief?"

"It is because it is *civilized*," I answered, feeling slightly irascible. "And I'm not a slave! British people shall never be slaves!"

"Oh, but Chah-lee," she whispered next to me. I felt her breast brushing against my arm, "I think you are such a strong man, and so handsome with your dark curls and hair on your lip. You must have many wives!"

"Not possible, I'm afraid," I said, mollified, "but it's gratifying you should think so."

When I rolled over, she was already on her back. Her kilt cast aside, one shining ebony leg bent with careless, languid carnality.

"I do think so, Chah-lee," she said in a husky voice, eyes glazed, "Oh yes, this I do believe."

I doubt that, in the annals of our nation's history, you will ever find a Smithers that might be rated as anything even remotely close to being a genius, but by God, I didn't have to be to pick up on this invitation. I was on top of her and inserted before you could say 'Jack Robinson'.

"Do you think I am beautiful, Chah-lee?"

"What? Oh, hell yes!" I growled, setting to, "Cute as a button!"

"Then show me!" She wrapped her long black legs around my torso, and raked her nails down my back, clinging to me while she whispered moistly in my ear. "Show me, Chah-lee!

138

Show me how beautiful I am! Show me with your big strong arms! Show me with your great broad chest and your…oh!…your *magnificent* manhood! Show me, Chah-lee! *Show me!*"

I had to admit there was something to this *emorata* business because, as I came to the boiling point, I was still taken with the heightened sensation of it all….again and again, and ever yet again. So wonderful was the experience, in fact, that by the time the act was completed – if she'd had even half of the pleasure I had – there was no doubt I had succeeded in convincing her she was very lovely, indeed…certainly by the sounds she'd been making, at any rate.

I was well spent when I finally rolled over onto my back, feeling one hell of a fine fellow. The sun was warm and the sand a delightful cushion. I doubted there would be any further traveling that day.

She cuddled up beside me.

"Chah-lee?" But already her voice seemed to be coming from far away.

Vaguely, like someone more than half asleep I heard myself say, "Mmm?"

Her words spiraled down with me into unconsciousness.

"What will your people think of me in Ingle-land?"

Chapter Twelve

We pulled onto the gravelled lane to Brampton Manor in a coach-and-four.

Everyone was gathered on the broad, stone-flagged steps of the entrance to greet us, all shouting and waving congratulations. I pulled the curtain aside with my silver-tipped walking stick and peered out at all the friendly faces beaming back at me.

There was dear old Mrs. Dyck, the cook, smiling toothlessly and waving her best lace hanky. Oh, and here was Maggie, the chambermaid, jumping up and down, ringlets bouncing like bedsprings, scarcely able to contain her enthusiasm. Over there was that young lad, whatsisname, the new ostler, knuckling his brow and grinning idiotically from ear to ear. Davis, the footman, immaculate as usual, was bowing gravely from the waist, right-angled to the ground. Oh my goodness! There was even redoubtable old Mrs. Kilns, the housekeeper, laying aside her glowering phiz for a change, the welcome of her smile contrasting sharply with the severity of her grey-haired bun. And old Tomkins, who had lost an arm at Waterloo, standing stiffly to attention, his remaining limb rigid at the salute.

And before them all, dressed in their very best coats and tails, were Lord Brampton himself, side by side with my guv'nor. Lord Brampton smiling amiably and my old man fit to burst the buttons on his starched front.

When Davis came forward to open the coach door, I emerged waving my topper amidst the warmth of all their cheers.

"Well done, Smithers!" Lord Brampton seized my hand, wringing it sincerely, "Jolly good show!"

"Now then, Charlie," my father piped his eye emotionally, but managed to give my back a good thumping all the same. "Now then, lad!"

And there was my mum, dressed up in her best calico, with the shawl that Dad had given her last Christmas draped over her shoulders.

140

"Ma bairn," she crooned, all five foot two Presbyterian inches of her enfolding me in her arms. "Ach, ma wee lamb, cum back frae the land o'the niggers tae see his old mither agin, has he no!"

"Mother!"

I held her close as I dared, being careful from force of habit to listen for excessive strain on her tiny bones. I breathed in deeply, filling my nostrils with the scent of the lye from her soap.

"Mother, I'm home!"

"Aye laddie, so y'ar. Fit to burst ma puir old heart w'the gladness of it, too!"

I held her for some time, and would have continued doing so for quite a bit longer, but the spell was broken by an expectant "Ahem!"

I looked up to see Lord Brampton fidgeting his eyeballs toward the coach like an over-excited child awaiting permission to open his birthday gifts.

"Aye then," my mother reluctantly extricated herself from my arms, smoothing out my lapels with little bird-like whisks of her hands. "Now, where's this bonnie lass we've bin hearin' so much aboot?"

"Yes, where?" cried Mrs. Kilns.

"We want to see her," Mrs. Dyck called from the step, peering short-sightedly at the carriage.

"Yes, do show us! Oh please!" Maggie piped.

Then there was a general uproar from all of them, even the townsfolk, assembled off to one side, all dressed in their finest, all eagerly demanding to see my new wife.

So, I released my mum and took proud station beside the carriage door.

"Everyone!" I cried, turning to face them all. I held my hand out in preparation for assisting her to dismount. "It is now my very great honour to present to you…Mrs. Charlie Smithers!"

I felt her tiny satin glove embrace my hand.

But for a slight creaking of the weathervane over the stables, the silence was instant and absolute.

141

All eyes were huge as saucers, all mouths gaping in unabashed astonishment.

Then from the quiet, came a single reverent exhalation.

"Cracky!" quoth the ostler lad.

Then, as if that were a signal, all was pandemonium, everyone cheering, laughing, wildly shouting for joy. Starlings that had come to roost on branches of the sturdy old oak, in which Lord Brampton and I used to play, took flight with a startled flurry of feathers. Over in the paddock, King William, the old earl's ancient charger, well past even his stud years, reared back, front hooves pawing at the sky, neighing joyous hosannas. At heel by Tomkins' side, Canute, the grey-whiskered old mastiff, bayed lustful bliss to an appreciative sun. Out in the meadow, little lambs cavorted and frolicked, while their mothers gathered as their ancestors had gathered at a manger, eager to bestow their blessings.

For here, emerging first with a dear little foot encased in softest calfskin, then in a sky blue dress of purest silk brocade, with strings of flawless pearls enclosing her own sweet throat – which yet failed to approach her own natural beauty – was my wife, Mrs. Charlie Smithers. My Loiyan.

"Well done Smithers!" Lord Brampton had once more seized my hand and was pumping it for all he was worth. "Oh, good show! Simply smashing!"

"Thank you milord," I replied with smug modesty. I turned to smile at my darling; to share in this moment of triumph. The smile that she returned was warm and sparkling, full of love...

...and...

'Oh my!' I think.

Without releasing my hand, my lord was busy gesturing with his other.

"Everyone! To the new Mrs. Smithers! Let's all give her three cheers and a tiger, shall we! Hip! Hip!"

....and she...

"HURRAH!" Everyone roared out in unison.

"Chah-lee!"

"Hip! Hip!"

...and she is....

"HURRAH!!"

"Chah-lee!"

"Hip! Hip!"

…and she is…

"Chah-lee, wake up!"

"HURRAH!!!!"

…and she is…

"Chah-lee!"

White!

I pried open my sleep-smudged eyes and was confused to see that, instead of Lord Brampton, Loiyan was shaking me for all she was worth.

"Chah-lee!"

For quite some time, nothing seemed real.

"But you're black," I said, although not yet believing it, "and where's your beautiful dress, your pearls?"

"Wake *up*, Chah-lee!"

"And the coach and…and my mother…and Lord Brampton…and…" I looked about myself in dazed stupidity, "Brampton Manor? Whatever has become of Brampton Manor?" Unreasonably, I suppose, I accused her, "What have you done with it?"

"Listen Chah-lee! Listen!"

Still not master of my wits, I at first thought she wanted to say something of importance, but then, with astounding obtuseness, I very gradually shook myself to some state of wakefulness after which, to a degree, I was able to cotton to her meaning.

Even so, it had been such a lovely dream that I found I was quite reluctant to thrust it away from the present. Everyone I held dear had been gathered to rejoice with me upon my good fortune. All was happiness! All was bliss!

It was while I was pondering on this genial state of affairs that the night sounds of Africa began to permeate my brain.

I must have been sleeping soundly for hours, because a bright full moon was high in the sky, and the fire had long since died away, leaving cold white ashes in its place. Cicadas sang in their hundreds amongst the nearby grasses; dozens of bullfrogs

143

croaked lustily by the water's edge. An owl softly hooted in the depths of the jungle, and then, over the gentle chuckle of ripples washing upon the shore, I heard it.

A woman screaming.

And then another, and another, and perhaps because it had been more constant that it formed a background of noise, I deciphered the roars and yells of many, deeper, voices. As my mind catapulted towards total wakefulness, I realized that it was a sound I'd come to recognize many times in the Crimea.

Men struggling in combat!

"Oh Chah-lee! I am frightened!" Loiyan gripped my bicep with both hands. Strong though she might be, only fear could make that grip so like a vice.

"The *Laibon*!" she wailed, "He has sent more warriors to find us!"

While I highly doubted that – even at our leisurely pace, we must have far outstripped the possibility of any pursuit from the Maasai Mara – but I couldn't be sure. The struggle – whatever it was – was coming from the direction of the village we had just passed earlier in the day.

Then, over all, came the distinctive sound of a gunshot, followed by several more reports hard on its heals.

Not Maasai then – I was surprised at how relieved I was about that – but who?

Quick as a wink, I realized what I would have to do.

"Now look, Loiyan," I said, gently prizing her fingers from my arm, "I want you to take the spear and all our supplies into the jungle. Erase all traces of the fire, or that we were ever here. I want you to hide. Can you do this?"

For reasons I couldn't fathom at the time, I had thrown Sabore's spear into the canoe after the battle with the *Laibon*'s war party, and thank God I had. It was quite possible she'd have need of its protection.

Her eyes rolled, white in the moonlight, but she brought herself under a measure of control.

"Yes, Chah-lee, but what about you? What are you thinking?"

144

"I'm taking the canoe, and I'm going to find out what this is all about."

"Oh no, Chah-lee!" She was about to relapse into hysterics.

"Now look here," I cajoled as forcefully as I dared, "we've got to find out who these people are. Don't you see, perhaps they're a danger to us, but perhaps they aren't. If they are, we'll have to take precautions; but if they aren't, well, we won't have anything to worry about then, now will we?"

She was still trembling. "But Chah-lee, the guns!"

"Maybe there's just a dust-up between villages or something." That seemed unlikely; up to this point none of the communities we'd passed had shown they possessed firearms, "Or maybe – oh, I don't know – something else. But one thing's sure, if I don't go and see for myself, we'll never know for certain."

"But they will see you and…and…and *shoot* you! Oh Chah-lee…!"

"No they won't, neither. I'll be careful, you'll see. They won't even know I'm there, I promise."

That seemed to settle her, at least to the point where she could concentrate on the task at hand. She pulled herself together somewhat, though there were tears streaming down both cheeks.

"Come back to me soon," she said, "and please-oh-please Chah-lee, please be careful!"

I promised her I would, but she still insisted on embracing me one more time before I left.

Then, all that seen to, I slung the elephant gun over my shoulder and, racing to the shore, launched the canoe out into the dark waters of the lake.

"I'll try to be back before first light," I said, hopping aboard, "but if I'm not, stay hidden, I'll get to you somehow."

She nodded that she understood, but made no further reply. What was understood, in fact, but what neither of us dared say was that, if I wasn't back come morning, the chances of my survival would have diminished significantly.

She stood by the shore, waving silently with one hand, the other covering her mouth to hold back further entreaties, until I was out of sight around the bend.

145

Once clear of the promontory, the littoral curved gradually in a long, shallow, concave arch that stretched far into the distance. Even from a mile away I could see the flames reflecting off the stone walls of the village, outlining tiny forms running to and fro in the night, interspersed here and there by sharper flashes followed by the reports of the musketry.

I halved the distance with all speed before slowing down, proceeding from that point with more caution. I had thought, at first, to approach in the canoe right up to the village, and darting away again into the shadows if sighted, but the moonlight was so bright that I soon discarded this idea as being impracticable. For sighted I almost certainly would be, and long before I would be able to discover anything that might be of use.

Instead, I steered the canoe towards the shore, and hid in a small inlet, tethering the craft to an overhanging branch instead of hauling it onto the beach. This was a precautionary measure to allow for a faster escape, should the need arise. Next I cut some boughs and used them to cover the sturdy little boat, hiding it from any casual perusal. Then, gun in hand, I stole silently into the forest, eyes and ears alert for signs of danger.

It was much darker in the jungle, of course, and necessitated my proceeding accordingly. Contrary to what I had told Loiyan, my chances of discovery were rather too high for my liking, but I was still not overly worried. Years of stalking in the craggy northern forests had conditioned me to making my way through the undergrowth with the utmost silence.

It wasn't long before I heard a groan and so came upon the first victim, an old man lying amongst some brambles, shot through the torso. It was evident from the broken path of foliage in his wake that he had crawled to this point while trying to escape.

There was still some life left in him though, so I knelt by his side and unstoppered the water gourd I had slung over my shoulder. The old codger drank gratefully, but then, when he took note of me, his eyes widened with surprise, and he broke out into a gasping babble that I could make nothing of. Whatever the lingo, there was nothing in it that was Maasai.

146

Then he did two things that surprised me. First, with ebbing strength, he pointed an accusing finger at me.

"Baggara!" he gasped.

The second was that he drew himself up as high as he could and with the last of his strength, spat in my face; whereupon, with a despairing gasp, he expired.

This confused me, you may be sure, but after I wiped my face and closed the old gent's eyes for him, I continued on towards the village to see what more I could discover.

Before having gone too far, what I found were more and more bodies. Every age and gender, there seemed to be no bias as to who these mysterious invaders desired to kill. Most were shot, although others appeared stabbed with spears, and still others displaying fearsome wounds from sword cuts. The smell of blood and excrement was heavy in the moist night air, and I realized, with some sense of gratitude, that I had found only a small fraction of the victims who had made their way into the jungle hoping for escape, but finding their deathbeds instead.

By now, I was quite close to the walled enclosure. Although the fires still raged, and the screams and wails of anguish continued on, seemingly without end, there had been no sound of gunfire for some time. Whatever fight there had been, it now appeared to be all but over.

Still in the jungle, I paused at the edge of the small clearing surrounding the walls. Parting the long grass, I could peer out and see the crumbled and burnt timbers that were the remnants of the fort's gate. From a narrow angle, I could even see flames licking up the side of a hut lying within the walls themselves. Scattered here and there in no particular pattern, more bodies lay, frozen in grotesque contortions in their final act of dying. Some lay around the walls, many more lay between the fort's entrance and the lakeshore. Craning my eyes in that direction, I saw, drawn up on the beach, row upon row of canoes. Also, I now perceived the shadowy shapes of men – two of them – standing guard.

Quite close by, a twig snapped.

I'm afraid it was more from fright than any sort of martial training I had ever received that was the cause of my freezing, stifling a surprised shriek in the bare nick of time. He must have been standing motionless at the edge of the clearing when I'd approached. Otherwise I could scarcely have failed to notice him. For there, not ten feet from my right front, was a man standing with his back to me, dressed like his comrades, in the flowing robes and burnoose of an Arab.

Although I had no way of knowing the meaning of 'Baggara', I thought I could make a guess. Seeing little difference between the colours of our skin, and knowing only that I was not black like himself, the old fellow, now lying dead beneath the brambles, had mistaken me for an enemy. Indeed, after months under this merciless sun, I had to admit that there *was* little difference. With a few more whiskers and in similar dress, I daresay I could have passed for one quite convincingly.

I had seen many such people in Cairo, naturally, and again in Mombasa. Of all that was uniform about them, I couldn't help being struck by their malicious features. And as this one casually turned to survey the jungle behind him (perhaps I had made some small sound, after all) I saw, by the light of the moon and the flickering flames of the dying village, that he was no different.

His long forked beard – dyed red with henna – seemed to pull the corners of his mouth down into a hard and merciless frown. The luxuriance of his mustaches further accented small, coal-dark eyes as hard as flint. While scanning the trees, he seemed at one point to be staring directly at me, malevolence emanating from his beady gaze with every instant, before finally moving on without having perceived my quaking form in the still shadows.

His robe was belted at the waist, and in the belt was thrust a scimitar; some jewel of questionable value glinting dully in its pommel. In the crook of his arm, he held an ancient long-barreled musket, the stock liberally adorned with the intricate carvings of oriental design.

I felt the weight of the elephant gun in my hands. By maintaining pressure on the triggers whilst easing back on the hammers, I was able to bring both barrels to full cock without making a sound; but apparently satisfied that the jungle was empty of any living human, he turned once more with his back to me, although I was able to relax only by a slight degree. He was close, dreadfully close, and cautious as I had been, I knew it was only by a miracle he had not noticed my approach. But though I didn't consider myself to be trapped – not *quite* – I was frozen in my position. I didn't dare try stealing away with him so near. What was more, I had no way of knowing how many others of his kind might be lurking close by. I had failed to notice this one; how many others had eluded me?

Unseen and unheard, a clock ticked away in my mind while the moon traced a leisurely path across the sky. Some fifty yards away, the two guards by the boats lounged and chatted in a language I could recognize as Arabic, yet did not understand.

Meanwhile, the tearful mourning and shouts of command emanating from the smoke and flames of the village continued with relentless repetition.

I was able to shift my weight with only the greatest of care, and then only dared do so when cramp threatened to seize hold of my muscles. Consequently, much of that time was spent in considerable discomfort while the clock in my head ticked on.

Finally, just as the moon was dipping below the horizon, there came from inside the enclosure one final authoritative command, closely followed by the unmistakably evil sound that has never failed to send shivers down my spine ever since – the cracking of a whip. Whereupon a great wailing of the most abject misery I had ever heard burst forth from the village. The whips cracked, and cracked again, demanding order, but the plaintive cries never ceased. A shot was fired, someone screamed in agony, then all was quiet. Presently the whips resumed, momentarily followed by a weird, low sound that could only have been the tramping of a great many bare feet in the dust, interspersed, here and there, with a solitary wail.

At this point there grew an air of expectation from the fellows without the walls – a heightened sense of alertness – as presently, reflected in the flames, shadows began to form at the entrance, followed closely by the solid forms that were people. At first there were more guards, some Arab, but as the procession filed out, I was surprised to note that most others were blacks, hoisting their firearms any old how, in a way that would have brought my old drill sergeant to tears. Then finally came a sight I had never thought to see. For emerging from the ruins of their village, stripped of every stitch of clothing – of every belonging they had in the world – and bound together at the neck with stout rope in columns of twos, in a long, awkwardly wormlike human chain, came a coffle of freshly-minted slaves.

Yet even as I stared, frozen with wonder, once more there arose from them such a pitiable howling as to rend your heart in two, whereupon one of the black guards, in evident ill humour, placed his musket against the temple of the prime instigator – an old greybeard – and pulled the trigger, spraying his brains over others in his immediate vicinity. The corpse dropped like a stone, dragging others down with him in an untidy heap, and of course the coffle was brought to an immediate halt.

That shocked me, I can tell you. For although by now I had seen my fair share of Africa and, I think, more than my fair share of its cruelty, I had never even remotely witnessed anything so casually barbaric. But if only I'd known what was in store, perhaps I'd have accepted this more easily and considered myself fortunate.

Meanwhile, angrily howling guards dove into the tangle with their whips, intent on restoring order and cutting the dead man free. One Arab, in even worse humour, strode forward and delivered the overzealous black such a terrific blow with the back of his hand that it sent him sprawling into the dust, all the while jabbering at him in the fiercest of terms, presumably over this unthinking loss of chattel.

When the darkie regained his feet I thought that he might retaliate, but all he did was grin and bob his head like a demented monkey, I presume to assure the Arab that such a breech of judgement would not happen again.

At last all was ready, and the coffle, now cowed into submissive terror, moved off towards the boats without further ado.

It was here that I was finally allowed some breathing room, as those guarding the perimeter, as well as the boats, came forward to lend a hand.

Still I remained, as though transfixed, while the long line of blacks was divvied up and stowed aboard. This process took less time than you might have thought, and I could appreciate the professional efficiency for what it was. For after counting off a dozen or so, an Arab drew his scimitar and cut the rope, herding those he'd told off into one of the canoes. Then another twelve – *slice* – and another cargo set to board, and so on. Still, by the time they were finished, the sun was just beginning to rise, and a full score of the vessels had been filled with their erstwhile owners; as sad an armada as you could ever hope to see. Then all were cast off, the captives flanked on all sides by the raiders in their own boats.

The course they set was to the north – to where Loiyan and I had made our camp.

I was up and bolting back through the bush like a whippet, unmindful of the brambles slashing across my face and body, trying to ignore the pins and needles shrieking for attention in my legs. I cursed myself for a fool. I should have been away as soon as it was safe to do so. I had to get to the canoe before they reached its hiding place. If they found it I was sunk, and though I had directed Loiyan to stay in hiding, just the mere thought of that satanic procession bearing down upon her while she waited, unknowing and all but defenseless, was enough to make my innards shrivel, let me tell you. Yes, I should have taken my leave much sooner than I had, but you see, I suppose I'd been struck with some sort of morbid awe at the hellish sight of it all, and could not have moved for a pension. But now the spell was broken, and I was bound no longer. I was crashing through the thickets with never a thought to the racket I was causing. The flotilla would be creating enough din of its own to be able to hear overmuch ashore.

I reached the canoe's hiding place before them, but only just. Even as I paused to consider the risk of casting off ahead of them, the first craft came into view – mostly Arabs, muskets bristling like a hedgehog. I immediately discarded the idea, and hoping the raiders would be too preoccupied with their captives to take much notice of what lay hidden in the shadows, I set off at a run back to our camp.

By great good fortune, I soon stumbled upon a well-trampled path through the bush roughly parallel to the lake, such as the numerous hooves of cattle might have made through similar terrain back home. This one must have been caused by wildebeest or eland, or perhaps a well-traveled route by all creatures coming down to the water. Yet, whatever it was, and whosoever had made it, I wasted little time on dwelling, but instead, dove myself upon it for all I was worth, picking up speed with the lack of any further hindrance.

I tried not to think of what might happen if I failed to arrive before them. I tried not to worry about all the things that might befall should Loiyan – alone and frightened – feeling the need to venture from hiding just long enough to come down to the shore, searching nervously for a glimpse of my return, at precisely the wrong time. I tried not to think of the shocking story Kakenya had related, about the cruel initiation of a beautiful captive – tried not to see Loiyan's face in her stead, cornered, surrounded, utterly without hope of rescue. Angrily, I chased away the vision of that first, filthy Arab hand as it reached out to seize her, but it came back again as surely as though it was bound to me, and I put my head down and sprinted forward with reserves of energy I had not thought to possess.

I had hoped the convoy of little boats would not be able to make maximum headway, as the fisher-folk, even as accustomed as they were to the water, would find the unfamiliarity of being bound together a crippling obstacle too great to overcome in so short a time, all threats from whips and guns notwithstanding. Perhaps such was the case, for a canoe, properly handled, should have been able easily to outdistance a man on foot; yet from the odd break in the trees, I caught glimpses of them a few hundred yards off the shore and could see that, although they were not pulling away from me, neither was I from them. Indeed, the situation appeared to remain unchanged as it had from the start, with myself slightly in the lead.

I recognized the headland shielding our site from the village. The path veered from here, so without breaking stride, or pausing to consider, I left it and crashed into the undergrowth, charging along without thought for my own safety.

152

Again I cursed myself. I had acted so precipitately, leaving her without knowing where she should choose to hide. Now there was no time to waste, yet no time to find her.

I broke through the jungle with mere moments to spare, and could have cried out with relief when I failed to see her on the beach. Then I dove back into the bush just as the bow of the first boat came into view.

Something cracked me a terrific blow on the scull and I was down like an ox. I found myself on my back, gazing with interest while the tops of the trees spun round and round over my head. Immediately, they were blotted out by Loiyan's concerned face mere inches above my own.

"Oh Chah-lee! I thought…"

I managed to hold a cautionary finger to my lips, although the effort caused my stomach to lurch uncomfortably.

She asked in a worried whisper, "Are you hurt?"

I shook my head to the negative, even though I wasn't sure if I was or if I wasn't. Instead, I took her by the hand and, cautiously testing the effectiveness of my motor senses, led her to the edge of the clearing.

The flotilla was in full view. As before, most of the guards were constantly patrolling the perimeter in their little craft with all the captives confined in the middle. Others of the raiders were close alongside them, darting in here and there, catching a sluggard with the whip's end or the butt of a musket.

And then, even while we watched transfixed in horror, one of the Arabs jabbed at a buck in the stern of one of the canoes closer to the shore. The fellow must have been faking a state of shock – Lord knows, it would have been simple enough to do – for when the blow came, he was ready.

Quick as lightning, he grabbed the musket by its stock and gave a sharp tug. What his plan was after that, there was no way of knowing; I doubt that he knew himself. This show of defiance was probably nothing other than the thought of going so meekly into bondage being more than he could bear. But of course it was futile.

The gun's hammer must have been accidentally drawn in the struggle, for suddenly there came a flash closely followed by the crash of a discharge. The Arab's face blossomed crimson even as he shrieked and spun away over the side.

The raiders' reaction was as immediate as it was pitiless. All their boats converged on the offending vessel, everyone firing indiscriminately.

The first to be hit was a young wench, her breasts mere nubs, scarcely more than a child. The ball shattered her shin just below the knee. I saw her mouth open wide to scream, but the roar of the musketry was so loud as to drown it out. The second, another woman, was shot through the chest, her body convulsing in its death throes, causing those before and behind her to struggle mightily to keep from going over the side. The next was an old woman. She clapped a hand to her neck. Even from such a distance, I could see thin jets of blood spouting from between her fingers.

A buck was whirled around by a ball to the shoulder. A second caught him in the fleshy part of his other arm. A third took away most of his jaw, and he was over the side. The ones coffled closest to him were a young boy and an old man. For a moment they were able to hold their own while they struggled to keep the boat upright, but then the man was overboard, shot through the heart, and one by one, the entire human chain – now weighed down by more and more bodies – was pulled in after.

I had thought it might end there - prayed that it would be so. After all, there was no longer any threat of resistance, but the raiders continued to bear down upon those unfortunate souls, firing as they came.

The lake must have been deep in that spot because those who survived that first onslaught had to struggle to stay above the surface even as the water boiled all around them from the lead balls. One or two actually managed to gain hold of their overturned canoe while they fought the weight of the others not so fortunate. But they, too, were shot away before all was mercifully hidden by the slavers' craft as they milled about, still firing down upon their heads. This continued for some time until there were none left alive, all having been dragged down to the bottom.

With no more targets in sight, the slavers ceased their firing, and went about the business of herding the rest of the blacks into a cluster. The villagers, no matter what their feelings, complied with silence and alacrity, for they had learned their lesson.

Soon the convoy was reassembled, and the course continued. In a very few minutes all were gone from sight, leaving in the placid waters of its wake no sign of the terrible slaughter we had just witnessed.

Although I couldn't speak for Loiyan at that instant, I could scarcely bring myself to believe I had actually seen what my eyes were telling me had just taken place. Certainly, but for the most minute of rills rolling out from the scene of the slaughter, there was not a scrap of evidence anything untoward had ever happened at that spot. No bodies, no charred remains, not even a child's broken toy to mark their graves.

I found myself clinging to Loiyan, and she to me. Then, as improbable as it sounds, our trembling lips became locked in a frantic kiss while, at the same time we were tearing at each other's clothing in an effort to be as close as possible.

I soon had her pinned to the ground, and was in the act of wresting her legs apart, but she surprised me, both with her strength and inclination. She pushed me over, and flung herself astride my hips. I grappled for her breasts while she impaled herself, and began to pump away like a demon.

At such a feverish pace the business was consummated quickly, and perhaps unsatisfactorily. Neither was there any effort made to lie basking in the afterglow, the presence of which was felt only by its absence. Rather, we both avoided meeting the eyes of the other while we shuffled about, slowly gathering the tatters of our clothing, and for my part, trying not to feel ashamed.

Macabre? Well might you think so, and even now there is a strong urge in me to agree with such an opinion. But let us not forget: I had been through the very worst of war and several other dangers since that time, and I can tell you that, amidst the stench of violent death – of the heightened aspect of fear – at the end of it all, there is no substitute for finding oneself alive. It therefore stands to reason, at some primordial level, there is a subsequent desire to prove to oneself that such is, indeed, the case. The senses are scarcely to be believed – so much horror cannot possibly be accepted by the mind – it is only by the most physical of acts that the body can be convinced it continues to exist. It can be a feverish affair, I'll grant you, but once achieved, all else begins to fall into place, thus making it possible to carry on.

I believe such was what happened to us that day. If you don't believe me, or if you're revolted by what I just told you, I suggest you ride with mad Lord Cardigan when he's within smelling distance of a Russian battery, or lie hidden, quivering with fright, while Arab slavers slaughter a baker's dozen or so of helpless darkies. Then come and tell me how you feel; and if it don't affect you, well then perhaps you should be looking more to yourself than to me.

Anyway, so endeth my sermon. It can be a bloody awful world sometimes.

Chapter Thirteen

We gathered our provisions with as few words as possible, and set off to where I had hidden our boat. I suppose it might have been easier to retrieve the canoe first, *then* come back to pick up Loiyan, but like our first campsite at Ukerewe this place, too, had lost its enchantment, and neither of us wanted to stay any longer than need be.

Thankfully, neither did Loiyan question me about the state of the village. She had seen enough, and I certainly wasn't going to volunteer to enlighten her further.

As for me, I had my own thoughts: to whit, what was to be done now?

To the north were ruthless Arab slavers and their happy gang, which put some doubt as to the wisdom of progressing any further in that direction. To the south bloodthirsty Maasai were itching to free their lands from the evil clutches of the demon Red Man, and if that didn't play out, there was still Musa's idiotic scheme of relinquishing Parsayip's responsibility of his herds – that is to say, if the mysterious disappearance of two of his brothers could be explained away with any satisfaction, not to mention the slaughter of a good few of the village's other warriors. No, on the whole, I decided that south was not the direction to be going either. To the east, even before we could reach those faraway snowpeaked mountains, there looked to be hundreds of miles of impenetrable jungle with all their attending hazards. To the west lay a vast body of water as big as the ocean, and nothing to cross it in but a canoe.

Given our state of mind, even the mere act of deciding where we would spend the night might prove to be a bit of a chore. Even if it was acceptable to Loiyan – and I didn't for a second entertain the idea that it was – I myself couldn't bear the thought of camping out in the middle of so much carnage. Our old site, with its awful memories, and horrid secrets hidden beneath the waters, had already become intolerable. On the other side, as the sun rose higher in the sky, anywhere near the desecrated village would soon become equally unsuitable. Where could we go? The carefree life of yesterday now seemed as unreal as my dream the night before.

We found the canoe tethered and unharmed as I'd left it. Loiyan helped me drag off the camouflaging foliage, and we deposited our meager supplies. By the time we had stepped aboard and settled in position, I was still undecided as to our destination. The only thing I was sure of was that I wanted to be away.

There were no words spoken, but Loiyan seemed to be of the same mind as we lost no time in casting off, and headed far out into the waters of Ukerewe.

No doubt it was a damn fool thing to do, running so far out until the shore was just a narrow, green ribbon halfway up the horizon. But we'd been reacting more or less instinctively ever since witnessing the murder of the villagers. Now it was telling us to be gone from that place of death; and Loiyan having drawn no clearer conclusions than I had myself, we just took ourselves off as far as we could, trying to run away from all things evil.

Hours passed, clouds were gathering in the west and the sun had long since reached its zenith when I called a halt. At last I realized that to go on was madness. A few weeks spent hugging the shore in a canoe didn't qualify us as old salts, no matter how much we wished that it might.

"We have to decide," I said.

From the sag of her shoulders, and the fact she didn't ask what needed deciding, I knew Loiyan was thinking the same thing, although that didn't make the decision any more welcome.

"Where will we go?" she asked.

"Look," I said, bracing myself for an argument, "we have to follow them."

She spun around so quickly the small craft very nearly capsized.

"No!"

"We can do it, if we're careful."

"No!"

She sat there, eyes wide, lower lip trembling.

"It is too dangerous, Chah-lee!"

158

"But, if we're careful…"

"No!"

"They know where the great river is," I said quietly, "the one that will take us to Cairo."

She hesitated. "But those horrible men…"

"We'll be very careful," I said, and patted the elephant gun, "and we have this."

"They too have guns, many guns."

"This one is better."

It was no idle boast. The heavy piece had rifled barrels – trust Lord Brampton to bring along nothing but the best – and could fire the heavy conical slugs at least four times the distance that the Arabs' lighter caliber smooth bores could send a ball, and with ten times the accuracy. In addition to that, it used percussion caps, making misfires far more unlikely, while I was willing to bet Johnny Arab was still making do with flintlocks. True, it could be a cumbersome thing to load, not nearly the rate of fire as a smooth bore, but the other advantages more than outweighed this single drawback. Our fellows had proven as much at Inkerman.

In spite of all that, she seemed about to object still one more time, but instead she slumped, the very picture of misery.

"I am frightened," she said softly.

"So am I." I admitted it. There seemed no point in declaring otherwise.

She looked up, surprised.

I smiled. "We will be *very* careful."

This prompted a timorous smile of her own.

"*Very* careful?"

"Yes." I felt I had to ask, "Will you come with me?"

She gave me a look that might have been despairing affection, and crawled to the back of the boat to sit beside me. "Oh Chah-lee," she said, laying her head against my chest, "sometimes I think you are *dorobo* in the head."

"Eh?!"

"Yes," she confirmed, "*dorobo*. Even now you do not know that I would go anywhere with you."

159

She turned her face up to me, her eyes soft in the duskiness of her skin.

"Anywhere in the world."

I was touched, and thought a kiss might be in order. After that – who knew – we had never tried it in the canoe before, but the day had grown suddenly darker. When I looked up, I saw the sun had been blotted out by angry looking clouds the colour of charcoal. Far off in the western horizon, a flash of lightning snaked down from the sky, extinguishing itself in Ukerewe's placid waters. A second later there was another, and then another. Thunder rumbled its way to us across the flat distances of the lake.

"*Olodoyiorie*," she said, her voice soft with apprehension, "the great rains are coming."

"We've got to get to shore," I quickly took up my paddle, hoping we had not already tarried too long.

I had us heading back towards the distant streak of land by the time Loiyan clambered back to the bow and taken up her own paddle. By now, she was almost as proficient as I. She would have to be, if we were going to make it back.

We set off like a shot, both paddles digging in earnest, the bow cutting through the glassy surface of the lake like a rapier. I doubted it would be smooth much longer.

Half an hour later the first fat drops started to come down. I checked nervously over my shoulder. There was a flash of lightning. I faced my front and had counted to five before a wild crash of thunder burst over us. Although it could only be shortly after noon, already the towering clouds made it seem eerily like evening. Peering into the gloom, I thought the distance we had covered thus far was pitifully small.

Then the wind began to rise, rilling the surface with hard choppy waves. Yet there was one good thing about that wind: it was directly at our backs.

It was raining harder now, great fat drops pounding down all around us like grapeshot. Then, suddenly, howling like a steam whistle, a great blast of wind tore the water into whitecaps a foot high. Raging, it continued on unabated, and soon they were higher still. Two…now three feet high, with the rain coming

160

down in sheets, hiding the distant shore behind a curtain of water – only visible through flashes of lightning.

The sturdy little craft was becoming difficult to manage. I looked down. Small wonder, it was filling up faster than you could say a prayer for the Lost Mariner.

I called out above the roar of the wind. "Loiyan!"

She looked over her shoulder, wide-eyed with fright.

"Grab the bowl! You'll need to bail!"

She received this news with dumb incomprehension.

"Bail!" I cried, "You'll have to take the bowl and…"

That's when it dawned on me that she wouldn't have a clue what I was talking about. Why would she? She had never even seen a boat before until not much more than a month ago, so the word meant nothing to her.

"You'll have to take the bowl and…." I made scooping motions with my hand.

I always said she was a bright one. She nodded immediately, reaching for the goatskin bag the bowl was kept in. After digging around for a moment, she brought it out, and set to with a will.

I paddled for all I was worth, but now our propulsion was halved. Considering the weight of the water we'd taken on board, perhaps even more than that.

Loiyan was bailing frantically, but the waves were breaking over the stern, drenching my already soaked skin and threatening to founder us. I thought to help her, but was afraid lest, devoid of steering, the little craft should turn sideways to the waves. If that happened, it was certain we would capsize. It was a damnable crisis; while it was vital I lend my assistance, I daren't leave my post. All seemed hopeless.

Then, seized by an idea, I took my belt and lashed the paddle to the gunwale like one of those steering oars I'd seen pictures of on those old Greek ships. I let go my hold, testing it, and was relieved when the course remained true. Next I grabbed a pot floating around in the bottom and began to bail for my life.

"Chah-lee!"

I stole a precious second to look up and couldn't believe my eyes.

161

Here we were, being tossed about the water like a cork in a barrel, expecting every moment to be our last, and I saw that the woman was actually laughing!

"Wot?!"

She'd been bailing on her knees, but now her arms hung useless by her side while she was contorted, helpless with laughter.

"Oh Chah-lee!" she pointed, laughing still, "Your kilt!"

It was then I realized that, without the restraints of my belt, my nether garment had taken flight at the earliest opportunity, and was fast disappearing above the waves.

"Bloody hell!"

Plainly the woman wasn't quite right in the head, because she grabbed her stomach with both arms, and fell back, helpless, into the scuppers.

"Oh!" she crowed "Oh! Oh! You should – oh! oh! – you should see yourself, Chah-lee! Oh! Oh! Oh!"

I wasted another second to deliver a hateful glare before attacking the water again. It didn't matter if I was stuck out on a lake with a crazy woman. What mattered was that we survived.

Presently I was aware she'd taken up her bowl as well, and was once more lending assistance. But the next time our eyes met, she had to clap a hand over her mouth to cover her laughter and, foolish as it sounds, I found myself grinning in return. The silly chit actually seemed to be enjoying this, and what was more, incredibly, so was I!

There was nothing logical about it, of course, and seemed barmy as all get out. Yet, in a strange way, it did make some sort of sense, when you really thought about it. I mean, here we were: bloodthirsty Maasai to the south, sadistic Arabs to the north. To the east were unimaginable perils of the jungle and to the west…well, to the west there was this water, and a bit of wind – well, quite a bit, really, but all things considered, it seemed the lesser evil – which just goes to show how ridiculous things had got. Yet what really struck me – and I suppose epiphanies don't really choose *when* to make an appearance – was that with this woman by my side, it seemed possible to move mountains. Even though that may not have been *strictly* true, what was important

162

was that, whatever our fate, we would face it together. Regardless of how life has treated you in every other respect, when you got down to it, you really couldn't ask for anything more than that.

Not that we were content to go down with the ship, you understand. There was far too much to live for. So we bailed, and we bailed, and we bailed until we became hypnotized by the very act. But all the while, in a peripheral sense, we were aware of monstrous winds and towering waves, of flashing lightning and terrible crashes of thunder. It was pretty unholy out there, let me tell you, and as the evening dragged on and turned into night, it grew unholier still.

The little boat was tossed about unmercifully, yet miraculously, the steering oar continued to work like a charm, providing a dependable rudder, keeping us tail-on to the wind. Still, we had no time to worry about that. All throughout that long and terrible night, there was but one function, and one function only, to occupy our minds in our close little world.

We bailed…and we bailed…and we bailed.

Come morning I was bailing still, all sense of elation having long since left me. My body had ceased to ache, or – outside of a primitive need to survive – my mind to function. All that existed for me was to scoop out one bowlful at a time, as quickly as I could, one after the other, until it seemed to the very end of time.

I don't know at what point it dawned on me that I was standing in water up to my knees or why I should think it strange to be so. I believe it was a gradual sort of thing, stretching over a period of hours, permeating my brain in the reverse to the way that frost will eventually seep its way from the ground.

But by and by, it came to me to wonder that, if the sides of the boat were only so high, how could it be I was standing in water which was so much higher still? Surely there was something scientifically wrong about that.

That was when I gazed with dull uncertainty upon the grey-green rollers – almost without a doubt waning now – and realized I could no longer see the boat. It took a bit longer to comprehend that this was because I was still standing in it – I could feel it beneath my feet.

But if such was the case, then surely it was inundated, and if inundated, certainly it must sink?

The calculations required to prove this were difficult to a mind so numb, but as near as I could tell, such should have been the case

All the while, but with an ever decreasing concentration, I continued to bail.

So…if I was on a sunken boat, why was the water only coming to my knees? Surely, by this time I should have been drowned?

Hmmm.

I continued to bail, but my efforts became ever more desultory.

If I was, in fact, drowned, as seemed probable, and if this was some sort of afterlife, would it not be correct to think that, should I cease my efforts, nothing untoward would happen?

In the spirit of empirical study, I paused.

The water rose no higher.

I tried to stand straight, but a paralyzing shock of pain in my lower back made its presence felt to the extent that I was unable. Indeed, it propelled me to my knees.

Thus it was that my tired mind – reasoning that as I must have drowned, and it being well known there was no pain in Heaven – could only conclude that I was now residing in Hell. That didn't surprise me overly; I'd done some desperate things in my time.

Gazing about me with over-tired eyes, I thought Hell not unlike where I had come from. In fact, considering my last moments on earth, this was a definite improvement.

The sky was a thin blue with low flying skeins of light-grey clouds skimming towards me at quite a clip. Waves were washing in, but not so badly; I was on my knees, yet they rose only as high as my chest. The single difference being that, instead of washing over my back, as they had when I was alive, they were now splashing up against my front. No, on the whole, this wasn't all that bad.

But there was one thing, of course.

"Loiyan?"

164

I called her name, but was too exhausted to shout. If she were with me, she would hear.

There was no reply.

I felt the pain go through my heart; still I tried to be brave about it. She was probably in Heaven, or even possibly still in the land of the living. There had never been any reason to expect that she would be down here with me. Still, I knew it would be hard to carry on without her.

Perhaps that was what Hell was – being parted from someone you loved.

And I did love her, I realized that now; couldn't understand why I'd never considered it before. She'd just always *been* there, I suppose, always cared for me, always – yes – always *loved* me. It had been such a natural thing that I had never given it much thought. Now that I had, it was too late.

Oh, it was too cruel!

I felt a self-sympathetic tear roll down my cheek, and was vaguely surprised that it was possible to weep in Hell. I could even taste its salt when it came to rest on the corner of my mouth.

She was beautiful, and she loved me…and now she was gone.

A hand touched my shoulder. A mango appeared before my eyes.

"Would you like something to eat?" Loiyan asked.

Wide-eyed with hope, I craned my neck (I could swear that I heard the muscles creak). And there she was, a tired smile wreathing her face, and slightly unsteady on her legs, but it was her, there was no doubt about it.

"Loiyan!" It was music to breathe her name. "My dear, sweet Loiyan!" I fumbled for her and grasped her to my breast with all my strength which, I admit, was not much.

"You're here! You're really here!"

"Yes, Chah-lee, I am here."

"But…." still holding her, I pushed myself away, "but why are you here? Why are you in Hell? Surely there's been some mistake?"

She frowned. "I do not know this 'Hell'."

165

"The place bad people go – you know – after they die."

Slowly, her brow began to arch.

"Do you think you have died, Chah-lee?"

"Why – why yes. Yes, of course."

Now her forehead began to wrinkle.

"Why do you say 'of course'?"

"Well it's obvious, surely."

I seized my pot and scooped up some water. "You see? It makes no difference, and if I stop..." I stopped bailing, "again, no difference. Can't you see, darling..."

"Darling?"

"Yes, it's a – oh what do you call it – a...a pet name...a term of endearment, but can't you see darling that we..."

"What is 'term of en....en....?"

"Endearment," I said. "It means that I love you."

"You.....*love* me, Chah-lee?"

"Yes," I said, "I love you, my beautiful, dear, sweet Loiyan." Then sadly, "Only now it's too late."

"But why?"

"Well, because we're dead, of course. Darling, haven't you been listening?"

"Oh, yes," she seemed interested, "continue, please."

"Well, as I was saying, it's obvious we've drowned, and...and my back aches like the very devil so we must be in Hell."

"But why do you say we have drowned?"

I sighed.

"Listen, darling, it's really quite simple." I was so weary that formulating the words had become quite a chore. Instead, I splashed some water about, "See? No difference."

"And....?"

"Don't you understand?" I must admit that my voice was becoming a bit shrill, "If the boat is swamped – and it is" with the last of my patience, I splashed my arm about in the water so even a fool could understand what I was talking about, "- then we must have *drowned*. Now do you see?"

"I'm beginning to think so."

She had dimples. Why had I never noticed that before?

Gently, she took my hand. "Come, Chah-lee."

I looked out over the vast panorama of endless water.

"But to where?"

She stepped out of the boat. The water continued to come only as high as her knees. I puzzled over this for a moment – surely she should have plummeted straight to the bottom? – but then I saw what she had been shielding from me with her body.

There, not a hundred yards from where I was standing, was a beach.

I don't suppose she'd been hiding that from me on purpose...I don't suppose.

I felt my eyelids flutter while my mind struggled to process this rather radical transformation.

How long had I been desperately trying to keep the boat afloat in water that was, at most, some twenty inches deep?

"It was still dark when we come," she explained. "But when there is lightning, I see land. I try to call you, many, many times, but you seem not to hear me. You just keep with the...." She made scooping motions with her hands.

"Bailing."

"Yes, with the bailing, and I cannot make you understand. Finally I am tired. I must go on land to sleep."

"Sleep?"

"Yes, I sleep."

I was trying my best not to glare – I really was – but it was a hard go.

"And did you sleep.....well?"

She smiled. "*Very* well, thank you. Many hours."

"I see."

"Yes, and when I wake I see you are still," she scooped with her hands, "with the bailing. I think you must be hungry so I get some fruit." Once more she smiled and offered the mango.

"*Are* you hungry, Chah-lee?"

167

Chapter Fourteen

"But what shall we do, my love?" Loiyan asked over the pounding of the rain.

It was three days later, and much had been accomplished. First the canoe had needed salvaging, together with as many of our supplies as was possible.

In this we were fortunate. Most importantly, the sealskin game bag had kept the precious cartridges dry for the most part. I was sure what little water did seep in hadn't got past their protective grease wrapping. The fish hooks and net hadn't broken free of their bindings, either, and while our pot of coals had been soaked, and a few nonessentials gone missing, but for the disappearance of my kilt, all else seemed well enough.

Being exhausted, we had slept out on the beach without benefit of a fire. We had done this many times before, and had thought it no great hardship. What we had forgotten in our fatigue, were the rains of *Olodoyiorie*. Still, I suppose we were fortunate. This time there'd been no great wind, nor were there mighty crashes of thunder, nor blinding bolts of lightning; but we awoke in the evening to torrents of rain streaming down by the bucketful, instantly soaking us to the skin.

I had thought, being English, I knew something about rain, but I'm here to tell you I'd never seen anything like this before. It poured without letup for most of that night, so much so that you could scarcely imagine all that water being suspended up in that *nothingness* of the sky. We spent it huddled in the forest, under a covering of old date palm leaves. I couldn't remember ever feeling quite so miserable. I suppose the previous night had been worse, but there wasn't much I could remember about that time, so it didn't count.

Next morning found the canoe full of water again. Perhaps this was fortunate. Otherwise, it might have floated away without our noticing, because – and I'm not telling a stretcher, neither – it rained so hard that Ukerewe's level had risen a good *three inches*! As it was, we had to tip the boat over and drag it well up the beach – not an easy feat at any time, but trebly hard when you were soaking wet and tired in the bargain. For outside of a few hours I'd allowed myself that first day before seeing to the salvaging, and perhaps an hour or two that evening before we were rudely woken, sleep had proven elusive.

Yet seeing to the boat was but the first problem to hand. Next we had gone into the forest and fashioned a crude shelter with deadfall poles woven together with a wickerwork of vines and saplings, all of which required thatching. This had taken much of the remainder of that day, but the rains had come before we could finish. So a second night was spent with conditions only minimally better than the preceding one.

We were up bright and early on the third morning, and out on a short neck of savannah where the long stalks of the elephant grass could be harvested for our thatching project, but scarcely had we started when we had to take to the trees to avoid a lioness who happened by for a visit.

It was fortunate the parting stalks of the long grass had given away her position, allowing Loiyan time to give warning. It was also fortunate that the old girl didn't seem all that hungry either, but merely curious. That was indeed providential, for in my tired frame of mind, I had forgotten to bring the gun with me. Still, it was vexing to be perched up a tree while that tawny monster wandered around below us, poking her nose here and there, and eating up precious daylight.

She wandered off after an hour or two, however – there not being much to capture her interest – and we scampered down to finish gathering our thatching material…with the gun never more than an arm's length away, you may be sure.

When the shelter (the word 'hut' seemed too grandiose) was finally completed, Loiyan set about making a fire the old fashioned way – by virtue of rubbing two sticks together. Meanwhile, I waded offshore and tried my luck with the fish spear. By the time the rains came (you could set your watch by them) I was able to enter our warm and dry abode with some feeling of accomplishment. In answer to Loiyan's enquiring gaze, feeling something of the Mighty Hunter, I proudly held out my catch – three perch-like creatures about six inches long and a couple more at the girth.

Gad, but it felt good to be providing some of the food for a change, let me tell you!

It was a man's work, after all.

But I have to say I was a bit disappointed with Loiyan's lack of appreciation. Far from being impressed with the fruits of my skill, she seemed more amused. Although, later, while the rain was pouring down outside, having dined and taken our leisure by a cheery fire, I had to admit it was just possible my sense of well-being might have been augmented somewhat had my stomach been more full.

"Tomorrow I will do the fishing," she said.

I was cleaning the rifle now, being careful to provide a liberal coating of oil after the dunking it took, and comforting myself with the thought that, if I couldn't be the main supplier of meat, at least I could play the role of protector.

"But what shall we do, my love?" Loiyan was now asking.

It had been a topic of conversation, off and on, for the past few days. Being caught by the storm out on the lake had not only been unforgivably stupid, but now we were quite possibly lost as well, for this shore had not looked familiar to either of us. While it was logical to assume we were further north of our last location, we didn't know how *far* north, but more importantly, neither did we know the position of the slavers. If they were in front of us then all might be well, but if they were coming up behind....

"I'll hide the boat first thing tomorrow morning," I said, cursing myself for a fool yet one more time. Our shelter was safe enough, tucked back well in the jungle, and a fire was no worry if it was only lit during the rains, but the brightly painted vermillion canoe was lying high and proud up on the beach. Only by lighting a bonfire could we possibly make our presence more known.

"But, my proud *orinka*, I will need the boat. The big fish are farther out."

Ever since I had introduced her to things like terms of endearment, Loiyan had taken to them like a Scotchman to whiskey, referring to me by anything that took her fancy. Privately, I rather liked it for the most part, but I had to take

170

exception to one or two, the worst being that detestable blood and milk concoction of hers – *nailang'a.*

"Now you tell me," I replied, not *quite* indignantly.

"I am sorry, my lion," she said, smoothing my ruffled feathers, "but perhaps you could kill something with your gun?"

I was reluctant to do this, however. Outside the fact those heavy caliber slugs would make mincemeat out of any game that might suit us, I had to force myself to be miserly with their use. There was no way of knowing how far our journey was yet to take us, or what hazards we might meet along the way. There were a mere forty cartridges left, so it was necessary to string them out for as long as possible.

"Then I must fish, my *olaiguenani.*" ('Chief' to you)

"So I'll just have to go out with you, my dear, and that's all there is to it."

"But why, my beautiful one?"

"It's best I keep a sharp lookout," I said grimly, patting the gun. "We should've been doing so all along, but we were too complacent. So far we've been lucky, but that's bound to change. Yet, if any of those Arab rascals dares show his face around here, I'll be ready for him, mark my words."

Yet none of this was bringing us any nearer a conclusion as to what our next course of action should be. Long moments were pondered in silence.

At last I spoke.

"I think we'd best lay up here for awhile, at least until the end of *Olodoyiorie.*" Under the circumstances, it may not have been much, but at least it was a decision. "It's quite impossible to travel in this weather, and there's no reason why we shouldn't be snug as bugs until it changes. We'll just have to find a place to hide the boat so we won't always need drag it up on the beach. It shouldn't be hard to camouflage so it's safe from prying eyes. Perhaps we could even make some sort of shed, you know, with a roof and whatnot."

All rather cozy and domestic, you'll notice, and I won't try to tell you that wasn't part of my reasoning – the *unspoken* part, but what would you? Yet in spite of the guilt I was feeling for not

171

striving more heartily to be by my master's side, at least you'll admit it made sense, in its way.

Whether it was the right decision, or the wrong one, after all these years it's impossible to say.

So it was decided to settle in for a bit. We found another little inlet to hide the boat, and masked it from the lake side with a clever fretwork of boughs, making it safe from discovery. Next, at waist height, we lashed poles to trees on either side, topping it off with wickerwork and a layer of thatching, forming a very serviceable boatshed.

Every day we would take the canoe out onto the lake for Loiyan to cast her net, while I sat and tried to pay attention to distant horizons and not my naked companion. For even though I should have been used to her that way, I was still finding it next to impossible to ignore her sublime perfection – every delectable inch of it. As the fish were plentiful and Loiyan expert with the net, no sooner were we out than we were coming back in again. And even when you consider the rains came in the mid-afternoon, there was still ample time at our disposal for a different project.

For with the completion of the boatshed, Loiyan had now started to look thoughtfully at our own shelter.

It was decided that it was too small.

Well, I couldn't really argue the fact. It had never been intended for anything other than an overnight shelter in the first place. It was only due to our exhausting ordeal on the lake that had necessitated a delay while we regained our strength. But now the rainy season was well upon us, we would have to come up with something more spacious.

There was some debate as to whether we would build an addition onto our little shelter, or find another place entirely. When I pointed out that the present location wasn't exactly suitable (due to its low elevation, sometimes water seeped in) we opted for the latter course.

While I would have dearly loved to possess an axe, or at least a hatchet, sadly such was not the case. However, Sabore's spear, with its heavy thirty-inch blade – when wrested from its

172

haft – served admirably as a chopping tool. That was fortunate, for we would have need of it.

We used it to procure poles – not bent and twisted deadfall, but straight young saplings, eight feet long and as thick as my wrist. We used it, as well, to excavate holes in the ground so the poles could be affixed – six feet apart, in a circle with a diameter of some twenty feet or so, with the last and stoutest planted in the center. This one was about two feet longer, and would be needed to support the conical roof. Next, at half the height of my shin, were lashed other stout poles crosswise to these verticals and horizontal to the ground. This formed the foundation of our floor, to keep us high and dry in the very wettest of weather. It was this that took the most of our time because of all the digging and heavier materials required. After it was completed three weeks later, things proceeded much more quickly as it was the same old wicker and thatch business both of us were accustomed to.

All in all, it took some five weeks to finish, but by then it was a structure in which I could stand and move about with ease. Indeed, I found I was quite proud of it.

Now, I'm sure you're thinking, 'Hello, that's an awful lot of trouble to go to for a shelter that would only be used for a month or two, surely', and you wouldn't be wrong. but something happened shortly after we had started that changed our plans yet again.

Prior to this, I had some vague idea of waiting out the wet months of *Olodoyiorie* and *Oloilepunye* as comfortably as may be before starting out as early as possible to see how the land lay.

You see, I had reason to believe that a slaver's stronghold could not be far away.

That day we had headed so precipitately out onto the lake, we had taken a course due west, but when the storm came, the wind that blew us back again had been from the west-*south*-west. It seemed logical to assume we had come ashore at a place further to the north than where the blacks had been massacred. Although it was impossible to say how far north that was, by the more westerly bend of the littoral, and the lowering of the surrounding country – that is to say that those volcanic peaks, which – in relation to the shore – had always loomed so mightily on our right-hand side, were now at our backs, the consequence of which the country further inland fell away dramatically – I thought it was reasonable to suspect we had reached the top of the depression upon which the lake was formed. And as the surrounding territory continued to descend, there was cause to believe the close proximity of a mighty river spilling over the depression's rim, perhaps to flow all the way to Cairo, and some sort of civilization.

So far, so good, you may think, yet there were still other things to consider.

First, the slavers must surely have known that the rains were imminent, and though barbarously cruel, I had witnessed them to be efficient. Most certainly they had been aware of hazards attending any attempts to travel through such a deluge with a retinue of captives in tow – who would be at their throats, given half a chance. Would it not make sense, then, to surmise that the village – and consequently Loiyan and myself – had been within a few day's journey of their base? And second (and most important), where else would that base be but at the headwaters of that same river?

Now, this was all conjecture, of course, but I believed it to be sound. Indeed, it was my plan to prove it at the first opportunity, and if so proven, was an important step on our way back to all that was sacred – slipping past a nest of pirates and slavers notwithstanding; but, as I said, shortly after we had begun to build our new shelter – one that might rightly deserve the description of 'hut' – everything changed dramatically.

Olodoyiorie had shown up for duty at the usual time sending us scuttling under the protection of our old shelter. While the deluge did its worst, we settled in to wait it out, as had become our custom.

You'll recall I had devoted more of my time than was strictly necessary in the study of Loiyan's physique, and indeed, had done so to the point where I believe I could have recognized her while blindfolded in an entire harem of naked women. I studied every inch of her, over and over, and every inch of her I marveled over and worshipped. Yet lately, I had been somewhat

174

disturbed to note a certain – how shall I say – *swelling* in her hips and a *thickening* in the abdominal region. Now, I'm not suggesting that any flaw in her perfection would reduce my ardency for her, not at all, but I was concerned. After all, our diet was hardly one to place extra pounds, and the stress of our labours had kept the both of us in rather good shape, if I do say so myself. So I thought it best to inquire.

"Loiyan, are you feeling well?"

Our shelter was so constricted that there was little choice but to lie down, and so we were – she on her left side, supporting her head in the crook of her arm, and scant inches away, I lay similarly on my right side.

"Yes, of course." Her eyes were playing over me in a way I knew as a prelude to what had also become our custom, "Why do you ask?"

"Oh nothing really," I replied airily, "it's just…" slowly, I traced my finger along the length of her stomach, "well…you seem a little more…I don't know…a bit *thicker* – I mean…*substantial* – that is to say….*different*," I ended lamely.

She stretched luxuriously, like a cat, never taking her eyes off me, and asked, all innocent-like, "Am I no longer beautiful, Chah-lee?"

"Good God no – I mean *yes*…oh crumbs."

"Do you no longer desire me?"

"What! Course I do." With the absence of my kilt, surely she could see that plain enough.

Her bottom lip began to protrude. "You think I am fat and ugly."

"Now, that's utter nonsense," I was beginning to wish I hadn't brought the subject up, "All I'm saying is…"

There were those dimples again.

"What?"

At first her smile broadened to be replaced by something altogether softer. Then, almost shyly, or perhaps introspectively, she lowered her lids.

"I am sorry, Chah-lee, I was teasing."

"Ah…well good, then."

"Yes, but I do have something to tell you. I wanted to wait until I was sure."

Suddenly I had the premonition I was about to hear something that was catastrophic.

"Is it some horrible disease?" I asked, preparing for the worst. "Has some terrible sort of jungle bug got into you?"

She considered this. "Perhaps." although it seemed to amuse her, more than anything.

"We'll get medicine!" Stirred to action, I leapt to my feet...and smashed my head against the roof. Our shelter was small, but I had always been taught to build things to last.

"Oh Chah-lee!"

She was up and coddling my pate while I wobbled back and forth uncertainly.

"Your poor head!"

"Never mind that," I held her firmly by the arms. "Tell me, how bad is it? It is, isn't it – bad, I mean? Oh I know it is! But you mustn't worry, darling, panicking won't help anyone! I'll go to Cairo and bring back a doctor! No, that won't serve, neither! Tell you what, we'll nip off across the lake again; there's got to be a settlement somewhere! Blast! That won't work either! Or I know, how about..."

"I am going to have a baby."

"...we find the river and then....and then...What?"

She smiled, suddenly shy.

"I am going to have your baby." She said it so softly I doubted I'd heard correctly.

"A baby?" I croaked.

"Yes."

"*My* baby?" Lord help me, that's what I said.

"Of course *your* baby," she made a great show of looking around, to see if she had another lover lurking about somewhere, "who else?"

I'm sure it would have been quite amusing, under different circumstances.

But for some reason, I needed her to be very, very clear...so that there might be no misunderstanding.

176

"You…" I pointed at her to make this part perfectly comprehensible.

"Yes."

"…are going to have…" I gestured towards her stomach.

"Yes."

Then I made cradling motions with my arms, "…a *baby*?"

"Yes, Chah-lee."

"*My* baby?" Damn, I'd said it again.

"Yes, Chah-lee," she was speaking very slowly, enunciating as clearly as you could hope for, almost as though she were talking to a halfwit, "I am going to have your baby."

"*Our* baby." Somehow that sounded better.

"Yes, Chah-lee, *our* baby."

I sat back with a great thump, and wheezed, "Well, God bless us all."

"Aren't you happy, Chah-lee?" And suddenly I understood that she was unsure I would be.

But *was* I? I mean, this was all rather sudden, a downright dirty trick to play on a fellow, when you got right down to it – springing the news on me like that. Why, of all the irresponsible things to do out here in the middle of the jungle, she had to go and get herself pregnant. It quite simply had never occurred to me such a thing might happen. Surely a woman as skilled as she knew how to take precautions? Why I'd just assumed…And the child? What hope was there for him/her…it? Why, there would be a little black bastard as ever there was.

And then, quite suddenly, I was smitten with the thought: …with her eyes…and her smile…and her heart.

Yes, I was sure of it. Don't ask me how I knew, but I did, and suddenly all the arguments that might have been made to the contrary disappeared in an instant. This child, whatever the gender, would be the most fantastic of miracles.

I had to clear my throat so I could speak. Somehow it seemed to have become constricted.

"Now then, old girl," I took her hand like it was made of eggshells, "that's just fine."

"Are you sure?" she whispered, her eyes searching.

God, I was trying not to blub. "My dear," I said, "I've never been more sure of anything in my life, and that's God's honest truth."

Gently, she cradled my head again. I felt her lips brush the goose egg on the crown.

"I love you, Chah-lee."

We made love afterwards. I was a bit reluctant, I was frightened of hurting the baby...my baby...*our* baby, but she wouldn't hear of it. Said she was fit as a fiddle. Said there was nothing to worry about on that score, not for a long time to come. As usual, especially when it came to that sort of thing, she got her way.

Even still, I tried to be careful, but she could be such a wanton baggage at times – as she was this time – and I'm afraid I ended up being a bit of a beast myself. Still, she didn't seem to mind.

In fact, to listen to her you would have thought I'd quite outdone myself.

Chapter Fifteen

I suppose it was only natural that I began to have feelings that were, for lack of a better word, spiritual.

I had come through the horrors of the Crimea shorn of all such beliefs, or so I thought. I stopped going to church, much to the displeasure of my mother, who was convinced I was bound for the fires of Hell if I didn't show a proper respect. But the thing was, at some dark level, I felt I was doing just that – showing a proper respect, or to put it rather differently, showing all the respect that a god of blood and carnage deserved; and this was the philosophy I thought to follow for the rest of my days.

It's hard to say when all that started to change, but Africa was working her effect on me, and there's no use in denying it. I don't doubt it might have started that night out on Unkerewe, when the storm was doing its best to send us down into the Dark Continent's answer to Davy Jones' locker. I mean, the Bible's chock full of fellows finding religion in a boat in the middle of a storm-tossed sea, so who was I to be any different? I'm not saying that I fell to my knees and gave thanks for my deliverance, or anything like that – that's not my style. All I know is, when the odds are as rum as they were that night (and they don't come any rummer) and still you pull through – not one, but *both* of you – it's not natural if you don't start wondering if there's not something to it. Then you start thinking that words like 'miracle' aren't so easily scoffed at.

But I'd been through Balaclava, remember, and in many ways, that wasn't altogether different – perhaps even more so. From that horrible day onward, I was a changed man. It marked my life much the same as Jesus' birth marked the earth. That is to say that everything in my world happened either before or after 25 October, 1854.

And it's not that it wasn't a miracle that we (again, not one, but *both* of us – my master and myself) survived that too, because it was, in its way. So how was it that something so horrible could snuff out my faith as easily as a candle in the wind, and another event, no less frightening, to some measure, restore it?

179

Well, you'd probably have to go to the archbishop for that answer (and *he'd* have to go ask his mum), but there are things you pick up when you're lying awake in the long, still hours of the night, when there's just you and the Great Perhaps, and you try to piece it all together. The best I could come up with was this:

Yes, I survived the Charge, and yes, it seemed like a miracle, but the thing is, there were all too many of us to whom that simply didn't apply. They died, you see, blown to kingdom come, or torn to bits, or pierced by bullet, lance or sword (Oh we've a genius for killing, and no error) and still more others horribly maimed, their bodies shredded by war's machinery, left – by a grateful country – to beg for alms on London's street corners, or all the street corners in all the towns of Britain. So, yes, I survived, and it's not that I'm not grateful, because I am, but somehow the sight of all those cadavers of broken horses and men, lying there on the north valley with their guts spread all around them, and the thought of the politicians – safe at home – who sent us there in the first place….well, there just didn't seem to be too much that was holy about it, that's all. And like I said, it wasn't like I was going to take my oath for the Orders upon surviving the storm, or anything like that either, but I do confess, there was a feeling in me that we had been spared for some reason. I suspect I'm not the first to experience that sort of feeling, and I'll probably not be the last.

Yet, although, without a doubt, it was a series of coincidences that were the cause of our dallying so long on that little stretch of beach, I wonder how much I was influenced by the idea that He had saved us, and that He had cast us upon this shore? He had saved us for a reason, therefore He had sent us here for a purpose. I can't say with any kind of certainty that it had any bearing on anything at all, but then, I can't say that it didn't, either.

At any rate, all that was dressing for the salad, and was not anywhere near the main course. For, as far as I was concerned, the most spiritual experience imaginable is when you're an expectant father.

I mean, it's bloody awful!

180

"We're not going, and that's flat." I was putting my foot down.

"But Chah-lee, I am a strong woman. There is no problem."

"That's obviously not so. Why, just look at you."

A little round mound had begun to appear on her belly. It had been there for weeks, and seemed to be growing bigger by the minute.

"You can't expect to go traipsing around uncharted territory like that, now can you? Why, who knows how far we'll have to travel, or what desperate measures we'll need to take along the way."

"But Chah-lee, you must get to Ingle-land, to *Olaiguenani* Brampton, you said so yourself."

I held up a vertical and decisive palm. "It'll have to wait, that's all."

I had just finished helping her to her cushions – she declared she didn't need any help, but I felt I knew best – and was propping her feet so she could rest more comfortably.

"There now," I said grasping a thatch of grass we used in lieu of a broom, "let's hear no more about it, shall we?"

"But Chah-lee..." She was regarding me with something like exasperation, and amused affection, all rolled into one.

I interrupted, "Now see here, don't you remember saying you would go with me anywhere, anywhere in the world?"

"Yes, but...."

"Well," I gestured around our newly finished home, "this is it, at least for the time being."

"But I am not helpless!" she cried, slapping her palms on the floor for emphasis.

"My love," I said fondly, the very voice of manly reason, "no one's saying you are, but it just isn't on, can't you see that?"

"You keep me here like a...a...a prisoner!" All in all, I thought the exasperation seemed to be winning out over amused affection.

"Oh pish," I said, sweeping around the hearthstones, "that's not true at all."

"It *is* true, and now you say I am a liar!"

181

"Bollocks, you're just going through one of your episodes, that's all."

"I am not!" And to prove the point she threw a pot at me.

"Chah-lee!" She was on her feet and flinging herself across the room and into my arms, "I'm so sorry!" Then she burst into tears.

She'd been doing that a lot, lately.

"There, there, old girl," I said, patting her shoulders, "it's all right. See? You missed!" But it took quite a bit to calm her down.

Finally, she snuffled into my chest, "Chah-lee?"

"Mmm?"

Shyly, she asked, "Am I still your beautiful wench?"

I held her tenderly at arm's length and gently chucked her under the chin until our eyes met. Then I winked, and said, "Rather!"

That never failed to jolly her up. So, in the end, she even allowed me to cajole her back to her cushions, and not before time, either.

I mean, there never seemed to be enough hours in the day!

As you may have gathered, our new hut was finished and we had taken occupancy some weeks earlier. *Olodoyiorie* had passed and the drier but still quite wet *Oloilpunye* was now on the wane. Soon would come the verdure of *Arat*, and it would be once more possible to travel. Yet in spite of my desire to see England, and in spite of the knowledge I was lagging in my duty to Lord Brampton, I thought it best not to. Loiyan's opinion notwithstanding, I had meant every word I said. It would have been madness to try to make it all the way to Cairo in her condition.

If only I had known. But we don't, do we?

There's something about watching your woman's belly fill with your child that's altogether different from anything else I've experienced, and I suppose that's what I mean when I say it lies on the spiritual side of things. I mean, it brings a certain sense of peace and contentment that can't quite be found in any other situation – or if it can, it's in a place I have yet to discover. And if that isn't spiritual, I don't know what is.

I've often heard of women in a family way being described as 'having a glow' and I really can't improve much on that. Except Loiyan didn't glow so much as shine – just like the sun, and like the sun, she brought warmth and light to the coldest and darkest of days. And as *Arat* withered and became the month of light hail – of *Morusasin* – I knew the warmth of my contentment was due solely to her.

At this point you might be thinking that I never did intend to leave this place by Ukerewe, and I won't say you're wrong. Travel with a child in arms is very nearly as perilous as one in the belly, and I would have none of it, regardless of what Loiyan told me about Maasai women having been doing just that for centuries. But in my heart of hearts, I may have realized it was only an excuse.

You see, I knew something of the world, and had come to the conclusion that the only place in it for us was where we were.

You'll recall the dream I had, where I was returning to Brampton Manor in triumph with her as my beautiful bride? Only it wasn't her, exactly, was it? Not quite my beautiful Loiyan. You'll note that, even in my dream state, I knew better than to leave her as a blackamoor. Oh, there were many times when I thought, 'If they could just get to know her, and see her the way I see her, it could still work out,' but deep down inside, I knew that would never happen. All they would see was a darkie and that would be it, filed and receipted. Because, in England, such things just weren't done, and the worst of it was, had this not happened to myself, I probably would have shunned anyone of a mixed marriage as much as everyone else. I see now that it would have been to my everlasting shame, but it doesn't make it any less true. But be that as it may, although I'm not sure I can say it was *wrong* to return to England, or that we couldn't manage to carve out some sort of life there for ourselves, I will say it just seemed wrong for us.

Not that I admitted as much to myself, you'll understand, but down in the nether regions of my soul, I think it was acknowledged, and so acknowledged, that door had closed.

Oh, I realize now that I should have put the question to her and let her decide for herself, but I didn't. In the dark hours, with her lying beside me, and outside the night noises all around, I was able to reason I couldn't allow her to experience all that cruelty. I was sure it would change her – it couldn't *help* but change her – and into whatever person it would render her, she would cease to be the girl that I loved.

Yet the question I *did* shy away from, and still find it hard to face today, was this: was I reluctant because I was *ashamed?*

Of course, the question was ludicrous when applied there by the shores of Africa's great water, for there could be no man more proud of his mate than I was of Loiyan. But, with the utmost reluctance, I will admit that it might well have been something altogether different back in Britain, and I was loathe to put that to the test. Would she be the only one who changed, I wonder? It's a daunting thing to stand in defiance of the world – of friends and neighbours, of my family…of Lord Brampton, himself – and I wonder if I would have been as ready for that as I would have liked to believe? I wouldn't allow myself to think of it then, certainly, and I *try* not to think of it now, but I've become an old man these past years, and my mind seems to take quite a delight in letting out its darker, most haunting secrets.

Still, there were other reasons, and I suppose these were the ones I surrendered to most gladly. At best, they could be summed up in a phrase old Joe Tanner, the local blacksmith, was always fond of saying, to whit, 'If it's not broken, don't mend it'. As far as I was concerned – outside of being plagued with niggling doubts that my sense of duty to Lord Brampton might not be as strong as I'd hoped – it wasn't broken.

We seemed well situated. Food was plentiful, and the climate not overly stressing. It might have been different if Loiyan had voiced regret over the lack of human contact, but she never did. On the contrary, she seemed quite happy to be wherever I was, and only ever made mention of leaving when it was on my own account. So, even without her being with child, all things considered, it seemed best to stay where we were. The attending risks of having it otherwise were simply too great.

And don't forget, we were bound together, like that capricious boulder rolling down the mountainside. Call it intuition, call it what you will, but somehow I *knew* that Britain would see that journey's end.

Now, having said all that, I'll take the liberty of appearing to contradict myself by saying that I'm not suggesting we *never* would have left. For although the sense of urgency I felt to return to my duties paled when compared to my desire to stay there with her, it never left me completely; and who knows, if an opportunity had presented itself where I deemed the risks acceptable, perhaps we would have packed up and left. But such an opportunity never came, so we didn't. You'll note the paradox to what I stated earlier, but such was the state of my mind. I'm afraid it's a question I'll never be able to answer with any satisfaction. More's the pity.

Yet, be that as it may, once the decision had been made to stay, it seemed a great weight had been lifted from my shoulders. Although it was only a decision deferred until after the child was born and of a sufficient age to endure the rigours of travel, it encompassed a period of sufficient length whereby it made viable all efforts to make our situation more comfortable.

Arat is the month of greenery, when all things grow in abundance. Loiyan, having long ago rebelled and won her release from my overly attentive clutches – with strong assurances that she was well capable – had once again claimed her former position in the household, which is to say, she did all the work.

Well, not *all*. I insisted on helping out wherever I could, but even I had to admit to being a bit ham-fisted in some of the more domestic areas.

In the mornings we would go out on the lake where she would cast her net while I stood guard in the stern, noting silently to myself that her belly was becoming something of an obstruction for the task. As time went on, however, she became accustomed and never allowed it to effect her prowess. So we seldom had to rely on my lesser skills. It's not that I never tried to try to convince her otherwise, because I did, but I knew she loved playing that role, probably for no other reason than it was something that had always been denied her, and subsequently, was fiercely protective of it. And as I loved her, I would not refuse her.

185

As I've said many times, she was so good at mastering such manly skills that I often reflected that, while she might not owe her survival to me, the reverse might be far more debatable.

In the afternoon, we might sometimes venture inland to find plants suitable for food or medicine. For with the greenery at its fullest, Loiyan assured me that *Arat* was the best time to stalk up on her small pharmacy. Or we might gather the elephant grass with which to weave baskets or mats, or simply set out with no more than a sense of the joy of exploration. There was no doubt she was her father's daughter and often displayed the same curiosity that must have infected him since before the time of her birth. We never ventured far, however – the jungle, being nigh on impenetrable, would not allow it – and as her pregnancy progressed, and she became more easily fatigued, we travelled inland less and less. Outside of finding many useful exhibits of flora and fauna, we discovered that there was no simple egress from our small territory, and that on three sides we were completely insulated. The lake, as it had always been, remained our sole connection to the outside world, such as it was.

While still in the waning days of the rainy season, we had made a few timid forays of a mile or more up and down the coast, but it was unwise to travel far from shelter at that time. Still, we were able to ascertain no other habitation within those confined limits, nor was there other lake traffic within our view. Only after the rains had ended did we decide, one day, to pack enough provisions for an extended absence and venture further afield.

Our decision to do so had not been lightly made, for as I have stated earlier in these pages, this was Africa, and the potential of discovering another people was very nearly equal to discovering another enemy. But there could be no arguing that discovery was knowledge. Whether the intelligence we gleaned was fair or foul, we understood it was best not to be living in a bubble of ignorance.

Therefore, early one morning, just as the sun had risen, we set out, proceeding with caution, staying close inshore so as not to display an easy view of ourselves against Ukerewe's flat

186

horizon, and still far enough away from land to provide warning should attack threaten from that quarter.

As had always been our habit, we proceeded due north, except now it was closer to west-north-west, but expecting a clearer heading once we had passed what we thought of as a headland some few miles from our little strand. It took us the better part of the morning to achieve this, and upon having done so, it appeared that our supposition had been proven correct. But upon proceeding north for no longer than an hour, we discovered the land fell sharply away to the east.

"It must be an inlet," I reckoned.

"Yes, it must be," she agreed, and not without reason, for we could see land a short distance away. "Shall we cut across?"

I hesitated. "No, we'll be too visible. Besides, we're exploring, remember?"

She laughed, warming me like sunshine, "As you say, my love. Very well," once more taking up her paddle, "then let us explore."

I half hoped she was using some form of sexual double-speak as a signal she would steer us inland so I might thereby drag her into the bushes for further exploration of another kind. I knew it wasn't beyond her, but this time she maintained our distance from the shore, leaving me to simmer in my own juices, as it were.

For as hard as it was for me to believe – well no it wasn't, not in some ways – I was finding her more desirable than ever. The bulge in her stomach had me going to the point where I was quite shocked with myself. The allure of her breasts, however – once youthful with promise, were now magnificently swollen to maturity – made much more sense to me. But whatever the reason, the effect was that I was finding it quite a struggle to leave off her. Not that she ever complained, mind, but I had an uncomfortable suspicion I was making rather a pest of myself.

Yet, as the sun reached its zenith and continued to slide toward the western horizon – and taking note that our closest neighbours appeared to be a family of hippopotami wallowing in some shallows – our conviction of an inlet turned to doubt. In the distance, to our left – to our *port* – the land continued visible, yet appeared to be broken into a series of islands. To the starboard, of course, was our own shore, but to our front, the water stretched far away, unbroken, to the horizon.

"Why, we are on an island," she said, awestruck with unexpected discovery.

"So it would seem," I concurred with my own sense of wonder. In fact it appeared that ours was the westernmost of a vast archipelago.

An hour or so further, the land began to taper to the south.

"I think we must be alone."

After the denseness of the population we had seen on the lake's eastern shore the previous year, I had to admit I was surprised, although not displeased. Once more, I reflected on our being cast upon this unlikely place, and was becoming more and more filled with the conviction that there was some higher purpose at play.

Yet even as these thoughts were toying with my mind, we rounded the coast and saw the land fall away into a shallow, crescent-shaped bay.

Upon its waters – in every way similar to our own – rode some half dozen boats.

We back-paddled to a complete stop, regarding the occupants with startled amazement, while they reciprocated in kind.

My first instinct was to turn tail and run for it, but the closest might have been a mere stone's throw from us, and I had my doubts as to whether this would answer. Instead, we sat where we were and waited for events to unfold, contenting myself by making sure the gun was close to hand.

Presently, the fellow made a cautious approach, while his comrades slowly drifted in behind him. When he came too close for comfort, I made to back water to maintain our distance, whereupon he ceased to paddle, but lay it aside and held up his hands, palms outward, in the universal signal that his intentions were peaceful.

Sitting in the bow, Loiyan had, thus far, made no effort to move.

She said, "I do not think he means us harm."

I regarded him warily, for he was a fine specimen – tall and broad-shouldered with well-muscled limbs. If he closed with evil intent, it would take no small effort to overcome him.

Gradually, his compatriots drew near as well, and began to speak softly amongst themselves, every so often rolling their eyes in our direction.

I grew suspicious and seized the rifle, and was amazed when there was instantly much distressed shouting. One or two made to be away, while others more bold frantically waved their hands back and forth, palms down to the water, signaling there was no cause for me to take alarm.

I relaxed my finger from the triggers, but did not let down my guard.

These appeared to be the same sort of folk as those of the stone forts we had seen before, but whereas their cousins had always shown an inclination to run away from a stranger, these fellows – or at least some of them – seemed to be made of sterner fiber, exhibiting nothing more than a natural caution, as I did myself. I found that to be somewhat reassuring. What it also told me was, although they appeared to possess none of their own, they were no strangers to firearms, and held a healthy respect for their potential.

"We come in peace," Loiyan called out in Maa, but they shook their heads, indicating they did not understand her. They jabbered back something in their own lingo, with similar results from us.

I continued to give them the cautious eye, all the while making sure they maintained their distance

Then the first one, after much gabble and motioning for me to stay calm, reached down into the bottom of his canoe and brought up a string of fish. Jabbering some more, he pointed first to his catch, and then to me. When I showed no recognition as to his meaning, he patiently repeated himself, pointing first to his catch and then to myself. And then, replacing the string, he gestured: hands spread slightly, with palms facing up, shoulders

189

hunched, allowing his gaze to play with interest into the confines of our craft.

Loiyan spoke in a low voice. "I think he is asking if we want to trade."

Of course it wasn't possible that he understood, but the fisherman nodded encouragingly, beckoning for us to approach.

When I hesitated to comply, he grew puzzled and once more pointing at me, uttered a single, interrogative word.

Whereupon I felt a chill run over my body, and the skin shrink away from my scalp.

For inconceivable as it was, I understood what he was asking. I had heard that word once before, from a dying old man beneath the brambles of a thorn bush. It had been included in several of my nightmares many times since.

"Baggara?"

Chapter Sixteen

The rifle was at my shoulder, its hammers pulled back to full cock.

"Chah-lee!" Loiyan may have heard the gun being made ready, but more like she felt the tension coming off me in waves.

I had a bead on the blighter and was taking up the slack on both triggers. I could see the whites of his eyes quite clearly. I don't know whether it was surprise or fear, but I suspect it was both.

"Chah-lee, no!"

Her hand was at the side of the barrel, pushing it down and away. I shook it free and swung it around, once more bringing it to bear.

"No, Chah-lee, they mean us no harm!"

"Stay clear," I barked, "I'll send this one straight to hell!"

But again she took hold of the barrel. Calmly, she ordered, "Put the gun down."

The fellow remained frozen, his eyes bulging as though he'd just swallowed his tongue. I noticed a trickle of fluid running down the inside of his leg. But for the unified drawing in of an astonished gasp, his *confrères* remained equally frozen.

For a moment he wavered in my sights, then slowly, I let out my breath, lowering the weapon, returning the hammers to their rest.

Not a word was said, but they looked from one to the other, and then, once more, to me.

Slowly, in spite of the tension that still coursed through me, I raised my palms in as unthreatening a manner as possible to reassure them. Then, pointing to myself, I shook my head, and explained as best I could, "No Baggara."

To which the first one – he who had come so close to dying – shook his head in turn, seeking confirmation.

"No Baggara?"

"No."

He gave a slow, introspective nod, indicating he understood, but he continued to look puzzled.

Loiyan's voice spoke softly at my side. "What happened, Chah-lee? What is Baggara?"

"The Arabs," I said, not willing to face her, "those murdering slavers, and for all I know, those black bastards they had helping them were Baggara, too."

"Oh Chah-lee!" Gently, she took my face in her hands, her eyes searching, "Oh my poor love!"

Meanwhile the others had gathered around their companion and held an impromptu powwow. It took some time, but gradually they seemed to come to an accord. Once more the first separated himself from his friends.

"No Baggara?" he asked, making absolutely certain. When it was staunchly reaffirmed, he simply teetered one way and then the other, wiggling his hands to indicate it was of no particular importance. The gesture might have been comical had it not been for those dangerous moments preceding.

"Hai," he said, gesturing, then pointing to the shore, followed with something else I couldn't understand.

But of course, I did understand. For the first time, I became aware of a village lying inside the bay. Not a stone fort, as we had seen many times before, but simple huts, not dissimilar to our own. On the beach, there were more boats pulled up on the sand with, here and there, children darting about them in play.

He seemed to be offering an invitation.

I was surprised, for this was the first that I'd received since Musa had brought me into his village, and even then that hadn't been an invitation so much as a kidnapping.

"I don't know, what do you think?" I asked, never taking my eyes off the brute. True, I hadn't blown him to kingdom come, but that didn't mean we were bosom chums, neither.

But Loiyan had no such reservations. "It will be alright, I am sure." She was speaking to me, of course, but she was looking at the children.

Meanwhile the fishermen continued to gesture their welcome, perhaps inviting us in for their version of tea.

So, cautiously, I nodded our acceptance, gesturing that they should lead off and we would follow. Outside the fact that I'm a

192

naturally suspicious character, I couldn't help feeling it was all rather odd. I mean, there we were, meeting the neighbours, in a manner of speaking – not so different than if we were back in England, and me and the missus had decided to hop in the buggy to drop in on people across the way. It was the first time I had done so in my connubial life, and that our hosts should be a passel of fuzzy-headed blacks made it all the more exotic, I thought.

As our boat grounded on the sand, we jumped out and hauled it securely up the beach. I hesitated over the rifle. I didn't want anyone to feel threatened, but neither would I feel comfortable without its reassuring presence (which, you might agree, isn't perhaps *quite* the same as a social visit in England). In the end, I compromised by slinging it casually over my shoulder, before turning and following the others up the short stretch of sand to the village proper.

As soon as we came ashore, the children playing around the boats – being naturally shy, I suppose – had withdrawn a ways. But Loiyan, placing both hands on her knees, had smiled and twittered her fingers at them. One lad – a tow-headed imp of about ten, with a sty in one eye, who had that look about him that said his usual form was getting up to no good – hesitated, and then beamed back at her for all he was worth, followed quickly by his cronies. I shouldn't have been surprised; he reminded me of myself when I was his age. Probably we shared the same tastes in women.

Whatever the case, while I followed her to the cluster of huts, I couldn't help feeling amused when they all crowded around her and the impudent young juggins slipped his hand neatly into hers. 'Here, what's this,' I thought, chuckling to myself, 'I'll have to keep an eye on you, my lad.'

But she was like that, of course. It fair radiated out of her pores. It made me feel quite proud, I can tell you, and if my shirt had still retained any of its buttons, I have no doubts that, at that moment, I would have burst them clean off.

Loiyan and children: they seemed to go together like eggs and ham.

The vanguard of our party had let out a yell, presumably to warn the cooks and bottle-washers there would be guests for tiffen. Presently a funny old duck hurried out from one of the huts and presented herself. From the others' attitude toward her, I soon gathered that she was their chief.

I was very surprised, and had to look twice to make sure, but there was no doubting she was a woman – a little wrinkled, perhaps, but still plainly of the fairer sex. Evidently, these people weren't beyond letting a woman have a go at the reins of power every now and then, just like us and our dear old Vicky back home.

While the old bird waited for us to come closer she was fastidiously smoothing down the fabric of her skirt so as to make herself more presentable. I supposed there was something universal with guest receptions, and hard on that thought, my attention was uncomfortably drawn to my own disheveled attire. For since suffering the loss of my kilt, and after experiencing a painful case of sunburn on my more delicate parts, I had long since taken to wearing a sort of skirt fashioned from elephant grass.

Loiyan had claimed it made me look more handsome than ever, which was all very nice, but she would have sounded more convincing if her tongue hadn't been so thoroughly installed in her cheek at the time.

The greyhair was surrounded by our fisher friends and informed of the exciting new visitors that had come their way. Amidst all the chatter, I could just make out the words, "no Baggara", at which she caught my eye, smiling sweetly, albeit toothlessly, probably to set me at ease over my sense of fashion. Then, coming forward, she indicated herself and said, "Ajiambo." To which I bowed and replied, "Charlie Smithers," and turning to Loiyan, introduced her as well.

We must have arrived just at meal time for, behind Ajiambo, the rest of the women folk were spreading mats upon the ground, after which they began to pile on the grub. Presently, with gestures and smiles, we were invited to follow everyone's example and take our ease amongst them.

194

The viands were the usual affair you might expect, but with some interesting combinations I saw Loiyan take special note of. But the concoction they provided to wash it all down was a truly revolting substance that strongly smelled of fish. Still, it has always been my contention that there is no such thing as bad beer, only uneducated palates, and sure enough by meal's end, I was swilling it down with the best of them.

These certainly seemed an egalitarian folk when compared to the rigid society of the Maasai. I couldn't say if such was the case with their cousins back on the mainland, or if our island had insulated them from the rest of the world, leaving them free to follow their own course; but from what I could see, there was no segregation or ceremony during the meal. Except for the women serving us, both sexes were free to recline where they would, and to come and go as they pleased, none visibly subservient to the other. It relieved me that this was so, for I had been worried that the women must dine apart from the men. I was not yet so comfortable amongst them as to suffer myself to be parted from Loiyan's company.

Presently this minor feast was completed, and after much rubbing of our stomachs to sign that we were grateful for their hospitality, all was cleared away and, to my surprise, replaced with a profusion of various and sometimes curious objects, all spread out on the mats for our perusal.

Loiyan and I regarded one another uncomfortably, for it was evident these folk wished to trade. But, apart from our necessities, we had brought along nothing with which to respond.

I signed to the old woman that such was the case, and was happy when she smiled, waving her hand dismissively to indicate it was of small consequence. Instead, she leaned forward, towards Loiyan, studying her closely. Finally she made a sign, as though asking for some sort of permission.

Mystified, my love acquiesced – for there was no harm in the dear thing – and was somewhat startled when Ajiambo gently pulled aside her robe to reveal her engorged breasts, and swollen stomach. I must say, I was quite startled myself, and if it had been anyone else but that gentle old soul, I daresay there would have been trouble right then and there. But I needn't have worried, of course, for upon seeing the state of Loiyan's pregnancy, there arose such a cry of admiration from all those crowding around that it was obvious the birth of a child, any child, apparently, was occasion for much joy.

Ajiambo put her hand on my darling's stomach. Presently, her face was wreathed in smiles and she nodded, apparently satisfied that all was well. It was a moment I shall not soon forget. Loiyan too, although blushing furiously, seemed pleased, in spite of everything.

Meantime, her adoring urchin and his cohorts had elbowed their way through the throng for no better reason I could discern other than their wish to be close to her. You'll note that this flew in the face of the fact that, if there was anyone present who was novel – and thus more worthy of their curiosity – it was my own white-skinned self, and was, I think, a testament to the richness of her personality that she easily outshone me as far as children were concerned.

After the old woman was finished, and modesty restored, Loiyan gave the lad a smile. Then, slowly, it transformed into an expression altogether more thoughtful.

The boy's sty was swollen, and though it might not have been painful, it was almost certainly a cause for considerable discomfort. Motioning for him to remain, she went to the boat, returning presently with her medicine bag. Whereupon asking and receiving permission from the bewildered matriarch, she bathed the lad's eye with water before gently applying a salve. Next a patch was provided and, by first indicating the sun followed by the holding up of three fingers – thus telling him he should wear it for three days – the job was finished.

It was a simple sort of thing, not unlike countless treatments she must have performed many times before (many of them on myself), but the effect it had on these simple folk was amazing.

Of course the cure wasn't instantaneous, but I will say the young beggar was transformed on the spot, grinning away like a Cheshire cat. A healing touch can do that – I'd seen it often enough in the Crimea – but when the healer is a beautiful woman, and you're already half in love with her to boot, it can do it all the faster, you may be sure.

Ajiambo regarded Loiyan with something that could only be described as deep veneration (we found out later the lad was her grandson, and her favourite), the rest of the clan following suit. After which there arose a great murmuring amongst the villagers.

"Well done, old girl," I said, "that seems to have got them on side."

Loiyan returned my smile with a look of the utmost perplexity. "But it was nothing, really, just a very small thing."

"I don't know about that," I said indicating the crowd, "but it looks as though you're on to something."

And so it appeared. For there, as if by magic, was a little girl with a swollen cheek, indicating abscess of the tooth. Hard on her heels came an emaciated woman with sores covering much of her body. Then even as we watched, the crowd parted to allow a young fellow to approach, in the company of his mother, nursing a dislocated elbow.

Of course nothing would do but she should set up shop right there and then. But as, one by one, she doctored their sickness and injuries – with my fumbling assistance – the line seemed to grow longer with every passing minute.

At first, I had thought the village to be no more than half dozen households. Yet as I saw people making their way through recesses masked by jungle, I realized it was far larger, perhaps a thousand souls all told. Judging by the crowd assembling, it seemed a good percentage of them required her attention.

The sun was well westering, with but minutes of light left when, inevitably, her medicine ran out, and we had to call it a day. Those left untreated were disappointed, of course, but there was nothing impolite about them when they turned around and – some hobbling painfully, others needing to be carried – made their way back to their homes.

Naturally, the sight tore at my dear one's heart.

"Oh Chah-lee," she cried, treating me to a full display of her irresistible eyes, "we must help these people! Tell me that we can!"

I put an arm around her and gave her shoulders a hug. "It's not up to me, old girl. It seems you're the sawbones around here."

She smiled gratefully, and I felt another one of those pangs when I realized how easily she was pleased.

But, although happy, she was also very tired. The day had taken much out of her, and I cursed my own stupidity, for I should have long since seen to our sleeping arrangements.

It was then that Ajiambo came forward, signing her gratitude to Loiyan for having helped her people before miming the occasion must be marked with a celebration.

At first I was pleasantly amazed; for no one had ever done such a thing on my account in my entire life. Yet I reconsidered and, although I had no wish to give offense, thought to decline on the grounds that Loiyan was too tired.

But it was she herself who forestalled me.

"Oh Chah-lee," she pleaded, "it will be fun!" And as I have often said before, seldom could I gainsay her anything, and in spite of my concern, neither did I do so now.

A great fire was built, and much food prepared, but before getting down to the festivities in earnest, Ajiambo bade us browse amongst the trading articles, indicating we should take from them what we might in payment for our kindness.

I was struck by the nobility of that simple gesture. These were a poor people, yet they insisted upon paying their way. There was a simple honesty to it that quite humbled me, for I cannot say, with all certainty, I would have done the same.

I perused the goods, and thought to content myself with a remnant of a plain and cheap cotton material, for it would enable me to cast my grass skirt aside. But then Loiyan, smiling with pleasure, chose a necklace of blue beads. She held the string up, inviting me to admire them.

"Aren't they pretty, Chah-lee?"

They were that, although they were nothing but cheap glass you could find anywhere; from the stalls of a London market to the bazaars in Cairo.

"Very pretty," I said and, taking them from her, indicated to Ajiambo this was to be our choice before placing them around my darling's neck where, once placed, the beads became, not merely pretty, but beautiful.

Yet there was something which gave me pause to wonder. Where had these items come from? It was quite obvious these folk were, to some extent, familiar with goods from an outside source. What that source was, however, remained a mystery.

Having made our choice, the rest of the goods were promptly stowed away. Whereupon, as the sun gently dipped into the jungle, a bonfire was kindled and everyone assembled in a great circle around it. We, being the guests of honour, were led to our places on either side of Ajiambo and, once seated, were served food and drink. With that, it could be said that the feast *proper* began.

Between mouthfuls and through signs, I asked Ajiambo where the beads had originated.

She was a bright old girl because she understood immediately.

"Baggara," she said, pointing out to the bay.

By now, of course, I had overcome the fright the word had instilled in me earlier, but even so, it gave me quite a shock. Yet when I asked her again to confirm, she repeated, once more indicating the waters.

"Baggara! Baggara!" And then, pointing to the sky, she held up all her arthritic old fingers of both hands and then two more.

From this I devined that Arab traders, who were also known as 'Baggara', would come to the village every twelve moons, or once a year.

This confused me further because, as I have said, these were a poor folk, and of as modest value as these goods were, I wondered what they might possess to cause any self-respecting merchants to venture so far. But when asked, all the old woman would do was hold up the morsel on which she was gumming away as if to say it was the fish they sought, and then to my cup which seemed to suggest their rancid beer, also.

When, by holding up the food and drink, I suggested, respectfully, with a polite frown, that the trade seemed unfair, she merely shrugged.

199

It seemed odd to me, but I couldn't get any more from her. It was the Baggara who came to trade, and what they wanted was fish and beer. If they insisted on paying more than what it was worth, then that was their affair.

I couldn't comprehend it, not at all, and for some reason, it made me feel slightly uneasy. Still, it seemed a small thing and, as the alcohol worked its way into my system, I put it out of my mind, and it was soon forgotten.

Meanwhile two men had come to the edge of the circle, carrying in their arms a hollow log. This they then set upon short poles, effectively supporting it from the ground. Then, taking club-like sticks in hand, they settled down and began to beat upon it as they would a drum. While I won't say the sounds they coaxed out was music, exactly – at least not the kind we know – I will readily admit there was a sort of primitive pulse that was not entirely displeasing to the ear. In fact, as the beer gradually took over my sense of reason, I thought it quite appealing.

Evidently, others were of the same mind as, one by one, regardless of gender, they leapt into the circle and began to stamp and whirl in a savage sort of dance about the fire, while others, stomping time with their feet, and clapping their hands in rhythm, began to sing.

They had fine voices, I'll give them that, with a wonderful sense of harmony, too, especially when you considered how inebriated everyone was getting. And what, with all the stamping and clapping and singing, and – counterpoint to everything – the low pulse of the log drum, it was all I could do to keep from jumping in to join them.

I couldn't help noticing there was one chit – I must say she was rather attractive – who was dancing with a particular abandon. The reason I say I couldn't help noticing is because she chose to do so directly to my front, from all but a few feet away.

Did I mention the women wore no garments other than a sort of tightly hugging sheath that served as a skirt, while neglecting to cover their top half? Well, they don't, and as the strumpet became more and more abandoned, her udders started to shake in such a way that I began to suck on the grog in earnest to calm my nerves. I thought it best to look away, but saw Loiyan watching me with sparkling eyes, and her hand over her mouth to cover her laughter. In some confusion now, I returned my attention to the wench, and saw, to my horror, she'd now removed her skirt and was gyrating her torso rather suggestively, and with nothing on but a loincloth that could scarcely serve to cover the palm of my hand. To make things worse, she was staring directly at me; and such a nakedly frank and carnal stare it was, too!

What with all that nervous energy and beer churning around on my insides, I'm afraid I was becoming rather spiffled.

This went on for some time – the drummers pounding out that primordial sound, the singers voices mingling with the beer fumes in my mind, and all the while the firelight reflecting off this brazen tart while she continued to writhe and expose herself to me in such a way as to make a sailor blush – that the whole threatened to hypnotize me with lust, and required a great deal of will power to resist. Thus it was that, partly as an excuse to be away from this baggage, but I confess mostly because it had already been a long day, and with the booze now making my head spin, I had just enough sense in me to realize it was time to turn in.

"Loi – Loiyan, wanna go to bed." I told her, but when I was able to focus my bleary eyes, I saw she was no longer at Ajiambo's side – come to that, neither was Ajiambo.

"Where's my woman?!" I shouted to no one in particular, "Where's Loiyan?!" and went lurching off into the crowd to find her.

I had vague memories of barreling into people, and thrusting them rudely aside. There didn't seem to be any voice of complaint, however, and small wonder, for nearly everyone was in worse shape than I was myself. And if that wasn't bad enough, I could have sworn I saw more than one couple rutting in the shadows, drunker than Davy's sow. I wasn't sure what my old mum would have thought of her son lurching along in the middle of all this, but I doubt she'd have approved.

Then I saw Loiyan reflected by the flames. Somehow she'd got to the opposite side of the circle with Ajiambo, both busily engaged in miming a conversation with what I thought was surprising alacrity.

Suddenly I knew what I wanted. With all the puggle I'd taken on board and naked dancing girls shoving their tits in my face and whatnot, I'd become randier than hell, and nothing would do but I should have my wicked way with my own dear one.

I bellowed out to her and plowed across the circle, continuing to bowl aside anyone who happened to be in my way. By the time I was halfway through that milling, gyrating, and stumbling throng of drunken humanity my passion had become the equivalent of a holy crusade.

It was only when I came lurching up to them, panting away as though I'd never seen a woman before, that I noticed the cheeky strumpet had also joined them. Although this made me uneasy, it was with some relief that I noticed she'd since reclaimed her garment.

Loiyan smiled her welcome, and asked, "Are you enjoying yourself, Chah-lee?"

"Wanna go to....to the bed....to bed," I managed, nuzzling her. "Wanna take you to bed. C'mon, it'll...it'll be fun."

Her smile never left her, but she indicated neither nay nor yea. Instead, she gestured to the saucy piece and explained, "I have asked Ajiambo, and she has agreed that we be the honoured guests of Aboyo tonight."

I twisted my neck and the girl – Aboyo – hove into view, and somehow, even through the fog of drunkenness, a suspicion began to grow that all was not as it seemed.

Even though she was smiling friendly enough – perhaps *too* friendly – Aboyo was regarding me with the same bold, speculative stare which, in turn, was bringing back that old uncomfortable feeling. In addition to which, I caught Ajiambo and the girl of my heart exchanging strange, knowing looks, and wasn't sure if it was in any way to my pleasing.

Then, to cap it all off, as if on signal, the three of them began to giggle.

"What?" I asked.

"It is nothing, my love," Loiyan assured me, although her dimples were still showing, "Come, it is time for bed."

There didn't seem to be any alternative but to comply. Yet while following Aboyo, carrying a torch down a secluded path, I couldn't help but wonder if she was accenting the swaying of her hips more than was absolutely necessary. They did seem to be bouncing along in the fireglow rather disturbingly, as if they had a life of their own. It were almost as though…well…she *expected* I was staring at her bottom, or something! When I realized that I was, in fact, staring like a mesmerized fool, I shook myself and whispered to Loiyan.

"M'not sure I trust that one. I'd keep my eye on'er if I was you."

"Oh, Chah-lee," she chided, then spoiled the effect by giggling slightly, "you are so suspicious. It will be fine, you will see. Besides," she added sympathetically, "she is a widow, poor thing. Her husband drowned a year ago."

I must admit that I didn't care about that one way or the other. At the moment, all I was interested in was coming to grips with my woman, and said so whilst giving her bottom a squeeze. Loiyan simply smiled, and saying nothing, continued lending me her shoulder whenever I staggered.

At last we came to a hut that, in the gloom, seemed much like the others. Turning, and signing we were to follow, Aboyo doused the torch and ducked inside.

The hut was lit by the low glow from a charcoal brazier. Over in the shadows, three sleeping mats lined one wall. Cooking utensils and the widow's meager belongings were stowed neatly on the floor opposite.

I also noticed her hut had only one room.

"But this won't do at all!" I howled indignantly.

"But why, Chah-lee?"

"'Cause I…I want…I want us to…*you* know, that's why. Here, what's she doing?"

This was directed at Aboyo on the far side of the room. She was shucking off her skirt again.

"She is getting ready for bed, of course." Loiyan also began to disrobe.

203

"But she can't stay here!" I must have become mesmerized because, after disencumbering herself of her outer garment, Aboyo was now slowly unwinding her loincloth, and I couldn't seem to turn my head away.

Loiyan folded her robe and placed it on the floor. "This is Aboyo's home. Where would you have her go?"

Totally naked now, the widow stretched like a cat, then lay down upon the farthest mat, displaying a shocking level of immodesty as she did so.

"Don't care," I moped, tearing my eyes from the curves of a succulent haunch. "I just don't want her ogling us while we...while we sleep."

"She will not – how you say – *ogle* us." Loiyan claimed the nearest mat, leaving free the one in the middle. "I will ogle *you*."

Aboyo lay on her side with her head propped on one elbow. She seemed to be watching me with something like an air of expectation.

Slowly, her words leaked through to my fuddled brain.

"What?"

Loiyan regarded me with a fond, weary smile.

"Oh Chah-lee, do not be so *Ingle-ish*."

"D'you mean to tell me you want me to...to..." I gave up, and instead finished, "with *her*?"

"Of course."

"But I don't want her! I want you, dammit!"

Patiently, she held out her hand, beckoning me over. I went, but felt like a child approaching my guv'nor when he's holding a switch.

"Aboyo has not been with a man in a very long time." She had taken my hand in both of hers, "I want you to do this for her...and for me."

"But why? This is preposterous!"

She shook her head, very serious, her eyes sparkling with affection. "Because before I met you," she said softly, "I was like her."

Bewildered, I could only reply, "But you were married, and Musa's alive and well."

"There are many ways to be a widow, Chah-lee. Musa would not touch me because he thought I had a demon." She was reflective. "It was not a marriage, not a real one, just an excuse for my mother to remove an undutiful daughter from her village, nothing more." When she looked at me, I saw tears glistening in her eyes, but she was smiling when she said, "Now I have you, I have *so much*, so many things: a man, a child, and more happiness than I have ever known. Please Chah-lee, Aboyo has so little, it is right that we should share."

Then with eyes atwinkle, her dimples appeared.

"But there is one other reason."

"Oh, and what's that."

"Ajiambo has told me this village is of the Luo people," she grinned wickedly, "I want to know if my father's memory was true."

"But that's no reason....."

She placed her fingers over my mouth, becoming serious again. "Please Chah-lee, it was because of a Luo woman that my father allowed me to taste my life and escape the *emorata*. I am now repaying that debt."

Then she pulled me gently down beside her. "You are a strong man."

I was suffocatingly aware of Aboyo's presence behind me.

"You are a good man."

Feminine hands began to relieve me of my shirt.

"You are *my* man, and I love you."

I felt fingers working at the waistband of my grass skirt.

"Love you, too."

Her smile deepened. "I know, Chah-lee."

There were lips brushing my shoulders – a tongue flecking against my skin. I allowed myself to be pulled down to the mat, but whatever happened, I was determined not to take my eyes from her face.

Now the lips were kissing my chest...then my stomach.

I would not look away.

The lips continued to descend.

I looked away.

Nearing the end of it all, while I was labouring along, with Aboyo whimpering ecstatically against my chest, her voice came, husky and low, beside my ear, the way it was when I knew she was about to be overcome in the throes of passion.

"I am tasting life, Chah-lee! Yes! *Ooooh yes*! And…and it tastes *sooooo gooooooood*!!"

Well, I don't know about you, but that did it for me. Soon I was all over the place, bellowing like the town bull, and fit to bring the whole place crashing down around our ears. By the time I rolled off her, Aboyo was glassy-eyed and spent, her eyes rolled up inside her head – a merry widow, indeed.

But when I gathered the strength to lean over to kiss Loiyan, I found she was already sleeping peacefully.

With the smile of an angel.

Chapter Seventeen

We returned to our home the next day, but only so we might bring back more medicine to finish what Loiyan had started...in the doctoring end of things.

I had woken to lips brushing my cheek, and found Aboyo warmly smiling down at me. Then, with a significant look to Loiyan's sleeping form, and then back to me, she had twittered her fingers farewell, and left, presumably to be about her business.

I took her cue, and awoke my darling, before having at her until she was begging for mercy. You see, it was all very well lending me out like I was a prize stud, but it was only proper to show her there were repercussions. When I finally left off, she was gasping for breath like a landed trout, but revelling in the pure lechery of it all.

We had said our farewells to the villagers, promising to be back in three days time. As we pulled away, I returned Aboyo's pretty little wave, but chose to ignore the evil little snicker Ajiambo made behind her hand.

Continuing south, then east before once more heading north, we completed our circumnavigation of the island – by rough reckoning, I figured it to be about ten miles in length by three across the girth. Although we never spoke of the previous night during that time, more than once I caught her smiling secretly to herself.

It wasn't until we had tethered the boat in its hidden shed and were taking our rest that, with dimples once more on the rise, she asked:

"Well?"

"Well, what?" I knew what she wanted, right enough, but two could play at that game.

"Was my father's memory true? Are the women of the Luo people as remarkable as he had claimed?"

I chucked her under the chin. "He was a bright spark, all right. She did the home side proud."

She laughed and buried her face in my chest. "I am glad, for all of us." Then playful, "But Chah-lee?"

"Yes, my love?"

"I am still your beautiful wench?"

I kissed her and pinched her bottom. Then, with a wink, I said, "You'll do, old girl. You'll do."

We returned to the village in three days as promised, whereupon Loiyan treated the sick and infirm as before, except now she insisted upon having Aboyo help her. It was on-the-job learning, no doubt about it, but she was a bright girl, and took to the healing arts like a fish to water. Thereafter, every time we visited those folk, the two women could always be seen with their heads together, discussing a patient's symptoms, or the benefits of different cures...or the pros and cons of the *emorata*, for all I know.

We would return every other month after that first hectic week, but no more than that. As *Arat* turned into *Morusasin*, the sun became a factor, for it was a wearying trip for Loiyan in her condition. But she would always insist upon returning for as long as she was needed.

You may wonder why we never decided to settle down to stay with these people. Well, it's a fair question, and we did discuss it from time to time. In fact, it was decided that, when Loiyan was in her seventh month, we would pack up and move in with Aboyo so she might help with the birthing. That was something I had to insist upon, for to tell the truth, I was terrified of being caught with no one to deliver the child but myself. I had been through war and seen terrible things no man should ever have to see, but this was a different kettle of fish altogether. But as for the rest of it, it was Loiyan who said it best.

"We are free, Chah-lee. We are tasting our lives."

We had our ways, and they suited us. In the end, that's all there was to say about it.

I think Loiyan had expected an argument from me, and though happy, seemed a bit puzzled when I agreed we should stay on our own. You see, I think she half-expected I would take Aboyo for a wife, and I might flatter myself by thinking Aboyo hoped for that too, yet I never did. Not because I didn't like her, for she was a jolly girl, and with all the bounce of a randy stoat besides. But the truth of it was she just wasn't Loiyan, and never could be; and though we all continued to avail ourselves with one another regularly during our visits, it never went further than that. It wouldn't have been fair to any one of us.

It was the time of our visit in the month of *Oloiborraire* – the time of clear pools – that the Baggara came.

I was loafing about while the women were dealing with the usual queue of patients (although, as Aboyo's skills became more honed, never so long as the first time) when I heard the children playing on the beach cry out, "Baggara! Baggara!" and come running, in great excitement to fetch their parents.

Looking out onto the bay, I saw perhaps a half dozen boats being propelled to shore, each carrying a compliment of robed figures identical to the ones I had last seen in the carnage of that burning village. Yet before they could disembark, a sizeable crowd had already come running down to the strand to greet them, with Ajiambo to the fore, jabbering with animated anticipation, while more and more arrived with every minute.

I steeled myself, and unslinging the rifle, sauntered down to join them.

There didn't seem to be much cause for fear, however. One of the Arabs – a seedy little cherub in a green turban and flowered waistcoat – hailed the villagers heartily, leaping out of the canoe, and began to embrace several as he would long lost brothers. When he came to Ajiambo, he cracked his ugly face into a smile, revealing several yellowing teeth, and kissed the old woman soundly on both cheeks, much to her blushing pleasure.

As this was taking place, others of the visitors spread carpets on the sand, and began to pile it with their wares – cheap trinkets, for the most part: beads and mirrors, that sort of thing, but nothing of any real value. When this was completed some few moments later, these men stood back nearer their canoes, allowing the fisher folk to inspect the goods. In the boats themselves, close to hand, I saw the same type of ancient muskets I remembered from before, but these, you'll note, were not put on the trading carpets.

I proceeded further, catching up to Ajiambo even as she was surveying the crowd to find me.

"Ah, Charlie Smithers! She cried fondly, then clapping the fat little Arab on the shoulder, made the simple introduction, "this is Sheik Omar ali Digna, our friend of the Baggara."

The second he saw me, the little greaser's smile faltered, and his small pig-like eyes seemed to shade into dark hatred. But, an instant later, he recovered himself so quickly I couldn't be sure it wasn't a trick of the sun.

Then, wreathing himself in the same joyful mask he'd used to greet the villagers, he bowed and said, "Salaam, Smithers effendi."

"Likewise, I'm sure," I replied, pretty cool.

Whereupon, he startled me by saying, "So you are English? Why of course you are! For what else is a name like 'Charlie Smithers' but that of the English!"

He smiled a satisfied smirk when he noted my consternation. "I see you are surprise when you hear I speak the English, are you not? Why, for five years did I not attend your King's College in London? Yes indeed! Oh my, my! Much beatings of bare bottoms, you may be sure, oh my yes! Jolly good! Eh,what! Ha! Ha!"

He was chuckling fond reminiscence when his eye lit upon Lord Brampton's gun.

"A fine piece," he said approvingly. "May I?"

I held it closer to my chest. "I prefer not, if it's all the same to you."

There might have been another flicker of dislike before he rearranged his features into a sage smile. "I understand. It is perhaps wise to be cautious among the niggers."

There was something about his tone I didn't like.

"Oh I don't know, *you* seem to be cozy enough with them."

Digna spread his arms expansively. "Come Mr. Smithers, we are both men of the world, are we not? How else should a simple merchant comport himself but by affecting pleasantries?"

"Just like you're doing now, with me?"

"Mr. Smithers," he began, "or may I call you Charlie?" Then as though I had so permitted, he continued in the most reasonable of tones, "You and I are but two civilized men

210

amongst a sea of savage blacks, Charlie. We should be friends, yet I sense a certain…hostility from you."

He was a cool customer, right enough. With that wide-eyed open sincerity of his – with that look that said butter wouldn't melt in his mouth – he almost had me going…almost.

"I wouldn't know anything about that," I said, still pretty cool, "and as for *civilized*, I don't take much with slavers."

He must have been ready for that…or maybe he was being sincere.

"Why Charlie," says he, smooth as oil, "what is this talk of *slavers*? I am but a poor merchant, trading in simple goods, as you can see." He gestured toward the carpets upon which his goods had been placed. It was as I had said before, glass beads, mirrors, low quality textiles and the like.

But, low quality or not, they were already doing a brisk trade. The local fishermen were elbowing one another aside, holding up their catches for inspection while they beckoned and bartered with the Arabs over items on the carpets. Even while we watched, one of the Baggara – an evil looking brute with a sword cut scarring his forehead – laughed and slapped the back of the fellow with which he was dealing, as though to say he knew a good bargain when he saw one. Then he hefted a bolt of cheap cotton from the pile, and in return, took some of the catch off the man's string. Meanwhile a young woman, having shown up with some crudely woven baskets, was trading for a tin broach, and another with a jar of strong beer, purchased a full dozen strings of brightly coloured beads.

So it seemed that Ajiambo had spoken the truth.

"Your fellows don't seem to be driving a very hard bargain," I observed, "and I thought Muslims didn't drink alchohol." I had learned as much from the Turks at Varna.

Omar chuckled, "Truly, we do not drink it, Charlie, for Allah – blessings be to His name – has forbidden it. No, no. Instead, we trade it downriver to the locals there."

So I was right.

"Downriver?"

211

"Yes, the Bahr el Jebel. There are many tribes of savages along its waters who are ignorant of the ways of Allah – peace be upon Him – and not disinclined to this beverage."

"This Bahr el Jebel," I asked, trying not to show much interest, "it doesn't run very far, I don't suppose?"

"Ah, but it does, effendi, for truly is it not the king of rivers? Does it not run all the way to our lands far to the north, and farther still – some say all the way to the Turkish cities of El Iskandaria and El Qâhira – that which you unbelievers call 'Cairo'?"

But his shrewd ears must have picked up something of my excitement, for he appended, "Or so it is said. Truly, I cannot be certain, for I am but a simple merchant."

'Simple merchant' my eye, I thought. This Bahr el Jebel was the river Nile, or barring that, at least joined up with it at some point, or my name wasn't Charlie Smithers. If this sod had been educated in England as he claimed, he must have first sailed to Cairo in order to get there.

And there was something else about this El Iskandaria – which I took to mean Alexandria. Among other things, it was probably the busiest hub of the trade in human beings in all of Africa. In my short time there I must have seen ships with half the flags of the world crowded around those cloistered pens waiting to take on their cargo of slaves – willing to take their chances of running the Royal Navy's blockade.

So it appeared there was a conduit to the Mediterranean, after all – a trade route that stretched from here to all the distant points of the globe. What was more, it was a pound to a penny they carried goods far more valuable than fish and bad beer – those pens had said so.

"And you Baggara have a settlement at the headwaters of this Bahr el Jebel, I suppose?"

But Omar had become evasive and would answer with a shrug, or point in a vague direction when I asked where these headwaters lay. My old mum always said I wore my heart on my sleeve, and I could tell this chubby little bastard saw right through me. What was more, wherever this settlement was – and I was now sure it existed – there was no way in God's green earth he was going to tell me where it was. I could only guess at the reasons why he was so hesitant.

Although he never asked, Omar must have wondered why and how I came to be here. Perhaps he was guessing I was trading with the natives, just as he was himself, and didn't want the competition to see his setup. After all, even though I hardly looked the picture of a prince of commerce with my new kilt (I had accepted the material as a gift from Ajiambo on our last visit – I think the dear old thing had felt sorry for me) it was still possible he suspected I was trying to make inroads on his monopoly.

But wasn't it also possible that he didn't want me to see what lay within that settlement's walls? I couldn't be sure; and what of Omar, himself? Was he what he claimed to be, just a simple merchant eeking out a living, trading with paltry items for goods even more paltry? It seemed unlikely, yet here he was doing just that, and 'seeing was believing', as my gran used to say. After all, it wasn't beyond the realm of possibility that there were two types of traders in these parts, perhaps even two separate outposts. Obviously it would be counter to the interests of those with honest intentions to have those whose darker agenda would disrupt the people with which they carried out their commerce. If not solely humanitarian, it would be these mercantile interests that kept Ajiambo's village safe.

Just then I saw Aboyo run up to the milling crowd. In her hands were some jars and a few rude carvings of figurines she hoped to trade. This must mean the clinic had been closed for the day, or more like the patients were all down here anyway, so there wasn't much point in keeping it open.

That was confirmed moments later when I felt a hand slip into mine, and I turned to see Loiyan smiling up at me.

"What is happening, Chah-lee? This is all so exciting!"

"So," Omar leered knowingly at Loiyan, and her belly bulging beneath her robe, "I see you have taken a nigger wench, Charlie," then as though he wished to show off his knowledge of the English vernacular, "and pupped her, as well."

Casting further speculation momentarily aside, I thrust Loiyan protectively behind me. Then I was on him in two strides, and had driven my fist into his fat greasy face.

"I'll thank you to show proper respect to my wife," I growled.

There was instant commotion by the boats, followed by the sounds of dozens of muskets being cocked.

Omar had gone sprawling onto the sand with all the astonished surprise you might imagine. Now, as he lay bleeding from a split upper lip, there was no doubt he was glaring at me with unalloyed hatred.

The villagers had fallen into a perplexed silence. First they looked in wide-eyed wonder to Omar, and then to myself, unable to comprehend what had just happened.

"Charlie?" Ajiambo's face was creased with worry. Beside her, Aboyo looked as though she might faint.

The rifle was in my hands, both hammers at full-cock, the muzzles pointing at the outraged pathetic creature lying before me. I was hopelessly outnumbered, it was true, but if today should be my last, I was determined to take this vile dog with me.

The air grew heavy with tension.

Meanwhile, Sheik Digna, his desire for revenge struggling with the vision of those massive O's that were the muzzles of the elephant gun, must have been thinking along the same lines.

Suddenly, he burst out laughing: a high, giggling Arab titter.

Still laughing, he climbed to his feet, dusting the sand from his clothes, and waved down his men.

"Truly, you are right, Charlie Smithers, effendi. You must forgive me. It would appear that my manners have become somewhat...*rusty* in these backwaters."

"You'll have to apologize to the lady, not to me." I half hoped he wouldn't, I wanted to murder him that badly.

"Of course. Of course."

With his paunch straining, Omar bowed towards Loiyan – who was standing behind me, as wide-eyed and bewildered as everyone else. For there was no way she could have understood what had just taken place.

"My deepest apologies, madam, if my foolish tongue has offended you. Truly, I am at an utter loss as to how to explain my boorish behaviour. If it is your wish, may Allah – blessed be His name – strike me dead."

Loiyan huddled close to me, murmuring she didn't think that would be necessary. Then, laying her hand upon my arm, asked, "Chah-lee?"

I lowered the gun, easing the tension on the hammers.

"It's all right," but I wasn't sure it was. "Take Aboyo with you. Go to her place. I'll be along shortly."

Loiyan complied after only a small hesitation, signing for the Luo woman to accompany her. I saw Ajiambo watching me, her worried look unchanged.

I smiled as reassuringly as I could, and shrugged an apology for having disturbed what, to them, must have been a special day.

Omar shook off the mood more rapidly than anyone. He returned to the crowd and was soon laughing and clapping backs, as jovial as ever. All trading had stalled when he'd gone sprawling in the sand and appeared to be slow to recover, but he must have put the word around to slash prices for, after awhile, things began to pick up more rapidly.

For myself, I kept my distance so as not to make the Arabs over edgy, yet was reluctant to stray too far away. I wanted to keep an eye on things, just in case.

I needn't have worried, however. By the end of the day all business was transacted without further interruption, and the carpets all but bare.

Then, while the others were packing up and making ready to leave, I saw Omar part from the crowd and make his way over to where I was standing. I thought to turn away, but in the end, decided to hold my ground.

"Well, that is that for one more year," he cried cheerfully. But for his swollen lip, you wouldn't have known we'd been on the point of killing one another scant hours earlier.

"You're leaving then?" I tried to sound offhand.

"Yes, yes, there are many villages, much trading to be done." He grinned and shook his head wearily, the very picture of an overworked man with a heavy schedule to keep.

"But before I go, effendi," he reached into his waistcoat and pulled out a small hand mirror, "I wish to offer a present from my poor selection for your...ah...*wife* as a small gesture, in hope that there may be peace between us."

I hesitated, then reached out and accepted his gift.

"I haven't any axe to grind with you." And, when it was all said and done, I didn't...or at least I wasn't sure I did. "I'm obliged."

"Not at all, it is but a small thing. Yet, if it brings a smile to such a beautiful lady's face, perhaps it will still hold some paltry value?"

He was being so pally, I thought there was just a chance he was sincere.

"Perhaps," I agreed.

Omar smiled, and bowed. "Saalam, Charlie. We will meet again. May Allah – blessings to His name – be with you."

"Pleasant journey," I said, and thought I almost meant it.

He turned to leave.

"Omar – Sheik Digna."

He turned back, waiting.

"The fish you trade for, what becomes of it? I mean, surely you don't take it all the way back to wherever you came from; it would have to be rotten in no time."

Omar laughed easily, "No doubt you speak true, Charlie, but it does not travel with us to the other villages. Instead, it is Babar – my brother's youngest son, who is – how you English say – *learning the ropes*, poor boy, who must take it back to...to where we use it to fertilize our modest, ah, *agricultural* pursuits."

Spoken like a merchant, I thought, answering the question while giving nothing away. There were secrets, yet what merchant didn't keep secrets? As far as I could tell, it was plausible.

"And those tribes along the river, what do you trade the beer for?"

He made much of scrutinizing my face as though trying to divine my intentions for asking – or I wondered if he was doing so for show.

Finally, he said, "You are not, I think, in trade, perhaps?"

I shook my head, 'No'.

He made a further study of me before coming to a decision. "Mayhap one of those tribes is expert at hunting the elephant, Charlie – please, do not ask which tribe – and mayhap that same tribe has a lamentable weakness for this fish beer." He shrugged, "Perhaps it is wrong of me to sell it to them, yet I am but a poor merchant, and I have many wives and children to feed. What else would you have me do?"

I felt my body relax a good deal. In addition to showing me that his real profit lay in the ivory trade, he was allowing me to see he was a rogue, but a rogue with a conscience, which suggested he had limits…unless it was all lies.

He was gone a short while later, standing in the stern of one of the canoes, waving farewell as the boats pulled away – with Babar alone, and not looking very happy, in the craft with the fish for cargo. Standing on the shore, also waving, the villagers seemed saddened to see them leave.

I felt bad about the earlier incident, almost. These simple but good people obviously set a great store by these visits. It would be a pity if they should be deprived of them because of something I had done, as necessary as it had been.

I turned, and with mirror in hand, followed the path to Aboyo's home.

Chapter Eighteen

Oloiborrare passed without further incident, and as *Kushin* approached (in case you were wondering, "the month when the little black and white birds, which feed in the midst of the cattle, appear") life returned to normal.

Home again, we whiled away the time as before, and the ties that bound us to one another grew ever stronger.

I hadn't thought it possible. Indeed, I was often awed at how something that had plumbed so deep could go ever deeper still. Yet, minute by minute, hour by hour, day by day, it continued to grow until I felt I was drowning in its very essence.

I wondered if it was because carrying our child was causing her to blossom so, and decided that it might be. For indeed, such was the case. She wore her condition as regally as a queen would a crown, all the more as she was not aware of doing so, but behaved as naturally as the world around her.

At times she might be a girl, laughing and skipping across the strand, running to meet me, eager to share some treasure: a shell, or a feather from some exotic bird. Although such things lay about in some abundance, they were foreign to the world she had known and she never tired of rediscovring their beauty, nor did she ever tire of sharing her joy of them.

Other times she would sit, quietly content, with a sort of private inward smile. That was when I knew she was thinking of motherhood and what it would be like for her when the moment arrived. Was she worried? Not for a minute. Instead, she looked forward to that day as though she were running towards her destiny; as though she recognized this was something she was born to become; that her finest days were yet before her. And she yearned for that awakening as a flower yearns for the hummingbird, yet was loathe to miss a single moment in between.

Then too, she was the woman of my heart, and cleaved to me with all of the willing passion that only one who is truly in love might offer, filling me with wonder, over and over, that such a recipient should be myself.

I felt pride – oh yes, all of that. I was proud she was mine; proud, too, of what she carried inside her, so proud in fact, I thought it must know no bounds. But I also felt humbly grateful when I saw I'd made her laugh, and that at least part of her joy was born from the simple fact that I was alive.

She once told me that I was the sun, but I know better – it was she.

So, too, did she once claim to having too much, and felt compelled to share it. In time, I came to understand her as being no one other than who she had always been. Whether healing with a touch or a smile, or – in Aboyo's case – even myself, she gave what she could, asking nothing in return but that others' pain might be lessened.

At times, I found myself quailing before such goodness, and felt undeserving of it, because, if judged beside her, I was but a craven miser, for I could never share her as she had done with me.

She had chosen to taste life, and so she did, savouring every last morsel to its very fullest. She made of her world a banquet, while others – so many others – with infinitely more reason, contented themselves with gruel.

And so it was that, one day, we found ourselves upon a spot – a pleasant little glade – where she knew of herbs and such like to exist in some abundance.

Her pregnancy was now in mid-term. I was beginning to feel the creature must be a boy, for such a bulge in her midriff must surely be housing none but the most lusty of fellows, and feared he must emerge half-grown. Yet Loiyan cautioned that this was not always the case, for in accordance with their nature, there was many a lusty female, too, before sharing her secret smile with my happily blushing self.

We had discussed this many times, of course. What expectant couple has not? But it was a pleasant way to pass the time together....and to dream.

"But I think you are right, I think it will be a boy," Loiyan declared on this particular day. She was harvesting the seeds of the elodua tree and placing them in a basket, while I, under the

219

pretense of helping, was weaving a garland of wild flowers instead.

"He will grow brave and strong, just like his father."

I don't think she cared one way or the other for herself, but I think she would have preferred a boy because she believed that was what *I* wanted.

"And will he scratch his arse in the morning, as does his father?" I asked.

She laughed. "Yes, he will do that, too. He will be everything that you are."

As for myself, I couldn't give a fig what the gender turned out to be, as long as all the fingers and toes were present and correct, which was the main thing. Yet sometimes, in my heart of hearts, I would find myself musing about a world that held two of her before guiltily chasing the thought away.

It wouldn't do to wish for too much from the gods. They might be offended.

"Chah-lee, what are you doing? Aren't you helping?"

"Certainly," I said, hiding the almost finished garland under my own basket.

Well, t'wasn't *my* fault I'd fallen into the habit of loafing.

"What are these things for, anyway?" I asked, popping one of the seeds into my mouth. I bit down, and spat it out. "Ugh! Disgusting."

"They are for worms."

"That figures, it tastes like worm food." It did, too.

"No, silly! It should be ground and boiled with water, and then you drink it to get *rid* of the worms."

"*I* don't have worms…do I?"

"No, of course not." Then she laughed, "Well, one big one."

"But that's not a worm, surely!" I huffed stentoriously. "That, my good lady, is a fine English broadsword made of fine English steel."

"Maybe it is not such a big worm, after all," there were those dimples again, "but," she allowed, "it does *wriggle* most attractively!"

"You scamp!"

220

And then, of course, nothing would do but to give chase, with her squealing ecstatically every step of the way, until she found a suitably soft spot and allowed me to drag her down – to prove my metal, as it were.

By now we had reached the stage where we had to engage with some caution, but you know how such things go. She looked so damned fetching, with her knees and elbows cushioned on the moss, and her behind wobbling in the air – not to mention a smile of anticipation that rather reminded me of a child on Christmas Eve – and it was over before you could say 'Bob's your uncle'.

Aye me...memories....

"And what's this?" I asked idly, afterwards. From where I was lying, I could just reach another basket already filled. "Looks like tree bark to me."

"That is because it is tree bark."

She was lying on her back, catching her breath, arms folded behind her head. Little beads of perspiration beaded her brow, while others trickled enticingly between her breasts.

"What's it for?"

"For...." But she didn't know the word, so she held up her hand and said, "for Ajiambo."

"Arthritis."

"Arrr-thrrrrii-tisss," she said, testing the unfamiliar word in her mouth, then beamed at me.

"Very good. And this?" Another basket, this one of leaves.

"That is for me," she said, rounding her hand over her belly.

"Ah. And these?" Little green apples that were too tart for my taste.

"For the...." She made a great show of laboured breathing and coughing.

Pneumonia, perhaps?

Minutes passed in contented silence, at least on my part. Loiyan, on the other hand, had been thinking.

"Chah-lee?"

"Mmm?"

221

"When we were last at the village, you told that man I was your wife."

"I did, didn't I?" There was some pleasure in the memory.

"Yet you know I am Musa's wife."

I felt a twinge of unease. "But that's all by the board now, surely? I mean, you can never go back to him, even if you wanted to. And even *if*," I accented the 'if', "what you say is true – that Maasai wives can sleep with whoever they please – I doubt if the same generosity of spirit extends to the deaths of his brothers."

Damn! Shouldn't have said that. There was no need to remind her of that time. I suppose being reminded she wasn't really my wife, at least in the eyes of Maasai law, had caused a pang of jealousy, and had loosened my tongue more than was prudent.

But Loiyan had long since come to terms with what she had done. Armed with the conviction that it had been necessary, she had faced that demon and sent it away.

"No, I could never go back." Then, perhaps sensing my jealousy – which was rather odd, as she didn't possess a drop of it herself – she snuggled up to my side. "And no, I would not dream of wanting to, not ever. Musa is gone. He was once part of another woman's life. Now she is no more."

"And yet, he is still your husband." I was relieved that particular danger had passed, but my own jealousy was harder to shake.

"Yes." I was somewhat mollified to hear a trace of sadness in her voice.

"But what about this little chap in here?" I asked, fondling her stomach. "That would be rather hard to explain away, now wouldn't it?"

"Oh no, not at all. No one would ask me to explain. The child would be taken into Musa's household. It would be accepted that it was *his* child."

"The devil you say!"

"It is true."

She was such a guileless creature, so she was simply stating a fact, but now the jealousy worms were really beginning to take hold.

"Well, that's not going to bloody happen, now is it?"

"No, Chah-lee."

"I mean, *I'm* the little bugger's father, and that's all there is to it!"

"Yes, Chah-lee. Of course."

"No one's going to be taking no one away from *any*one, is that clear?"

"But Chah-lee, I never…"

"I mean, I *love* you, dash it all!"

"I love you *too*, Chah-lee!"

"And…and….I'll love that little nipper in there, as well – more than half do already."

"I know you will! I know you do!"

"Well then!"

"Chah-lee! You must calm yourself!"

"I *am* calm! In fact, I'm so *bloody* calm I couldn't *bloody* ever *bloody get* any *bloody* calmer, see! So don't tell me to be *calm*!"

"Oh, Chah-lee, I have upset you! I am so sorry!"

When she started to cry, I was able to get myself under some form of control again. I felt wretched whenever she did that.

"There, there. No need for all that. I was being a boor."

She snuffled into my armpit, "But you are unhappy."

"Well, it was all that talk of your still being married to Musa, wasn't it? I mean, what was that all for?"

Gradually, the tears had ended. Now, one arm was wrapped around my waist, her head resting on my chest.

"I don't know," she whispered, "I think I am a silly woman. I have so much – more than I can ever dream – and still I want more."

"Here," I said, watching her closely, "that ain't like you." Nor was it.

"I think I am being ungrateful for all that Enkai, or your god, or all that the gods who ever were, have given me, but I cannot help it. I thought that it did not matter – that I would be happy just to be with you, and I *am*, Chah-lee, I am so *very* happy. But sometimes I feel this follow me like a shadow – like a ghost – and I feel sad that it is not so."

Then she turned her head so she could look at me.

"I do not *want* to be the wife of Musa. I want to be *your* wife." And in a small, little voice, as though testing the sound of it, "I want to be *Meesus* Chah-lee Smithers."

I gave her a hug for that, for it had gone a long way towards setting my mind at ease.

"But I am still Musa's wife," and the tears threatened again.

I wondered if this wasn't just another one of those episodes she would have every so often ever since she told me she was expecting. You know…one of those *female* moments, but I wasn't sure. But I suppose what mattered was the poor duck was unhappy, whatever the cause.

"You might get a divorce," I suggested. Granted, it wasn't a perfect solution. In England, 'divorce' was a word seldom heard, and carried with it the censure of having sundered what God Himself, had joined. The disgrace would often brand such people for life.

"We have such a thing," she agreed, "It is called the *Kitala*. But the elders must grant it, and I must return to my village to live with my father."

I made no reply to that; it wasn't necessary. She had long ago burned the bridges that would allow a return to any aspect of her old life. Once more I was humbled by the realization of just how much she had surrendered in order to be with me.

That was when the idea entered my head. I'll admit it was something of a desperate measure, and perhaps even a bit deceitful, but what would you? She was so unhappy I would have done anything.

"Look here, old girl," I said chucking her under the chin.

"Yes, Chah-lee?" Her eyes were moist, but she'd stepped back from the point of blubbing.

"I'm going to tell you something I've never told you before."

"What do you want to tell me?"

"You must trust me," I warned. "*Do* you trust me?"

Wide-eyed now, "Of course I trust you, Chah-lee."

"Are you sure?" I asked sternly. "Because this is very important, you know?"

"I trust you with all my heart!"

I studied her closely, then reached a decision. "Very well, I shall tell you."

"Tell me *what?*" She actually gave me a little shake.

"That I," I told her in my gravest tone, "possess a very strong magic that will release you from your marriage."

"Say you so?" She breathed great wonder.

In many ways Loiyan was ahead of her time – in my world as well as her own – but the Maasai are the very devil when it comes to superstition and things going bump in the night, and though she might not have bought into all of that culture, it would have been rare indeed, if some of it hadn't become absorbed over the years. The fact that I was now going to use that strength of belief on her caused me a twinge of guilt, but it was for her own good…and mine too, of course.

"Yes, I do say so."

"But why have you never told me this before?"

"Because," I said as one burdened with grave responsibility, "it can be very dangerous. Only by trusting me *completely*," I paused for emphasis, "can I hope to keep you safe." Continuing in my most reasonable tone, I told her, "I had thought not to use this power as I had hoped there might be some other way, but, alas, such has not been the case. Now, if it is still your desire, we will perform the ceremony, and you shall be free of Musa forever.

"*Are* you willing?" I asked. "Answer carefully, for once having started," I finished in doom-laden tones, "there shall be no going back."

I think I'd hoped I'd talked her out of it. Because it was true: once told, the lie, however innocent, could not be taken back.

Loiyan spent much time searching within herself as I'd requested.

"Is there danger for the child?" she asked.

"No," I told her, "the child is safe. It is your mind that may be in peril."

At which, with great solemnity, she said, "Then it is still my desire."

225

"Very well," I squelched an inward sigh, and helped her to her feet. "We shall begin."

I stood facing her, my hands gripping her shoulders.

"First, you must look into my eyes, and never, *never* take them away. Can you do this? Because, if you cannot, you may see things – dark and *dreadful* things – that may cause you to be driven mad."

She nodded breathlessly, never taking her eyes from mine.

Then gripping her shoulders still more firmly, and regarding her with the utmost gravity, I began.

I thought to start with a chanted intonation once heard from one of Lord Brampton's more adventurous friends who, for a period of time, had stayed amongst the Esquimaux of North America, and had demonstrated their peculiar manner of singing.

It wasn't singing at all, really, but rather a lot of low, sonorous grunts interspersed with a regular inhaled inflection, if you can imagine such a thing.

"Nnnnah! Nnnnah! Nnnnah! Nnnnah! Nnnnah! Nnnnah! Nnnnah! Nnnnah!"

I held her gaze. The reason why I had chosen to use this form of incantation was because I'd always thought it hypnotic, and if repeated often enough, might induce an atmosphere sufficient to impress the superstitious mind.

Loiyan's eyes never left me. Instead, they seemed to reach across the space between us and fasten themselves to me as physically as an embrace.

"Nnnnah! Nnnnah! Nnnnah! Nnnnah! Nnnnah! Nnnnah! Nnnnah! Nnnnah!"

After some few moments, I was aware of the sunlight fading around us, as though it were a thing belonging to another world. It seemed as though it was no longer I who was chanting, but a disembodied sound, not even a voice, coming from a great distance.

Nnnnah! Nnnnah! Nnnnah! Nnnnah! Nnnnah! Nnnnah! Nnnnah! Nnnnah!

I felt an icy chill run down my spine. Shadows flitted along the periphery of my mind...dark dreadful things that threatened

226

to dash in and steal us away to where they dwelt in nefarious and murky depths. All that remained to me of our world were Loiyan's eyes, and without a doubt, I knew that to break that bond would see us both tumbling down into the pits of madness.

Nnnnah! Nnnnah! Nnnnah! Nnnnah! Nnnnah! Nnnnah! Nnnnah! Nnnnah!

We were in a chamber – a long, dark hall made of stone, and smoke-blackened beams. Still I would not let go of my vision of her. Wolf-like creatures lurked about, blood-red eyes glaring at us from shadowy enclaves.

Then suddenly, the chanting stopped.

A tired voice, incredibly old, shedding the dusts of the ages, roused itself enough to ask:

"Why have you come?"

Still from far away, another voice, eerily like my own, replied:

"Oh great god – um – Vishaka! We have come here before you so that this Okiek woman shall be free of the man to whom she was unjustly joined!"

To which the first voice enquired, *"And what reason do you bring that I should grant her this thing?"*

And the second replied, "Well, because it was *unjust*, and all that. The bride price was only a bullock and two goats, for starters. Then he never, you know, *touched* her, or anything like that, and to top it off, she fancies another."

"Fancies another, eh? Hmmm."

There was a longish pause, then:

"Woman of the Okiek, is it true that you wish to be rid of the ties binding you to this unjust man?"

Loiyan's voice came timorously from across the vastness of an ocean.

"Yes."

"What? Louder!"

"Yes!"

"And is it true that you fancy another?"

"Yes!"

"Do you love this man!"

"Yes! With all my heart!"

227

"*And will you wed him, and promise to cleave to him, etc. etc.?*"

"I will be his wife! I so promise!"

A very long pause.

Then as though having aroused from slumber, "*Very well then, I shall grant you your wish.*" I was aware of the gathering of great power, then, "*Ipso-facto! Mumbo-jumbo! Jibber! Jabber! Abbra Cadabra! YOU ARE FREE OF YOUR UNJUST BONDS AND YOU SHALL LIVE FOREVERMORE WITH THIS OTHER FELLOW! I, THE GREAT GOD* – uh – *VISHAKA SO COMMAND IT!!!!*"

A mighty storm descended and scooped us up, engulfing us in its angry vortex. There was neither sky nor earth, but only a vast sea of madness. I could hear the wolf-like creatures howl their eldritch cry, and something laughing maniacally all around us. My heart quelled with fear, and I sought to hold Loiyan protectively closer to my breast, but then there came a blinding flash of lightning, and we were sundered into a million pieces – scattered throughout the universe – disparate pieces of flotsam, lost in infinity.

Then…there was nothing.

When I prised open my eyes, it was with a great deal of gratitude that I saw we were once more in the light of our own world, the glade spinning ever more slowly around us.

She pitched forward in a swoon, and would have fallen had I not held her. Slowly, we both settled to the mossy floor.

"Loiyan!"

I chafed her wrists, and patted her cheeks, but her eyes were closed, respiration shallow.

I raced to the lake and brought back water. Supporting her head, I coaxed a few drops between her lips.

Her eyes fluttered, then opened. I could have wept with relief.

She looked at me. Her expression was of a deep knowing.

"I am free," she said.

I hugged her close, relief still washing over me in waves. "Yes, you are free."

She considered this in silence, allowing it to settle into her being. The sun cast twinkling shadows across her face, and for a moment, I wondered if I were holding a wood nymph instead.

That evening we spoke our vows under the argent hue of the moon. This, too, was done in the glade, for with obvious reasons, it had taken overtones of sacredness.

Her gift to me was a sprig of hibiscus, and mine to her the garland I had made earlier.

We honeymooned in the lake, and buoyed by its waters, made love to the music of the nightwind.

Then, hand in hand, we waded ashore, and with mats spread on the beach, lay under the stars to sleep.

Was it a dream? I couldn't be sure, yet somewhere between light and darkness, her face, glowing with magic, swam before my eyes.

"Thank you, Chah-lee," she said. "Thank you for your beautiful lie."

Then tinkling laughter.

"'Vishaka' indeed!"

Chapter Nineteen

I don't know what happened, and that's God's honest truth, but you may be sure I was damned careful to steer well clear of that Esquimaux mumbo jumbo from that day forward.

And was it just some beautiful lie, as Loiyan (or her dream self) had suggested? Well, if it was, then no harm done, because she'd bounced back to her cheery old form and never mentioned it again. And as for me, I thought of it as a kind of absolution for having told her the one and only untruth in our entire life together.

All in all, we came out the better for it, so 'nuff said.

Kushin had passed, and the rains of *Olgisan* could be seen in the far away highlands before we ventured forth, once more, to return to our friends on the far side of the island.

This time we were greeted with even more occasion than ever, for the time had finally come for Loiyan's lying in.

Ajiambo and Aboyo, and all the other women of the village, gasped in admiration, and made much of Loiyans's distended torso, claiming that only a great warrior would require so much room. Meanwhile, the men shyly thumped my back, assuring me I hadn't let the side down, and all those other sorts of things men say to one another at such times.

There was much feasting and rejoicing that night, for I have said earlier in these pages that the birth of a child was regarded as quite an event amongst these people. Although this was by no means a birthing – not quite yet, anyway – it *was* regarded as one step closer to the fact, so they might as well have a dress rehearsal – not that they ever needed an excuse to tip back a few in the first place.

Loiyan, however, even though the guest of honour, took no part in these festivities. Tired out by the journey and the ensuing excitement of our arrival, she had retired early, accompanied by Aboyo, to her hut. I would have followed directly but didn't want to seem impolite, and by the time everything got started, it was next to impossible to sneak away, so determined were the men on keeping me in their company. Therefore, to make a long story short, it was very late when two dear and bosom (and newly found) friends deposited me – all squiffy and happy, and thinking no end of myself – at the door to Aboyo's hut. I won't tell you what happened after that, because I can't remember a blessed thing.

I awoke the next morning to a raging headache and the feel of a cool cloth on my brow. I opened my eyes to see Loiyan's laughing face sparkling down at me.

"My brave warrior," she giggled, "back from the wars."

I gawped at her stupidly. My stomach felt queasy and my breath smelled rancid as all get out. From the far side of the room, where she had been preparing the morning meal, Aboyo, too, was regarding me with some amusement.

"Howjamean?"

Still laughing, she gestured with her hand. "I have but to look at you to see you have been in a desperate battle."

I goggled down the length of my form, and took note that my shirt was askew, or rather, upside down, my kilt was hanging by a thread and one of my sandals seemed to have come adrift somewhere.

Feeling nauseous, I managed to croak, "You should see the other fellow."

She must have thought that very funny indeed, for her laughter followed me out the door and down the path, all the way to the bushes where I could, at last, be decently sick in privacy.

Not that anyone else who had attended the soirée had fared any better, mind. It was a quiet village that morning, let me tell you. After rearranging my attire as best I could, I looked out upon the scattering of huts, and saw the place largely empty. But for a desultory fisherman out on the lake (looking as though he was about to go tumbling in at any moment) there were just the usual gaggle of children running about, and not another soul. But even they appeared to be under orders to keep the noise down while mummy and daddy grabbed a few more hours rest.

Some distance away amongst the huts there was sign of movement. Okello, one of my friends from the night before, managed a listless wave. I returned it with about as much enthusiasm.

231

I made my way down the trail, not stopping until I'd reached the beach – not stopping even there, but continued wading into the lake until I was up to my thighs. Then, with a silent prayer that it would help, I tipped over, face down, into the water.

It was wonderfully cool and refreshing, so much so that by the time I broke the surface, a year or so later, I was feeling vaguely alive again, and in time to see Okobel – Okello's brother and another of my cronies – wading out with my missing sandal in tow.

"Thanks," I said, spluttering water, "I was wondering where that had got to."

"I am amazed you could not find it, Charlie," he grinned, "for it was floating in a jar of *uki.*"

Uki was their word for the concoction which I'd imbibed upon several pleasant and (more or less) memorable occasions. Though I had discovered that instead of fish (thank God) it was made from honey just as the Maasai *enkiroret* was. How the former acquired its distinctive smell, I couldn't say except to guess that, as the village's main industry *was* fishing, after all, and that distinctive odour permeated everywhere, it would be surprising if their beer *didn't* smell of fish.

I was feeling quite a lot better later, when I ducked into Aboyo's hut for breakfast, only to find Loiyan looking sad and crestfallen.

"What's the matter, old girl?" I asked, instantly concerned, "You look down in the dumps."

"Oh Chah-lee," she wailed, close to tears, "I have forgotten the flowers you had made for me!"

She was speaking of the garland I'd fashioned for her. Not that particular one, obviously, for it had long since withered, but I'd grown into the habit of fashioning a new one for her every so often. It had become a sort of ritual with us – a token of our lives continuing together. It was a circle where old withered stems are replaced by buds fresh and new, and in time, replaced in their own turn, a symbolic rejuvenation, if you like, that portrayed the perpetuity of life, or rather, the perpetuity of *our* life together.

232

It was just a silly thing, really, just one of those stupid things that love-stricken couples do.

"Ne'er mind," I said, pecking a soggy cheek, "I'll fix you another."

But she continued wringing her hands and said, "It will not be the same. It will not be present for the rebirth and the chain will be broken." Now great pearls of tears were overflowing down onto her chin.

Well, that was true, all right. We'd always made sure part of the old wreath was woven into the fabric of the new one, hence your perpetuity. Fashioning a new one without bits of the old garland – still lying back in our hut on the other side of the island – just wouldn't be the same. She was right: the chain would be broken. That may not mean much to you or me, but to a Maasai, the superstitious implications were enough to make your spine shiver.

The trouble with young men with a romantic streak is they are, beyond a doubt, the most susceptible asses to a woman's tears that'll be found on the face of the planet, and I was no exception.

Well, I loved her, you see?

"It's all right, I'll go back and get it."

She looked at me as though I were mad – I'll give her that.

"Oh, Chah-lee, no that is too much."

"Now, now," I said, "nothing's too good for my missus. Besides, you'd feel better, admit it."

"But it is so far to go for…for…*flowers!*"

"But that's not what this is about, and you know it. There, it's settled. Come afternoon, I'll take Okello and we'll nip home and get it. We should be back tomorrow noon, and you'll never even notice we were gone."

There comes a time when your woman may give you a certain look, and if you don't know what I'm talking about, well, you have my sympathy, because there's really nothing quite like it. It's a sort of look that, I don't know, that can lift you up and make you feel you could fight dragons, or fly, or climb the highest mountain, or…or…oh just anything at all. When you see that mixture of worship and admiration – and let's not forget

233

love – when you see that shining from their eyes, you just try and tell me that whatever it was you'd done to deserve it, hadn't been worth the effort.

Anyway, that's the way she was looking at me now, and I was feeling gallant as all get out – more fool me.

In spite of suffering from a spirit-quailing hangover, it wasn't difficult to persuade Okello to accompany me. Probably he was curious to see our home. Odd isn't it? We had never thought to invite any of those people there, preferring to maintain our privacy instead. I suspect the fisher folk had sensed as much, and therefore, been too polite to impose themselves. But now that an invitation had been extended, however, the amiable young man didn't hesitate.

We met at the appointed time and dumped the meagre necessities required for the journey into our canoe. As he still looked like death warmed over, I let Okello take the bow.

Although I hadn't wanted her to make the trip down to the beach, Loiyan had insisted on seeing us off. I thought it too much of a chore for her. More and more her condition was changing her light girlish steps into something more resembling the swaying of a majestic ship upon the briny sea. I thought it endearing, yet I thought all things about her endearing. Still, I suspected it must be cumbersome for her to get about, but in the end, I wasn't really surprised to see her there. It was just her way.

So, with Okello huddled disconsolately in the bow, and myself, feeling more than ever like Sir Galahad, ensconced proudly in the stern, we had set forth on our quest to return with our version of the Holy Grail.

When we reached the headland, I turned for one last look back. There was Loiyan, laughing and waving us out of sight. I'll always remember her that way, with joy fairly bursting out of her, tasting every drop that life gave as though each and every one was a personal gift.

I smiled and raised my own arm in farewell. Before we were gone from sight, a passing cloud cast her in shadow.

Even though I was still in sunshine, a sudden chill caused me to shiver.

It was a perfect day for a voyage, and as Okello was not disposed to conversation, as of yet, I had time for my own thoughts.

There were those first relaxed pangs as absence made my heart grow fonder, even though we were scarcely a mile apart at that point. Then there was also a deep contentment of my mind. So long and winding had been my African journey, and to realize that it had brought me to this place, at this time, so overwhelmed my senses that gratitude showered over me, rendering me humbly abased before the kindness of whatever great entity it was that had contrived it.

For so too, was there a dawning awareness of the transformation of my spirit. From the frightened and shivering thing huddled within me upon my return from the Crimea, how little I had suspected the existence of such joy, and the possibility of such events that might lead to this blossoming of my soul. I reflected upon the vast change in my fortunes, and could no longer regret my past if it had served to heighten my appreciation of the present and the future.

And oh, what a future! Days without end – numbering in my mind as stars numbered in the heavens – with this woman by my side.

Okello perked up after awhile, willing to converse; he, in halting English, and I in even worse Luo. And as the demands of concentration precluded, my private thoughts were stowed away to be brought out later at a time more convenient.

At length, we came to our little beach on the opposite side of the island. Okello was much impressed with our boathouse, and how masked was our habitation from the water, although by now several months of living there had fashioned various trails through the jungle and numerous footprints on the strand. Perhaps the rains might change all that with the arrival of *Olodoyiorie*, but for now there were these markings of occupation…of home.

I found Loiyan's garland exactly where she said I might, beside a jug we used for water. Already partly withered, it seemed to me forlorn at having been left behind.

235

Okello much admired Sabore's spear, and as he possessed an axe, we agreed to trade upon our return to the village.

We ate our meal and talked into the night, speaking of nothing in particular, but comfortable in our companionship. Yet presently, we became tired, for though the past two days had been merry, they had also been wearisome. And so, anticipating an early start on the morrow, we took our rest.

I awoke with a start, feeling vaguely uneasy, but not able to discern why this should be. Night noises surrounded the hut, yet all was peaceful. Snoring softly a few feet away, Okello slept on undisturbed.

Then there came to me a wisp of dream, already fading like a washed memory. Even as it diminished, as windblown grains will diminish a footprint in the sand, I recognized the face of Omar, the Baggara merchant.

Why should this fat little man intrude on my dreams? And why should his doing so leave me so low in spirit? Yet as my mind was muddled from too much fatigue, no ready answers appeared and, with a discomforting conviction I would not do so for the remainder of that night, I fell back into sleep.

The sun had arisen when I next opened my eyes, and although I had grown out of the habit of using time as a sense, I felt an urgency to be away.

He never asked, but Okello must have wondered at our hurried breakfast of mangoes and cow peas. Nor did he complain when, with Loiyan's faded garland in one hand and the rifle in the other, I herded him impatiently to the canoe and cast off.

Perhaps he reflected on the reluctance of newlyweds to be too long apart. He himself had been married for several years (but had forgotten how many) and regarded our outing as a holiday.

There were a few attempts to converse from his quarter, but as I offered no reply, he lapsed into silence as well. I don't know if such things are possible, but I thought my sense of foreboding leapt across the distance between us, and seated themselves in his own mind, for after awhile, his paddle began to dip into the lake with more determination.

236

There was something deep and troubling in me. Although I couldn't make any sense of it, it persisted to dog my thoughts. And though there was nothing definite to formulate, the ghost of Omar's vision returned, over and over again, and would not leave me alone.

What of the Baggara?

Why should I feel so...*threatened?* The very word made me shiver, yet reflection said it was not incorrect.

I remember he had told me he was only a simple merchant, and I believed him...almost. Certainly Ajiambo, and those of her village, believed him, so should I not, too?

There was some comfort there, but it was cold.

Then, with a slow sense of dread, I began to understand that I had been reasoning like a fool. I had chosen to believe Omar because I had *wanted* to believe him. In the end, my conclusions were made simply because I'd been reluctant to disrupt the peaceful village. Due to my lack of objectivity, I may well have authored its destruction.

Oh, but surely I was being overly suspicious? That old conservative part of my brain – the part that didn't gladly suffer disruptions – was reluctant to let go its hold of me.

Then I thought of the cheap goods, the Baggara's affable claps on the back, the lopsided bargains made on the strand. Was it possible they were designed to win confidence?

It was possible. Hadn't Omar admitted as much?

He had.

Yet, instead of engendering faith in a simple merchant, might not the real design have been to allow the Arabs to place a viper into their midst?

That, too, was possible, and as I recalled the Baggara's contempt for the blacks, a certainty began to form in me like the face of a drowned man slowly rising to the water's surface.

Successive visits would have allowed them to map out the village until they knew the position of every last hut. With such intelligence, it would allow them to strike in the night – just as had been done to the village along the coast the previous year – at the same time ensuring that none would escape. Oh, Omar

237

may be a merchant, right enough, but there was nothing simple about this elaborate trap he'd been preparing.

The sun was rising higher by the minute, drawing moisture to my back. Yet it chilled even as it sprouted from my skin.

I plunged in my paddle, increasing the pace.

I saw them in my mind's eye. I saw their canoes approaching in darkness. There would be no alarm to a casual witness on shore. They were the same few boats with the same few Arabs they had seen many times before. The hour might be considered unusual, but there was no cause to flee.

Yet that witness would not see the dozens of craft moored a short way down the coast. Nor would they see the hundreds of raiders – blacks mixed with Arabs, glints of moonlight reflecting off their weapons – as they stole through the forest to take up positions cutting off lines of escape.

Then, on some prearranged signal, the torches would be lit, and they would start to close in.

It was at this point that I wanted to look away, yet I forced myself to watch, even while my paddle bit into the lake with ever more energy.

First, one raider would enter one hut and then another would another, and then more and more as the invasion began to spread throughout the village like a rising tide.

There would be silence.

Then a scream.

Then a bellow of outrage, and maybe the sound of a shot being fired. Again, the scene repeats itself, one after the other, more and more, until the entire night is a bedlam of crying children, of the horrified screams of their mothers and frantic shouts of their fathers and, woven through it all, merciless gunfire.

Bodies being dragged, struggling, out into the open – flames starting to lick the tinder-dry thatch of roofs, casting the night into weird shadows. Those who resisted would be struck down and subdued. Those who fought too hard would be butchered. Those who raced past that encircling snare would be seized or shot down.

Soon all is an inferno of shouts and screams and gunfire…and flames – much higher now – revealing scenes that even Dante must shrink from. An Arab with his foot on a man's throat, four others crowding around their struggling victim, their muskets rising and falling, battering him with the butts. Children being herded, wailing for their mothers, into a roped circle. One – a baby too young for bondage – is thrown back into what's left of its home, its screams mingling amongst a multitude of screams, silenced only when the burning roof collapses. The same happens to an old woman, and again to a crippled boy, and on and on until those who are of no use are dispatched with chilling disregard.

And even while the flames burn their brightest, yet another scene is played out until it must drive me insane to bear witness. But turning away is no longer possible.

Women being dragged by their arms, or kicking feet, or even their hair, are circled and set upon, often by two men at once – sometimes even more. They scream and they kick, and they claw, but are cuffed and beaten into submission. Sometimes, in their great excitement, the slavers beat them too hard, ruining the commodity with a single, careless blow, and the screams are cut short. Yet the cries of others not so fortunate lose power, their bodies being used over and over, as their minds recoil from the horror that is happening to them.

And there, illuminated by the flames of her burning hut, amidst a throng of cheering villains, is Aboyo on her stomach with her legs asprawl, head craned backwards, mouth gaping in a silent shriek. From beneath, a grinning Arab plunges into her, his knife gleaming at her throat. Another, a woolly-headed black, grabs her cruelly by her hair, and pumps into her rectum. I see the blood streaming down her legs.

And there, in the shadows…oh God, I must look away!…there in the shadows…..

Okello's cry brings me around.

It wasn't real….it wasn't real….oh dear God, let it not be real!

239

But he's pointing and shouting. He's concerned, very concerned, but there's neither fear, nor grief, not yet. He doesn't understand.

I recognize the headland we must round before coming to the village.

"Smoke, Charlie! Someone's house is burning!"

And with an ache of despair stabbing deep into my vitals, I see it – great roiling drifts of dirty black clouds cascading high into the air, from flames consuming what was never intended for fuel. It is too much smoke for one hut, too much for ten.

They were all burning.

Chapter Twenty

We burst past the headland in time to see the last of the slavers disappearing around the promontory opposite.

Okello sees them and twists in his seat, his honest, puzzled face hoping I can explain, but there is no time.

I grab the rifle.

"Change with me!" I shout, and lunge for his place in the bow. But Okello's movements are wooden and unsure; he moves too slowly. In my impatience, I seize him by the shoulders and point to the smouldering ruins of the village – here and there bodies dot the shore – then to the far headland.

"Baggara!"

I snarl it into his face, yet he doesn't seem to hear, for he too has seen what is left of his home – sees the bodies – and seems frozen with shock. I shake him, but still he doesn't move. I shake him harder, but his head only rolls on his neck, as if there is no life left in him. It is like shaking a doll. I slap him with the palm of my hand, and am rewarded with the blinking of his eyes. Slowly – too slowly – comprehension registers.

A horrible moan grows from somewhere deep in his throat until it bursts from his mouth in a terrible cry of anguish. He grabs a paddle and tries to turn for shore.

"No!" I shout, and keep shaking him until, finally, he sees me.

Once more I point. I force myself to speak clearly and calmly. I don't know how I do it, but I do. "We have to catch them."

He's listening now, but seems reluctant. He wants to be hysterical. So do I.

"We still have a chance to catch them! We still have a chance to free your family!"

I don't know if it's true, but we have to try.

The dead would wait.

At last I see hope nudging aside some of the fear in his eyes. He gathers himself, readies for action.

I point to the stern. He is the stronger; I have the gun.

241

He nods, determined now, and takes my place. I settle down in the bow, and we set off for all we are worth.

We round the headland and see the raiders' boats half a mile out on the lake heading north. We are like dogs to the scent. Our paddles bite into the lake with a vengeance.

Why hadn't I at least tried to warn them? How had I ever let it come to this?

But I know why.

I wanted to believe everything happened for a reason. I wanted to believe there was some sense to be made from it all. I wanted to believe we were saved from the storm and tossed upon this island for a purpose – no, not a purpose, a *reward*. I wanted to believe that this place was my reward, that *she* was my reward; that all the happiness I ever found here was my reward – my *compensation* – for everything that had happened before. I didn't want to convince myself that there was anything to fear. I thought – I *knew* – we were being watched over.

I wanted to believe that God must care, after all.

We halve the distance to the nearest craft. The raiders are tired and content to take their time. I must be tired, too, but I won't think about that.

I gauge the distance: two hundred yards. Close enough to be effective, but not close enough to be sure. As yet, none of them realize we are coming up from behind.

Five minutes later, we halve the distance again. I steer us slightly to the left until we are dead astern of the first of the slaver craft. Maybe two hundred yards beyond, the surviving villagers are huddled in a concentrated group of shock and misery. Here and there, Baggara dart amongst them. Even from this distance I can hear the cracking of the whips.

Would Loiyan be in there, I wonder?

I pray she is…and I pray my suspicions are wrong.

For, once more with my inner eye, I see men creep into Aboyo's hut – it would be a small matter to discover where the white man slept – but this time their purpose is not to capture, for these men will be assassins. Omar would recognize myself as the sole threat to his enterprise, and would thus attempt my death for purely mercenary reasons. That this should also coincide with his thirst for the settling of a score would only serve to sweeten the issue.

However, my absence would in no way thwart his plans. He could just as easily inflict on Loiyan the revenge that had been intended for myself.

With this thought struggling to take control of my senses, I set aside the paddle to take up the rifle. The first shot had to be perfect.

I sight down the barrel. The blue steel glows dully in a sun I had thought gone from the sky. I hold my breath. Because they are in line, all I can see of the raiders in this nearest boat is the dirty white burnoose of the man in the stern. I notice that its edges are frayed.

I squeeze the trigger.

The shot roars over the lake, the recoil slams into my shoulder. When the smoke clears, there seems to be no one left in the craft. Yet when we pull abreast, I see all – six in number – are lying in the bottom, dead. As we go by, I reach in and relieve them of any cutting tools – scimitars and knives – that are readily seen.

There's a shot to our right, but I don't see where the ball strikes. Another boat is bearing down on us. It's heading straight towards me, allowing only the man in the bow to use his musket. I see his face is recently scarred, as though by the claws of some wild animal.

I aim and fire.

That boat, too, lies dead on the water.

There is a great human roar. The captives have seen us, and taken hope.

While reloading, I tell Okello to head towards them, but a Baggara craft emerges from their midst, and turns broadside on. They have witnessed the fate of their friends, and will not make the same mistake.

I level the enormous rifle. They level their muskets. From this range, there will be little difference in accuracy.

My gun roars first. The bullet smashes into the side of the canoe, through the man behind it, and leaves an exit hole out the other side the size of a nine-pound shot. There's a scream – I feel

243

insane laughter welling inside me – and the impact of the heavy slug causes the canoe to capsize.

We dash in amongst the captives. I want to cut them free, but there is no time; another raider is coming at us from the front of the pack. I toss knives and swords to the nearest so they might cut their own bonds before we turn toward this latest foe.

These Baggara have not seen how powerful the elephant gun is and are coming head on. These are mowed down as easily as the others.

We forge ahead and burst through the packed craft in time to see yet another slaver bearing down. Omar himself is in the bow, waving a pistol and urging his fellows to close. My heart gives savage exultation. I'd feared he would have fled.

He should have killed me when he had the chance.

He sees me, and his face is a mask of hatred. He aims the pistol and fires, but he's a hopeless shot. I hear the bullet buzz past my ear.

I level the rifle and let loose with both barrels. His head explodes in a pink mist leaving a stump of neck. Blood fountains out before the corpse tumbles over the side. The rest of the boat is in carnage. Blood seeps from its sides as though the craft itself has been mortally hurt.

With their leader gone, the remaining slavers draw away. Never having anticipated this sort of battle, there is little fight left in them.

Yet there is still plenty left in me.

I throw down the gun and pick up my paddle.

We chase them until the sun is halfway down the horizon. Some – shamed that their many are pursued by one – turn to fight, and are shot or sunk and left to drown. Others that are too slow, we catch; still others – too many others – we don't. Those with insufficient speed are dispatched as thoughtlessly as when they had thrown babies into burning huts. Those too fast must live to tell the tale.

At last we come to the mainland and, in the distance, see a wooden fort jutting out upon the tip of a promontory. It is towards this place that the raiders flee. Over the sound of the bloodlust roaring through my head, I can hear the cascade of a mighty waterfall, and in some part of my mind not occupied with killing, I recognize that this is the headwaters of the Bahr el Jebel, the waterway to Cairo.

The first of the enemy's boats touches the shore, and I know we have done enough. I content myself with some parting shots, but see no results. We turn back to our island, leaving the Baggara to ponder upon the wisdom of ever again venturing from their stronghold.

It is dark when we finally pull up on that familiar piece of strand. The former captives, most still in a daze, are stumbling through the still glowing ruins of their village. Some call out names of loved ones. Others stare about themselves in stark disbelief.

The first corpse I see is on the beach. It is Ajiambo – her skull crushed by a musket butt. The crumpled little form is even smaller in death than she had been in life.

There is a cry behind me. Okello rushes towards the figure of his brother sitting among the ruins of his hut. Yet Okobel does not move, but stares sightlessly into the night.

I fashion a torch and light it on some glowing embers. I run up the path leading to Aboyo's home. All around me, flames reveal hellish visions of death and destruction.

I find Aboyo sitting by the entrance of what had been her hut, clothed in tattered remnants of what she has been able to find. Like Okobel, she, too, is in a state of dumb shock; yet when she sees me, she rises. I notice that it is painful for her to walk, yet she comes, hesitantly, into my arms.

Then she bursts into tears.

"Oh Charlie! Oh Charlie!" is all she will say.

I hold her for a moment but then disengage myself as gently as I can.

I need to know.

I find her a few yards off. It is not difficult, for it is where my imagination had seen her in shadows. Her lips are peeled back, teeth bared in a rictus, eyes sightless in death. Her hands are shaped as claws with long strings of flesh growing from the nails.

I remember the Arab in the bow of the second boat – he with a face clawed as though by an animal – and I regret not having known before I'd killed him. He would not have died so easily.

Her belly has been hacked open, the fetus strewn on the ground. The umbilical chord is a winding road leading back to her womb.

I kneel beside her, needing to feel the puncture wound in her shoulder, needing to trace the slash across her throat with my fingertips. A merciless voice whispers in my mind. It tells me they would have killed her only after the child had been torn from her body. They would have made her look upon it.

There is a hand on my back.

"Oh Charlie!" Aboyo is more subdued now, yet can still speak only my name. I feel I should comfort her, but have no comfort to give. I feel a cold numbness for all things living.

Instead, I cradle Loiyan's head on my lap.

I caress her cheek.

I am very tired.

I lie down.

I sleep.

The next morning, I take her back to our home– her and the little one. I think Okello is there to wave farewell, but I'm not sure.

We reach our shore, and I carry her to the hut and lie her down upon our sleeping mat, with the tiny bundle beside her. I want to compose her features, but am not successful. I want to see her smile, but the art is beyond me.

I take the wooden bowl and go down to the strand for water. I mean to bathe her body, but before I reach the lake, it occurs to me that this is the same old bowl she'd first used when so insistently tormenting me with *nailang'a*.

The memory brings me to my knees, and then to my stomach. Sand fills my nostrils and mouth. I feel I am surely going to weep, yet no tears will come. Instead, I lie prostrated before the waters of Ukerewe as though worshipping the place

246

where she'd brought me. But in reality, I am pierced by the knowledge that this will be her final resting place.

I try to rise, for there is much to do and time is short, but it is a long while before strength returns to my limbs.

Yet, at length, I am able to finish fetching the water and return to the hut. On the way back, I think I will find her sitting up, and see her smiling at me the way she had always used to. So strong is this vision that my own answering smile has begun to form. But when I enter, I see she is lying as I'd left her.

As I wash her limbs, I talk to her of things as we had always used to – our future, and all other things that gave us joy. Yet try as I might, I cannot coax a smile to her lips.

When I finish bathing her, I think to put the baby, so impossibly small, in her arms. I reason that she had hungered to hold her for so long, it is only fitting she be allowed to do so now. But once more my ignorance defeats me, and I must be content to bundle her closer to her mother. It seems so impersonal, like setting a rock next to a log.

Taking up the garland, I break off a stem, then leave the hut to follow the path leading to our glade. There is a bad moment when I notice a dimple in the moss. I recognize it as one that her knee had made, and I remember that day, that same day we were married. I place my hand upon the spot, feel the ridge's smooth surface with my fingers. I wait for the tears, but still my eyes are dry. After some time, I am able to reach the point where I can take the withered stem and weave it with fresh flowers. This takes more time than should have been required; my fingers seem not as nimble as they had once been, and need to be reminded how to complete the task. When it is ready, I bring this new garland back to her, and lie both – new and old – upon her breast.

Then I take up her medicine bag, meaning to put it at her side opposite the child, but when I smell the aroma of all those herbs and roots and leaves and salves, I am filled with her essence far more than the still figure lying before me can do. I am on my knees, hugging it close to me, wondering how on earth I can ever let it go. I will bring it with me, I decide, yet something tells me I must not. She would give me much – almost anything – but she would never give me that bag.

I place it by her side, and – trembling – force my fingers to let it go.

I survey my work. I am not satisfied; she deserves more, much more, but I think it is the best I can do. Then it comes to me. I go to the boat and bring out the casting net. I return to her and arrange it at her feet. I place the wooden bowl there as well.

I stand back, trying to memorize her. I fear I am too successful. Eyes once soft are staring and fierce. The mouth that had always smiled is an animal's snarl. Those hands that had so often caressed me with such tenderness are now feral claws. *Rigor mortis* has taken hold even before I found her, making a mockery of what I was trying to do – to give her peace, but there is none to be found here. I have to admit it...she has become something obscene. The *rigor* has completed the task of stealing every part of her away from me, and I am powerless to give her even this small dignity. She, who had always been there for me, through so much, is now utterly and completely gone.

I unwrap her torn and bloodied robe from her body. The process takes time for I wish to proceed with as little disturbance as possible. I try not to stare at the gaping wound where her womb has been cut open, but I cannot help myself. What had once been so round and smooth, so deserving of adoration, is now ghastly and torn – the edges of traumatized flesh puckered and swollen. I notice flies have settled into the cavity. I know they will be laying their eggs. Soon there will be clouds of them.

I use her robe to cover her body – to hide the offensive sight from my eyes. I study her face one last time, trying desperately to conjure the memory of who she was, but this, too, has been stolen from me. So I cover that as well.

I have made a fire on the beach with coals left over from the village. I leave the hut for the last time, and take up a brand from the flames. I pause, thinking I should say something, but like my tears, so too are words denied me. I find the thought of praying to an uncaring god offensive.

I throw the burning brand on the thatch and stay until I am sure the flames have caught. Darkness falls when I return to the boat.

I reach in and take up the gun. I check to see it is loaded and the caps are fresh. I sit down by the fire and shuck off my sandal. I cock the hammers, and place the muzzles in my mouth, my toe upon the triggers.

Once more, I am dully aware there should be some last thoughts, yet I am too anxious for it to end. I push down with my toe.

There is a loud double 'click'.

It must be a full minute before I realize both caps – usually so dependable – have failed to fire – a full minute I had supposed myself blessedly dead.

It is when I – moving in a daze – am replacing the faulty caps, determined to try again, that I feel her hand on my arm.

"No, Chah-lee," she says.

My heart swells with a wild illogical hope. I look up from where I am sitting, and can see her standing over me. Her smile is more beautiful than ever. Her body is, again, unscarred perfection. She holds our daughter to her breast. I can hear the sounds of her suckling.

She gazes down upon me with all her old gentle love, and it's more than I can bear. As I struggle to my feet, I am aware of the heat of tears on my face.

I try to embrace her, but she moves away, light as gossamer, then repeats, "No Chah-lee." Her voice is like a sigh on the wind.

Behind her – and perhaps, *through* her – I can see the raging flames of our home.

"Loiyan."

I breathe her name, neither capable nor daring anything louder, lest this, too, should chase her away. My strength deserts me and I fall to my knees. My eyes are now fountains of tears, but though my vision blurs, I can see her still in front of me.

"Loiyan!"

"You must not, Chah-lee." Her free hand gestures to where the gun lies forgotten on the sand. "You must live."

249

My words are twisted in anguish. "But I want to be with you!"

"And so you shall, my husband. Wherever you go, Chah-lee," she indicates to include the little one, "we will always be near. But, my love, you must continue to taste your life."

"I do taste it," I tell her with a grimace, "but the cup is bitter."

"Dear Chah-lee," she is close once more, I feel the warmth of her hand as it caresses my cheek, "it will not always be so. One day, you will learn to laugh again, and to feel joy, and taste all the goodness that there is to taste."

It seems unlikely, but I find myself humouring her. It is something I have always done.

I say, "That was always your thing, not mine."

In spite of everything, I find I am able to smile for her. Sad and pathetic though it might be, I am conversing with her in the manner which has always been so easy – so comfortable. A smile is a natural part of that.

And with that smile I know that, like a petulant child being cajoled into laughter, she has won. It is something that need not be acknowledged with words. It meditates, soundlessly, between us.

I will live.

As I come to accept, I understand this is why she has returned to me one last time – to tell me I must continue. Why, I cannot say, but it is her wish and that is enough. I would not carry such a burden for myself, nor for God, but I will do anything for her who had so selflessly done everything for me.

So too, even though it tears great gaping wounds in my already shredded heart, I must also accept when she begins to fade.

"It was always you who tasted." My smile must now be twisted and grotesque, but I will not let it go. She would have me be brave, so I do my best.

Her laughter is like the tinkling of little bells – that isn't quite right, laughter does not make such a sound, but it is as close as I can come…beautiful little silver bells.

"I shall, Chah-lee! I shall!"

I can easily see through her now, yet still feel her hand upon my face.

"This world, too...I...shall.......taste!"

Then, with the ringing of her laughter but a fading echo on the wind, she is gone.

I stand in that place for much of that night, trying to pull every last drop of her essence from around me while tears course unchecked down my cheeks. But there is no more to be had. I call her name, but even this is flat and tasteless; the very air has ceased to be alive.

In addition to the fading of her vision, so too are the flames that consume our home beginning to dwindle. There is no longer anything for me here.

I dry my eyes, and taking up the gun, climb into the canoe. I think to look back on where I had felt so much, but some ancient superstition prevents me.

It has become a place for the dead.

Epilogue

It was raining a cold drizzle the day the mail coach pulled up at the lane leading to Brampton Manor. I jumped down from my seat beside the driver, and caught my duffle when he tossed it down after.

"Ta, Jim."

"Good to see you back, Charlie." He touched his whip to the brim of his hat before clucking his tongue to the lead mare. "Up there, Bess, we've got a schedule to keep."

With the coach soon swallowed in the mist, I hefted the bag over my shoulder, and began the long trudge up the lane.

It had taken me a year to arrive after last leaving the shores of Ukerewe. As long as that may seem, exhausted and malaria ridden as I was, it's a wonder I got back at all.

I'd paddled the little craft through the rest of that night to the Baggara fort where, true to memory, there came sounds of a waterfall in the near distance. I continued without hesitation and disembarked on the far side of the headwaters of a vast river, where, after unloading the game little boat, I left it to the current to take downstream while I traversed the cataract on foot. Though watchful eyes must have seen me from the fort's palisades, none came out to hinder. I believe they were glad to see me go.

I caught up to the canoe some miles further downstream. It was capsized and water-logged, but this was soon put right, and I was able to continue on.

Soon I came to another lake. Though not nearly so large as Ukerewe, it was still some weeks before I discovered an exit, and then it was but a matter of days before I arrived at yet another.

It was here that something of note took place.

I had been preoccupied studying the shoreline, searching for a current that would lead me out of that lake, and had taken little notice of much else. Then, quite clearly, I heard Loiyan speaking directly into my ear. It was as though she was sitting at my very side.

"Danger, Chah-lee!"

It was then that I turned and saw the native craft stealing up behind me, to the point where I was now almost within range of their bows. They gave a shout and had chased me for miles, and should have caught me, for they had several paddles to my one, but I was infused with an urgency to survive and somehow managed to keep ahead until I heard:

"Quickly, my love! Over there!"

Although I could not see her pointing, my head turned of its own accord until I saw a break in the jungle, and felt a current begin to pull me in that direction. I shot down that avenue with those howling natives hard on my heels. It was only when we had come to some rapids that they pulled up, while I – left with little choice – had ridden on through, testing my skill to the utmost.

Since then, it had been several weeks of ducking out of sight of traffic, or running in the face of arrows and other missiles coming from the forest – for this was still a savage land where a lone white man may be regarded as prey – and more than once she had whispered a warning in my ear, shying me away from trap and ambuscade. Afterwards, there was never any indication she had ever been, yet now I knew I was not alone. Had she not been watching over me, I am convinced I should have left my bones upon that river.

Gradually the weeks passed, and the surrounding jungle gave way to grassland.

Soon I was discovering villages, and then towns, with domestic herds to augment those of the wild which also made use of these plains. In a way, I was reminded of the Serengeti, for as well as the cattle, even the people here had the look of those tall, fine boned Maasai warriors, and may well have been their distant cousins.

With that in mind, I'd made a point of avoiding all settlements until I came to a sizeable town called Reng. It was here that I discovered a small garrison of Egyptian troops, and when steeled with enough courage, had presented myself at the gates.

I was escorted into the presence of their commander who was a sort of minor pasha. Even though he spoke some little English, I thought him a disagreeable fellow because he had little, shifty eyes that reminded me of Omar. He kept telling me I was now in the Egyptian territory of the Sudan, and what did I mean by it? I rather thought he was tempted to throw me in the clink for a spy.

Yet I was an Englishman – something not to be lightly dismissed in the world – and I'd maintained a bold English front. That – together with my hand upon the rifle – had persuaded this petty fool his best policy was to send me on my way unmolested. So convincing was I, in fact, that – with only a minimum of physical persuasion – I was able to cajole him into issuing a letter granting me passage all the way to a place called Khartoum, some two or three hundred miles further downstream.

Once in possession of this document, however, I thought it safest to bind and gag the fellow before taking my leave through a convenient back window, lest he be tempted to renege on its contents. As long as I maintained a steady progress, there was little to fear from pursuit.

Some weeks later, I discovered that Khartoum was a real city with tens of thousands of inhabitants, and stank to high heaven. But the governing pasha was a decent old stick, with a smattering of French, who *sacre bleu*-ed the evening away over a bottle of excellent port while I related my adventures. It seemed that all Mohammedans weren't impartial to a cordial nip every now and then.

I must have caught the bug further upriver, but it was at Khartoum where I came down with malaria, and when I threw that off some weeks later, was in time to catch a rather nasty case of dysentery. The pasha really was a kind old thing because he sent me his personal physician to ease my suffering.

I'm sure the be-spectacled old medico was of some help, but I rather thought that the wraith which visited in my delirium – forever coaxing until I drank of that putrid *nailang'a* – was what caused me to pull through. For even though I was left weak as a kitten afterwards, neither disease was the end of me.

After a month or two of recuperation, I felt well enough to travel with a detachment of soldiers who were carrying dispatches all the way to Cairo. From there, it was but a short trip

254

to Alexandria where I loitered for a week or two until I was able to work my passage home on a mail packet.

I apologize if – outside of those strange visitations – you find all this rather boring. To be sure, I wouldn't have bothered to relate it but for one reason. I was the very first European to make that journey, and in so doing, had proved that I had discovered the source of the Nile. Anyone who could place that sort of thing in front of the Royal Geographic Society was bound to be smothered in fame and fortune for the rest of his days.

Why, there could even be a knighthood in it for me. '*Sir Charlie Smithers*' – I thought it had rather a ring to it.

I was reflecting on all this when I entered the stable yard. The ostler lad was much as I remembered him. He was burrowing a digit into the furthest reaches of his left nostril when he saw me. Although I called out a greeting, he just stood there with his finger up his nose, gaping at me as if he'd seen a ghost.

I continued on, crossing the stableyard to the little cottage where my parents had taken up residence. I set my bag down and rapped my knuckles on the door. Presently, there came a sound of shuffling footsteps and it creaked open to reveal a wizened narrow-faced creature.

"Hello, Mother, I'm home."

She regarded me with dark suspicion for a minute, then by way of welcome said, "Aye weel, Ah expect yoor hungry. Ther's porridge ow'er the fire." Then she turned and led the way into the kitchen.

Once settled at the table, I was trying not to feel too crestfallen, when I heard the gruff old voice of my guv'nor coming from the other room.

"Who was at the door, Mother?"

"'Tis Chairlie!" she called, shuffling over to the fire and ladling porridge into a bowl, "Back frae the land o' the niggers!"

At least that part of my old dream had held true.

I heard the rustling sound of a newspaper being put down, and then there was my father, poking his grizzled napper around the corner.

"Hello Dad."

"Well, so it is!" he cried. "Charlie lad, by all that's holy!"

I got to my feet and held out my arms – and then adjusted quickly when he offered his hand instead.

"We thought you'd gone to your maker. Isn't that so, Mother?"

"Aye," Mum gave a single, severe nod, "'tis a hard life."

"His lordship said he searched high and low for well nigh on a week."

"Really?" I felt my heart warm to my dear master.

"Well, a day or two, anyway, but he said you'd vanished into thin air."

"Aye," Mother agreed, nodding sagely, "Ah told 'im yoor took by faeries."

"Now Mother…" my dad admonished, rolling his eyes at me.

"Ach! Weel, did Ah no have vision of the laddie wi' the likes of an angel an him no daid?"

"Well, that's true enough," the guv'nor had to concede. "She did tell me that, you know."

"Aye, Ah saw her!" Mum cried, warming to the memory, "Dark as shadow, she were, an' such beauty as to be too great for th' realm o' man. So Ah ken richt away she were faerie princess!"

That gave me a start, I can tell you, and my heart lurched with that old familiar ache whenever Loiyan's memory was invoked. I couldn't help thinking it odd that it should happen on this cold and dreary northern day in my parents' kitchen – so foreign to anything she had ever known.

I was grateful when further conversation was prevented by a knock on the door.

"What again?" Dad wondered aloud, "We're like Paddington Station the day."

It was Davis the footman, who, after gravely welcoming me home, announced that his lordship wished to see me in the gun room directly.

"Well. That's it then," my father said, hiding his disappointment, "mustn't keep him waiting. Off to your duty, lad."

Pausing only long enough to change from my stained and muddied travelling garments into more suitable attire, I crossed the back courtyard to the manor and let myself in at the servants' entrance.

I dashed past the kitchen, pausing to cry out a cheery hello to Mrs. Dyck, but cutting it short when the dear old thing gawped in so much amazement her teeth fell into the soup she'd been stirring. Further on there was a more respectful nod to Mrs. Kilns' severe features, and later a gladsome exchange with Maggie, fair bubbling all over herself to see me back. Finally, after polishing my boots on the back of both pant legs, I was scratching a respectful knuckle on the gunroom door.

"Come!"

True to family tradition, Lord Brampton was ensconced in his favourite room, affecting not to notice the scarcity of trophies adorning its walls, nor to show how offended he was by it. He was seated comfortably before a cheerful log fire, reading *The Times*, and taking an irritable sip from a snifter of brandy.

"I see the Frogs are at it again, *and* the Eye Ties, too," he growled without looking up. "Couple of spaghetti's tried to blow up Napoleon III. Missed though. Not surprised. Incompetents, every last one of 'em.

"Then there's this *common* girl in Lourdes, claims to've seen the Virgin Mary. Bunch of papist nonsense, of course."

"Indeed, milord," I ventured.

"And those fools have finally got the sepoys under control in India. Not a moment too soon. Wouldn't have done in my day, I can tell you. Hang the lot of 'em." His lordship, you'll note, was my senior in years by a total of eight weeks, yet upon his retiring from military service had got into the habit of viewing those still in uniform as pimply faced upstarts.

"Quite, your grace."

He looked up, his piggy little eyes burning from beneath fierce bushy brows. His innards rumbled an ill-tempered greeting.

"Smithers."

"Yes, milord?"

"You're back."

"Yes milord."

"Finished gallivanting all over Africa, have you?"

257

"Indeed sir. In fact I've made some very interesting disc...."

"Yes well, never mind that now. See that my hunting togs are laid out for tomorrow morning. Ghillies tell me there's a stag up on the western fell, rack of antlers big as a horse."

"But..."

"You brought my gun back, did you?"

"Yes, sir, it's at my fathers."

"Still in one piece?"

"Oh, yes, sir."

"Good. Cost me thirty guineas from a smith in London. Specially made. Irreplaceable, of course. Must fix the sights, though. Can't hit a bloody thing."

"I'll clean it and put it in the rack, milord."

"See to it."

I quelled my disappointment. Never mind, there would be time to tell him, later on.

"Certainly, milord."

"That's all." He dismissed me without another word, and went back to his paper.

I was almost at the door when I thought I heard him say something, but it was uttered in a tone too low for me to make out.

"Milord?"

"What? Oh, nothing. It's just this fellow." He peered short-sightedly at the page, "This John Speke."

"Speke, sir?"

"Yes. Been to Africa, too. Claims to have found the source of the Nile, and all that."

"Has he, sir?" My heart did a flip.

"Mmm. Big lake, it says. Named it after the queen, it says." Then, as is his habit, his mouth worked silently around an unpronounceable word.

"Uk....Ukeee....Uk....."

"Ukerewe, sir?" I suggested with spirits plummeting.

"Perhaps, hard to say, that's what the natives called it, anyway."

258

He put the paper down and riveted me with his monocle. "By Jove, Smithers, that's British spirit for you, what!"

"Indeed, milord."

Then, with a jaundiced eye, "Pity you couldn't take a lesson from your betters when you had the chance."

"Your grace?"

"A real discovery, man! Something useful instead of running around doing...whatever it was you were doing.

"It's interesting that you should mention it, milord, because..."

"Oh well, can't be helped. Guns at eight. Make sure there's plenty of brandy in the game bag."

I could feel my face begin to flush with anger.

It had been I who had been the first to see what no other white man had seen! It had been I who had acquired languages as alien to our own as would be that of the Man in the Moon to one of his *bloody* lordship's *bloody* fox hounds! It had been I who had first ventured out onto the African steppe, been chased by rhinos and crocodiles, survived falls from dizzying heights, and fought untold desperate battles with nothing more than a battered old rifle and two broken ankles...and...and...!!!!

And shining through it all had been those tender loving eyes, and that sweet gentle smile, walking beside me every step of the way, and I saw that it was no good.

Even assuming I'd be believed in the first place, if I caused controversy, such things couldn't help but degrade into something ignoble – no more than a mudslinging match. I realized I wasn't prepared to put her memory through anything like that. Maybe it wouldn't have meant much to anyone else, but it would have to me, and that's what mattered.

Let 'this Speke fellow have the plaudits. Let him have the knighthood, too, if that's what it came to. What worth had they beside memories like mine? I was by far the richer man, for I had known *her*.

In that time, she had been many people, and yet, curiously, had been all of them for my sake alone: a domestic, a rebel, a warrior, a fisher, a healer, a companion, a lover, a mother...even a murderess – yes, even that – and though it was she who had

259

tasted all of it to the very utmost, it was *I* who had tasted *her* to heights quite as equal, not he – not John Speke.

When you got right down to it, knighthoods and recognition were but paltry things in comparison.

I bowed.

"Very good, my lord."

I left, closing the door quietly behind me.

Though, in my mind, I could hear the faint soft sounds of laughter – the ringing of tiny little bells in the distance – at long last, I felt a surety of the world around me, which had been lacking for quite some time.

I was home.

The End

Acknowledgements

Writing a novel often starts as a lonely business – just one person and an idea. It ends quite a bit differently, and you find that there are people that you would like to thank, because each in their own way, somewhere along the road, has made the finished work possible.

Friends and family go without saying (you know who you are). From the first time I showed any of you one of my stories, you didn't laugh in my face, but actually encouraged me. Thank you.

Then there's the talented and patient folks at Wild Wolf, who never once told me to stop acting like a ninny, and just get on with it…and then, of course, there's my very close friend, Amber Clark, who did…*more* than once, when I needed to hear it.

Thank you all.

CWL

Biography

C. W. Lovatt lives in Canada where it's quite cold.

This is his debut novel, but don't hold that against him.

www.ingramcontent.com/pod-product-compliance
Lightning Source LLC
Chambersburg PA
CBHW020823260626
47169CB00003B/809